GLASSPIER

Thayer Yates

This book is a work of fiction. Names, characters, businesses, organizations, places, events and incidents either are the product of the author's imagination or are used fictitiously. Any resemblance to actual persons, living or dead, events, or locales is entirely coincidental.

Printed in the United States of America.

Book design by : Thayer Yates
Cover art by : Susan Bin
Other art by : Kaitlyn Speigl

ISBN - Paperback: 979-8-8690-2439-8
ISBN - Hardcover : 979-8-8691-9321-6

First Edition: April 2024

Contents

Chapter 1 - Letters

Leon

Sept. 13th 1947
Saturday
Glasspier,

Foxglove Killer Strikes Again! Second Victim Poisoned!

The headline of The Glasspier Herald screamed at me from the coffee table. We'd just been discussing this latest rash of Glasspier charm before moving on to more pleasant subjects. The rain pattered dully upon the sill as I sat back with my three best friends – Thomas Langston, Dottie McFarlane, and the bottle of Old Forester on the coffee table between us. Friends might be a strong word for the three of them, but they provided distraction enough from day-to-day life in the city.

North of here, in the heart of the city, the nightly chorus of others too looking to forget the troubles of the week would be singing out into rain slicked avenues from crowded nightclubs and dingy bars. But as far as I was concerned, when dusk closed in on Glasspier, a good night was one spent staying in. This was a city of bloodstains and chalk outlines after the sun went down.

Here at the agency, I reclined in the lamp light of the main lounge as Dottie recounted a particularly well received performance of hers at The Blind Tiger – her parents' bar.

"When I went up on stage, well, the area we've set aside as a stage, one of our regulars actually requested a song of mine!" she effused, smoke curling above her dark hair from a nearly spent cigarette.

"Well, we may have a star on our hands yet after all, eh Leon?" Thomas smiled, raising his glass. "To Dottie then. And at least one of us making something of ourselves in this damned city."

And so we drank, while a warbling jazz number crackled over the RCA Victor in the back corner of the room. After a moment's pause, and presumably sensing a lull in the conversation, Thomas leaned forward and I could tell we were perched on the brink of another night of tales either of adventure or academia. His attire today consisted of a diamond patterned sweater pulled over a dress shirt and blue tie, so my guess was the latter. With a familiar gleam from behind his circle-rim glasses he began:

"Did I ever tell you two about the research we did on the S.S. Martin off the coast of Puerto Madryn?"

So I was half right. A meeting of worlds was in store for us this time.

"We were aboard the Martin, and I of course would have preferred a smooth gliding sloop of some sort, but anyways-"

He was cut off by the sound of a fist rapping at the front door. Dottie made a small start of surprise and I rose slowly from my armchair, trying to remember if there was an appointment I'd forgotten. Peering through the security aperture installed on the door revealed a short, wiry man wearing a faded navy work shirt beneath stained overalls. He had dark charcoal eyebrows and sandy hair peeking out from under a flat ivy cap and looked to be in his middle to late twenties; like myself and the rest of my company that night. There was a wild, fieriness to his eyes and demeanor that made me feel a slight twinge of regret that my *.45* was nestled safely in my desk drawer and not nestled in my side. Not wanting to make the poor man wait any longer in the drizzle and with my curiosity getting the better of me, I let the door swing wide.

"Do you have an appointment? It's after hours," I said, as the man looked me up and down and then past me into the sitting room.

“This McCreary Investigations?” the small man bluntly inquired, likely rhetorically given the sign posted above the door. I noted a slight Irish accent.

“Yes.”

“And are you Mr. McCreary?” A fair question.

“I am. And you are?”

“Conrad O'Malley" he stated simply, extending his hand which I shook, unsurprised by his multitude of calluses, given his workman’s appearance.

I motioned him inside. He stepped in and shut the door, his gaze panning about the room, moving quickly over Thomas and landing firmly on Dottie. This was nothing new to me, Dottie had that effect on most men. Her dark hair, light complexion and currently cherry-red lips all combined to flatter her naturally alluring figure; making for a striking combination that often overshadowed anyone else in the room. It certainly didn’t help that she had a cabaret later tonight and had pulled out all the stops with a slim red dress for the occasion.

Finally breaking his stare, Conrad paused in the entryway and began digging into his pockets, eventually producing a slightly damp and crumpled piece of paper which he unfurled and passed my way; revealing a well curated collection of scars and burns along his hands and arms in the low light of the room as he did so. Looking sidelong between Conrad and Dottie, I took the page and brought it over into better lighting.

512 Belmont St. -McCreary Investigations
Be there, evening Sept. 13th for something that will become of interest to you...

Machine typed. Today's date. My address.

“This mean anything to you, Conrad?” I questioned.

“No sir. Just fell through my mail slot sometime this mornin’ before work.”

“Which is… where?” I had a hunch.

“Down south of here, at the steel mill.”

So far, I was unsure what interest a millwright might have in anything going on here tonight – beyond the liquor of course.

"Come over and have a seat." I motioned for the chair nearest the front door.

I'd have offered him a drink, but I wasn't sure I wanted him that close with my friends just yet, not knowing his nature. He had a way of talking that made me want to trust him, but that's what I was worried about; alongside the fact that he looked about as scrappy as a stray bulldog. I was about to start asking Mr. O'Malley a bit about himself, when we heard another knock on the door. Softer this time.

"What in the blazes-"

I strode evenly again to the front of the lounge and peered once more through the aperture. This time, what I saw outside was in stark contrast to Conrad's work-worn form. A lady, slightly older than the rest of us there that night by my reckoning, but still very attractive by all conventional means, stood beneath a large black umbrella and toted a cream-colored purse. She wore a hat and a neat looking tan overcoat, underneath which, a pinkish blouse surfaced just below the curls of her blonde hair. I hesitated once again while reaching for the doorknob.

Despite Conrad's more intimidating demeanor, I knew there was a good chance this woman would be more trouble. She looked expensive. Alas, the door swung again and the lady looked up at me from beneath her hat with soft eyes like a lost puppy hoping for somewhere warm to stay for the night.

"Detective McCreary?" she near-whispered.

I nodded, sighing. "You'd best come in."

My guests were looking as confused as I felt. The woman entered, glancing around my lounge with mild interest. I didn't notice any flash of recognition from Conrad.

"I'm not interrupting anything am I?" she asked with an air that gave belief she didn't really mind if she was.

"Just afternoon tea with some friends," I replied, and Thomas took a sip from his glass in corroboration. Her mouth showed a brief flicker of confusion before smiling, as she delicately procured an envelope from her overcoat.

“I was recommended your services by someone in regards to a problem I’ve found myself in today,” she began lightly, “I was recently contacted by my older sister whom I’ve not seen in nearly twenty years. I received this letter entreating me to come visit, but earlier this morning when I went by the address it seemed as though no one had been there for years! It looked quite dreadful and abandoned, I do hope you can help me figure out what’s going on…” she trailed off, extending the envelope towards me.

Taking it, the envelope looked like a standard affair and featured the address 451 Lenox St. New Hampshire on the front along with the name ‘Jenny Baurle’ for delivery instructions; dated on the 5th of last month. The letter read:

Dear Jenny,

It is regrettable how many years it has been since we've had any correspondence, a stretch of time that I now hope to rectify or at the very least, attempt to. When I eloped with Lester, I didn't intend to establish a rift between us. Now if there would come a day where old wounds could be healed, I believe it is that time. Lester and I recently came into a sizable fortune and I have included some money to aid in your traveling here. I hope to further bring you into this fold of wealth and celebration upon your arrival. My address is 201 Carmen Ave. Do come by on Sept. 13th and I will explain more upon your arrival.

Love,

-Charlotte

I read it over twice, aloud the second time. “What ‘wounds’ would she be talking about?”

“Well… Lester wasn’t exactly well liked by our family, especially by our parents. So when he whisked her away to the big city, they were less than thrilled I suppose, but I did come to miss her dearly…" she let her words trail off again.

I returned to where I'd been sitting peacefully just minutes prior, before my night of relaxation had been upended. I placed the envelope on the coffee table and lit a smoke while the others waited in restless silence. I wasn't planning on taking a new job tonight, but I could use a way to keep the leaser off my back for another fortnight or so, and besides, who knows how in depth this would end up being? Could just be a simple case of having the wrong address. Jenny had a look that I'd attribute to those used to being chauffeured and having her meals prepared for her, so I figured she was just the type of client whose patronage I couldn't pass up.

"Thirty a day plus expenses," I said with some finality. Let's see what kind of a person this Jenny Baurle was. I could see the reels turning over behind her eyes as she hesitated for a second, fidgeting with the dainty silver watch on her pale wrist.

"Deal," she finally announced.

Across the table, Thomas shifted in his chair and Dottie hid a smile, snubbing out her cigarette in the ashtray on the end table nearby.

"Conrad, you'd better come with if you don't mind. I have a feeling somehow that you're involved in this, though just *how* escapes me currently."

Jenny regarded Conrad again with some evident interest this time.

"And Thomas, you're welcome along as always, if you wish," I added, heading for my office door.

I never turned down having some extra muscle and Thomas never turned down a chance at an adventure that might make a good story. While I don't necessarily trust Thomas fully yet, given that he and Dottie are both the leftover remnants of a job I'd worked half a year ago and not employees of mine; I do, however, trust the military training Thomas had from his time in the Navy. I disappeared into my office. Walking over to my desk, I pulled my *.45* automatic from the side drawer. Ever since my time overseas I'd sworn that I'd never take another life, so now I just keep my pistol as a conversation piece: I point it at someone and the conversation starts flowing. I tucked it into the shoulder holster beneath my jacket and re-emerged back into the lobby. Dottie was whispering something to Thomas, but leaned away as all eyes turned back to me.

"Jenny, you can wait here in the lobby 'till we get back, or I can recommend a hotel."

"How long will you be?"

"The address isn't far, less than an hour total to look around. Maybe longer depending on what I find," I said, lifting the envelope from the table.

She finally took off and hung up her overcoat as I walked over and pulled my own from the rack.

"I can wait," she decided, with a subtle edge to her voice that suggested that while she *can* wait, she wouldn't enjoy it.

I grabbed my keys and stood in the doorway. "Mind keeping her some company 'till we're back, Dottie?"

"I suppose," she said, straightening up a bit, but not doing well to hide the hint of disdain in her voice at the idea.

"Well? You two coming or not?" I directed at Conrad and Thomas, who both glanced at each other before rising in unison towards the door. Outside, the twilight sky was the color of steel and twice as heavy. I walked out into the rain.

Chapter 2 - Pictures

Thomas

We stopped in front of 201 Carmen Avenue, headlights from my motorbike and Leon's car struggling to pierce through the rainy night to faintly illuminate the dilapidated craftsman style house before us. Leon and Conrad exited the black sedan as I shut off and dismounted my motorcycle. It was nights like these I pined for a car, but the ease of taking a motorcycle onboard a ship outweighed the discomfort of being cold and wet for someone like me who spent half his life on the water. It did always seem to be raining in this damned city though. I joined Leon on the front walk, who was eying the house number with some suspicion. Somewhere down the street a dog barked. 201 Carmen Avenue was west and slightly north of the agency and in a decent neighborhood. The house was situated on the corner of the block with only one neighbor to the right, whose lights glowed behind thick curtains. 201 however, was completely dark.

"Whaddya think?" Conrad asked in a low voice to Leon.

I laughed to myself inwardly. He wasn't used to how Leon operates; I knew better. It usually wasn't worth asking too many questions while in the field with him. Leon grunted in response and began walking along the right side of the seemingly abandoned house. Conrad and I followed. The planters out front were neglected and full of weeds and upon closer inspection I could see that the peeling paint on the house had been neglected for even longer. We walked between the decaying house and the neighboring one until we emerged into the small backyard and stood before the back porch, Leon glancing over the house's rear facade.

It was a simple porch leading up a couple of steps to a faded white door, on either side of which there were prairie frame windows. The difference in the two being: the window on the left was open, the glass missing. Leon had procured a large flashlight and was looking around the porch area, while I walked over and peered into the stygian darkness of the house. Conrad struggled to light up a smoke behind me in the rain and leaned against the exterior of the house after some success. Not being able to see much from my current vantage, I deftly clambered through the sill into the building. The soft crunch beneath my feet clued me in as to where the glass had gone and I was barely inside before the dim street lamp light behind me was blotted out by Leon in the window.

"*What are you doing*?" he hissed at me in a whisper and I turned back towards the sill which he was now leaning into.

"Getting some answers. Don't tell me you were planning on admiring the woodwork of the porch all night?" I drawled, pulling out my lighter. I didn't smoke, but it was handy for fusing ropes. And illuminating abandoned buildings.

"Thought we might at least ask around at the neighbors place before committing a trespass," Leon retorted flatly. He sounded annoyed. I didn't care. I knew he was just as curious as me and would be inside momentarily. It's what made us such good pals.

I stepped forward and took in what I could of the grimy interior of the house while hearing Leon curse under his breath and clamber ungracefully over the sill as well. The area we'd entered appeared to be where a sitting room once would have been, the only thing here now was trash and other detritus littering the floor. Further beyond, which I could now see thanks to Leons flashlight, was the front door and entryway. To the right of us was the backdoor and a wall that wrapped around to a hallway. Leon glanced at me and went right, I opted to follow. We walked a little ways down the hallway when I became aware of a sound from behind me. Turning sharply, I realized it was Conrad, following us with one hand in his overalls and the other holding a cigarette. I swore softly and shook my head, surprised at how quietly he'd managed to enter the house.

Leon stopped before a pair of doors. One to our left near a small kitchenette and the other across from it on our right. Didn't that letter Jenny had say something about a fortune? I wasn't getting the impression of great wealth from this tiny, dump of a house. Leon leaned and put his ear against the door on our left and we were all silent. Slowly then, he drew his pistol from within the left breast area of his jacket and I let my right-hand rest gently on the pocket in which I kept my own small revolver. With a 'prepare yourself' glance back at me, he handed me his flashlight and then pushed the door open and let its momentum carry it the rest of the way as he entered the room, gun at the ready. I followed behind. Immediately there was a flurry of motion and shuffling sounds, as a form on the other side of the room struggled on the floor. I drew in a startled breath at the sudden commotion and let my flash beam fall onto the man across the room, as Leon let the muzzle of his pistol do the same.

"Please, don't shoot!" a scruffy man who I could now see had been struggling to get out of a ratty sleeping bag pleaded with both hands above his head. Leon immediately lowered his gun and held up his free hand in a show of peace. The man staggered to his feet, still displaying his palms to us. He was young, with disheveled long brown hair and was draped with a ragged green jacket above gray pants and heavily worn boots.

"I was just lookin' to get outta the rain somewhere, Glasspier is startin' to get awful cold these months. I'll get out, I promise. Please just let me go, I've got no trouble with the police, none at all, I swear."

It was clear that the man was a squatter, looking only for a place for the night and not for trouble. Leon tucked away his pistol and instead drew out his private detective badge, flashing it with some authority towards the man.

"I've got no problem with you taking a load off here for the night, but I do have one with the case I'm working. Do you know anything about this house, its previous residents, or how long it's been in this state?" Leon questioned.

The man relaxed a bit and allowed his hands to fall to his sides, no longer looking as worried about ending up spending a night in the pen rather than here. “Been staying here occasionally since I got back from the war,” the man started. “I’ve had trouble keeping a job. It’s hard act’n like anything matters after the things I seen over there. This house has been abandoned for years s’far as I know. It’s a known spot for people like me…” he said, looking at the floor as though some solution for his situation would be rising out from the dust any second now.

On hearing this, Leon's expression softened a bit. I know that he’d seen just as much horror in the war, if not more than this poor man. I myself was lucky, never saw real open fighting, just some far off bombardments while aboard the old USS *Atropos.* Leon seemed to be mulling things over, when Conrad stepped forward between us and walked over to the man. He smiled and outstretched his hand.

“What’s your name son?” Conrad asked, taking the man's hand in a firm grip.

“Was Private Jason Fullom. 717th tank battalion,” he said, with what I thought might be a slight sense of pride. “Just Jason now though…” he waned, releasing Conrad's hand, eyes sinking back down to the dust.

“Well Jason, it’s good to meet you. The names Conrad and I apologize for any fright we may of caused. I’m head of the union down at the steel mill. You come find me if you ever want to turn things around for yourself. We take care of each other down there,” he said, sounding very genuine and pressing a card into Jason’s hand. Leon looked over at me and shrugged and I lowered the flashlight.

Conrad began to enthusiastically explain to Jason the various roles he could fill and the involvement he could have in the union at the mill, which Leon seemed to take as his cue to look around elsewhere in the house. Not having a particular interest in the workers’ rights issues Conrad was explaining, I elected to follow Leon back into the hallway. We entered the door across the hall from what appeared to be the master bedroom that Jason had taken up residence in for the night and found a smaller room that was completely barren. I cast the light around as Leon examined the walls and floor.

"Bed was here," Leon stated very matter of fact, motioning towards four uniformly spaced scuffs in the wood panel flooring near a broken floorboard on the right side of the room. Pale light from outside filtered through the dirty glass of the window on the back wall of the room and faintly illuminated the left-hand wall which Leon had moved to inspect. I saw a marred section of the drywall and Leon too was looking at it with sudden interest. I moved closer with the flashlight.

"Is that-"

"A bullet hole?" Leon cut me off. "I'd say so." He leaned back on his heels, as though pondering the house anew.

I continued to stare at the hole in the wall, trying not to imagine what might have happened here. It was around waist level and appeared to go quite deep, through drywall and timber. Leon had begun scouring the rest of the walls in the room, I assumed in search of further holes and apparently finding none, set his jaw and said 'follow me,' as he walked back into the hall.

He thoroughly inspected all the flooring and walls of the house and I pointed the flashlight where he directed as he did so, eventually making our way back to the would-have-been sitting room. We continued our search, and upon looking at the furthest most wall of the room: sure enough, Leon spotted another hole. No words needed to be said, I glanced sideways at him and he nodded in confirmation. It seemed to be another firearm caused wound to the drywall, around midriff level this time.

"Maybe head or chest level, had someone been sitting," Leon said, reading my thoughts. He looked around the room as though envisioning what had taken place.

I speculated myself. Maybe this wasn't related to Charlotte. Maybe it was a deal gone bad between rival gangs, or a violent encounter between two random Glasspier citizens down on their luck like Jason. Maybe it all happened years after Charlotte and Lester had moved out and had continued living happy lives together in some well-to-do neighborhood up north. I tried to convince myself such a thing was possible in Glasspier, and that a happy ending was possible for anyone in this city. I didn't buy it. After all, if that was what'd happened, why did that letter tell Jenny to come here? Could it be a simple mistake of putting down their old address in a moment of wandering thoughts? Maybe. My own thoughts were interrupted and my attention re-focused by the scrape and squeak of Leon pulling down a built-in overhead ladder that we'd walked beneath twice earlier without noticing. A cloud of dust came down with it and I suppressed a cough as we peered up into the darkness above.

"Do you think we should tell Conrad where we went?" I asked.

"He'll see the stairs. Besides, I can still hear him talking Jason's ear off," Leon said dismissively and began ascending the rickety, dust covered steps. I did the same. The attic was a triangular low-ceilinged affair and unlike the rest of the house, appeared untouched. Remnants of some previous owner occupied the space. An old lamp with a moth-eaten shade stood in the back left corner, alongside a wooden chest beneath a small circular window. To our right, a few sagging cardboard boxes sat wearily by. I moved forward towards the chest and Leon went for the boxes. As we walked, half crouching, dust kicked up into the space and resembled a phantasm of some kind with the wane light from the window shining through its particulate. The whole space had an eerie quality about it.

"You believe in ghosts Leon?" I questioned, half joking because I was sure I knew my pragmatic friend's answer.

"Of course I do," came Leon's sardonic reply, with a shadow of a grin, "after all, you're speaking with one right now".

I responded in the form of a hollow laugh. It was general knowledge to Dottie and I, that Leon had been severely wounded and all but dead before being extracted from where he'd served in the war. It wasn't all too uncommon for him to refer to himself as a dead man walking.

"You?" Leon asked simply in return.

I thought for a second. What did I believe in? Not in any gods, that was for sure. At least not in the form that they were commonly thought of. Despite not wanting to, I couldn't help but think back to the village I'd found in the Congo so many years ago. I'd been chasing a lead in my free time with some money I'd put away for pleasure, and what greater pleasure was there than the thrill of a good adventure? The locals had told me about a village, cursed and containing some dark power. I didn't believe in ghosts then. And I didn't believe in that either. But I had to see for myself. I tried to push that place from my mind again, but as always, the memories flooded in from my subconscious, drowning my present thoughts in their muddied waters. I was searching for that village for days, lost in the jungles and delirious with hunger and thirst, but eventually I found it. Or I thought I did. I'd woken up in a tent hospital some days later and was out of time and out of money. I had to go back someday, I had to put my curiosity to rest. It's why I was working with The Blight after all, to fund a return trip. Did I believe in ghosts? I certainly believed there were things out there beyond what we currently understood with modern science.

"Thomas?" Leon's voice cut through my thoughts, with a slightly concerned edge.

I wiped a drop of sweat from my brow that had defied the chill of the September night. "Ghosts? Of course not. I'm a man of science after all!" I joked back weakly, while Leon rummaged through the handful of cardboard boxes. They appeared to be full of women's clothes.

I continued my crouched walk over to the wooden chest and opened it gently. Inside, I found a handful of dusty things. A few old children's books such as *Tarzan of the Apes,* which was in rough shape, and *Outlaws* which appeared to be about wild west gunslingers. More interesting however, were two framed photographs. One was in black and white and featured a pale, dark haired boy of around maybe five or six years old. The other was, surprisingly, in color. It pictured three women, in their twenties if I had to guess, dressed up in finery and sitting on what appeared to be a velvet chaise lounge in a rather opulent looking room. From left to right there was a blonde, a tall redhead, and a woman with black hair. They were all quite beautiful and seemed to know it. Flipping the first picture over, I found a name scrawled on the back: 'Jake'. The picture with the women on it also had writing on its back, two names- 'Alyssa' and 'Charlotte'. Damn. Good chance that this *was* Charlotte's house then. At some point at least.

"Just a bunch of old clothes in those boxes, might take some back to Jenny and see if she can identify them as Charlotte's size."

"I don't think you'll need to do that," I said, passing the photo of the women to Leon. "Seems as though Charlotte may have had some money after all."

Leon flipped the frame over and read the back and then did the same with the one of the young boy. His expression hardened.

"I want to look around the master bedroom, then let's get Conrad and get out of here," Leon said, tucking the pictures into his coat and beginning the descent back down from the attic.

Chapter 3 - Payments

Leon

I walked the gray stone path leading up to the neighboring 199 Carmen Avenue with Thomas and Conrad in tow. This time it was me knocking on someone's door and disturbing their Saturday night. The three of us stood expectantly on the front porch in the damp air outside, until the door opened a crack. The man inside kept the chain lock in place and talked to me through the opening.

"What do you want?" croaked a gravelly voice that rattled like a beggars' cup. The voice was rattling from the shell of an older African American man with graying hair and thick eyebrows. He seemed a bit cagey so I figured a second show of authority was necessary for the night.

"Detective McCreary," I stated, flipping my badge out for him, "just want to ask you about your neighbors."

"What of 'em?"

"Mind if we come in?" I said, looking up at the water dripping down the brim of my hat for emphasis.

He nodded hesitantly. The door shut and I heard the chain rake across the back of it before reopening again. The three of us filed inside. Conrad shook the rain from his hair, then slicked it back and replaced his flat cap on top. Thomas removed and hung his leather jacket; I did the same with my trench coat and hat, placing them neatly on the rack to the right of the door.

I could see now that the man leaned on a cane as he walked and wore a burgundy smoking jacket. He beckoned us over to the Chesterfield that sat across from a chair he stood in front of. The inside of his home had what I thought to be an excessive number of potted ferns and books scattered here and there, and the house overall appeared to have its styling cues left over from a few decades' past. We all took a seat, a bit cramped sharing the same settee.

"Can I get you anything to drink?" he asked, not sounding very hospitable.

Conrad began to speak up. "Sure. I wouldn't mind a -"

"No thanks, we're fine," I cut him off, "we won't be long."

The man sat down. Conrad looked miffed. I tried to ignore it.

"Frederick Banks by the way, but you're not interested in me of course," he grumbled, leaning back in his chair with a cigar he'd lifted from the table beside him. "You just want to know about poor Charlotte and her kid next door right? Or were you maybe hoping to hear about the boring old Sullivans at one-ninety-seven?"

"Only if the Sullivans were involved in what happened with Charlotte," I replied evenly.

Mr. Banks leaned forward again. "I wondered if someday someone might come looking into all that business again. The police sure gave up on it fast enough, not sure what luck you'll have some twenty years later."

"Were you at this address when it happened?"

"Sure. Just up those stairs, sleeping you see." He pointed toward the stairs leading up to a second floor to our left. "I heard the gunshots and woke up. My wife did too. Never thought something like that would happen here, it's not a bad neighborhood, not like down south of the mill."

"Charlotte was murdered then?" I stared.

He took a puff from his cigar and laughed through a cough, his eyes darkening quickly. "My, my, you are a bit behind on the times. Charlotte and her son Jake were both killed over twenty years ago in their home next door. No trace of the killer, no known motive. Just a line in the paper, a quick funeral on a rainy day like this one and that was that. It's why I had that installed." He gestured towards the chain on his door.

I hated breaking news like this to clients. Why couldn't I just have one easy job goddammit. One where the neighbor says something like: 'Oh, Charlotte and her family moved years ago, but we're still in touch, here's the address!' But no. Murdered and a cold case. Although maybe there was still an angle here. Something I could find.

"What about Lester? Her husband?"

"Gone. Long before the murder. Things didn't work out between the two of them. Not sure what happened. Charlotte was always rather private after that. Came and went at odd hours of the night. Never saw much of her son," Mr. Banks said dismissively, leaning back once again into the cushions of his chair as though this conversation was taking a lot out of him. Maybe it was. He looked ancient, and the events had obviously scared him enough to take security measures.

"One more thing," I said, standing up and walking over to my coat and pulling the pictures from where they'd been stowed. "Do you recognize any of these women?" I placed the frame in Mr. Banks' lap.

He looked at it for a second. "Just Charlotte," he said, pointing to the blonde on the left. "Don't suppose you could tell me what this is all about? Some kind of new evidence come out?"

"I don't suppose I can. Client confidentiality and all that."

He didn't look surprised and handed the photo back to me. I jerked my head at Conrad and Thomas, a signal that they both understood and rose from the Chesterfield. We donned our coats as Mr. Banks watched and puffed on his cigar.

"Come on back if you have any more questions. I don't have a lot going on," he said, looking around wistfully through the smoke.

We stood on the porch and heard the chain slide across the back of the door, then made for our respective vehicles; with Conrad once again in my passenger seat. Before I even got the car into gear he started talking.

"So what the hell was I here for? Don't think I've got anything to do with a murder that happened twenty-some odd years ago when I'm only twenty-five myself. And who decided you were calling all the shots in there? I don't work for you. Maybe I wanted a nice glass of scotch from Mr. Banks – I saw he had a fine collection. Would've been the only 'something of interest' as that letter put it, that I've seen tonight! Although I suppose I did get to meet Mr. Fullom and he seemed interested in what I had to say, so maybe it wasn't all a waste…" He cooled off and finally seemed to run out of steam. I kept driving.

"And what exactly *did* you have to say to Mr. Fullom?" I swerved to dodge a particularly nasty looking pothole. "You're some kind of union boy? Think that might have anything to do with that letter being dropped through your door?"

"Don't see how it could. If I can think of a connection, I'll make sure you're the first to know; *detective,"* he said icily.

I reached into my breast pocket with the other hand still on the wheel and retrieved a card with my information on it and held it over to Conrad. He went to take it.

"Ah, not so fast." I grinned, pulling the card away, warranting a glare from him. "Haven't you ever traded baseball cards? I want one of yours in exchange."

At this Conrad awarded me with a small, half-grimace smile and rummaged into his pockets, producing a slightly crumpled piece of paper as another fell between the seat and the door. This seemed to escape his notice. We made the trade as my black sedan hurtled through the puddles of Glasspier's endless streets and back to McCreary Investigations.

It was a little past 21:00 when we arrived back at the agency. Conrad and I went inside and Thomas joined us shortly after, shivering from his ride back. Jenny stood quickly from her seat, threatening to spill her glass of wine.

"Well? Did you find her?" she asked expectantly. I tried not to let my face betray any emotion. It wasn't too hard.

"In my office. I'll explain there. The rest of you, wait out here. I might have some parting words."

I hung my coat and hat, hopefully for the final time that night, taking the photos out as I did. Walking past the tense crowd in the lobby, I led Jenny into my office, shutting the door behind us. I sat at my desk, and Jenny, in one of two simple chairs I kept across from it. Her delicate fingers plucked at the equally delicate band of her silver watch. I stared ahead, bracing mentally to give her the news. Maybe I should pay Dottie a retainer of some kind just for things like this; she was much better at dealing with affairs of the heart. I decided on a direct approach.

"Jenny, your sister is dead. It happened over twenty years ago. It was quick and painless. I'm sorry."

Jenny seemed to think that over for a bit and came to the conclusion she didn't like it. I couldn't blame her. It wasn't my best performance. Tears welled up as they always tended to do once this city got under your skin – and it always did one way or another. I spent the next few minutes sitting still and trying to look compassionate while she cried, occasionally throwing another 'I'm really sorry about your loss' into the room to see if it would help, along with passing her tissues. After a little while she composed herself as much as she could with streaked makeup and a running nose.

"What happened?" she choked out.

"I'm not fully sure," I elaborated as gently as I could, while keeping honest, "what I do know is this. Charlotte and Lester split up, and sometime later she was shot in her home along with her son. Not sure by who, or why just yet."

That set her off again. Dammit. I shouldn't have mentioned the kid so soon. She looked more distraught and tried to pull herself back together again.

"I had… a nephew?" She managed shakily, and I figured now was as good a time as any to show her the pictures. I laid the frames on the desk for her consideration. She wiped her eyes with the backs of her hands and squinted to have a look at them.

"His name was Jake," I said softly and gave her a moment to take that in before continuing. "Recognize the other two women?"

She shook her head, then suddenly looked up from those remnants of her sister's life with something dangerous in her eyes. "I want you to find out who did this. And why. And I want you to make them pay. The more you make them pay, the more I'll pay you. You understand?"

"Trying to," I replied, a bit pleasantly surprised by this new Jenny. "If you're serious, I have some things for you to sign." I reached into the steel-gray filing cabinet beside my desk and brought out some papers. She extended a shaking hand out for them and the pen I also provided.

"Do need to tell you though, I won't be killing anyone. I'm not some contract killer for hire. If I find out who did this, I'll be bringing them in by the books and letting Glasspier Penitentiary do the rest."

She lowered her chin in understanding, hunching over the papers and staining them with tears as she wrote. She finished, pushing them back over to me and slumping back into her chair.

"Will you be staying in Glasspier?" I asked. "Who knows how long this could take. I've got a couple small leads, but until I follow them I've no real estimate for how deep this one goes."

"I understand. I'll stay a little while, I think."

We went back into my lobby. She composed herself one final time and walked as dignified as she could over to where her purse hung with her coat. I looked to Thomas and Conrad.

"Conrad, I'll phone you if anything comes to light that might concern you, otherwise keep an eye and an ear out for anything that might be relevant and call me if you've got something." Conrad made no visible reaction to this order.

"And Thomas, you can be as involved as you'd like to be. I know you're between jobs at the port right now; it won't be much, but I can provide some small compensation for your time."

I knew I didn't even need to add that second bit, there was already a gleam of excitement at the prospect of a mystery showing through his expression.

"Gladly," he nodded and paused before adding, "just not on Tuesday nights."

"Of course."

Thomas had a midweek dinner with an old friend every week on Tuesday nights for as long as I'd known him that took precedence over anything else that was going on. I didn't know the details, and he never shared them, so I didn't press him about it. I just knew it couldn't be missed for anything. He and Conrad collected their things and left. Before doing the same, Jenny paid me $210 to cover the first week of investigation. That was enough to make me forget any worries about accepting a case twenty years gone stale.

Only Dottie remained. She rose gracefully and intercepted me on my way back to my chair.

"I want to help," she said, in a tone blunter than I'd ever heard her use. "If I can get you useful information, will you honor the same offer you made to Thomas?"

I thought about that, a little taken aback. "Suppose so, but I'm not even sure what angle to chase for this case yet, seeing I've only got a couple names and some pictures to go on. Finding either Lester, or the other girls in the photo with Charlotte is probably where I'll start."

"So Lester is still alive?" she questioned, looking excited at being privy to more information.

"As far as I know, he could be. I'm going to look into public records tomorrow and see what became of him. Supposedly he and Charlotte split before she was killed."

I filled her in on the details of the case somewhat hesitantly, after all, the trail of a double homicide was hardly a place for a young lady like Dottie – especially in Glasspier. She fiddled with the ring around her neck for a second or two, looking lost in thought.

"Well, I really must be getting to my show. Don't want to disappoint the fans," she finally said, and then leaned in towards me, whispering through a wane smile: "Next time though, I'm coming with, and you're hiring a sitter."

I offered as sincere a smile as I could muster in return. "Best of luck with the show."

She went for the door, leaving me wondering about her sudden interest in snooping around with Thomas and I. A minute later I heard her car rumble begrudgingly to life amidst the soft sound of rain continuing outside. I lit a cigarette and finished the glass I'd started on over an hour ago, while recording the events of the evening in my journal. Then, locking the journal in the drawer of my bedside table, I turned out the light.

That night I dreamed of crimson spattered across white flashes of snow; a lion tearing its claws and teeth into a golden stag as two gunshots rang out in the forest. A cloud of dust rose into the form of a ghostly German soldier and searing pain shot across my stomach. Whoever said you can't feel pain in dreams was full of shit.

Chapter 4 - The Blind Tiger

Dottie

I departed Leon's place a little annoyed at being left out of all the fun again as usual and having to make small talk with Jenny in his absence, who I'd quickly found very little in common with. My mood wasn't improved by the beat up old 37' two-door my older brother and I shared refusing to start without a fight. I bargained with it and eventually after some protest it sputtered to life, sounding as though the puddle it sat in was deeper than it appeared and it was struggling to stay above the waterline.

I drove by the rundown apartment that I also shared with my brother on Charo Lane, wondering if he was out yet for the night. Seeing no lights behind the faded curtains, I kept driving. He must have been picked up by his friends. A slight smile reached the corners of my lips knowing the car was mine for the evening. I drove further north towards the heart of the city, and its pale, yellowed street lights reflected off the sunken hollows in the road where pools of water coalesced and splashed beneath the worn-down treads of the car. Rainy nights like this in the city always had a kind of surreal magic to them.

Arriving at The Blind Tiger, the car groaned to a stop and sounded relieved when I shut it off. It was a decent establishment: a bar and restaurant turned legitimate by my parents at the end of prohibition. It was where I performed for scraps on nights such as this one when I'd failed to book anywhere more lucrative. I double checked my appearance in the car's cloudy rearview mirror and, being satisfied, stepped out into the yellow glow of neon light cast down by the sign overhead. Entering the bar to the sound of conversation and clinking glass, I smoothly donned the version of myself that I hate. The version that was suggestive and demanded attention. The version that sways through the crowd towards the microphone on slender legs and makes the men turn to stare with beady eyes. The version that I hate, yet also need. The one that although loathsome and false, pays for gasoline and a place to live. The one with which I planned to secure my independence.

I took my place now behind the tarnished silver microphone, a mouthpiece through which I spoke directly to the lovesick and debauchers alike. And there in that moment before my performance, a place where the air is laden with the sweltering hum of anticipation, I reached up unconsciously and held the white-gold ring looped through my necklace chain. I remembered a time when I'd dreamed of white picket fences, bouncing babies, and cooking in a two-tone kitchen. A time before my husband Charles McFarlane had become *PFC Charles McFarlane* and gone overseas, swearing to come back to me before the year was up. My dear husband Charles McFarlane, who died in France just two months after our wedding, leaving behind just a burning memory of the life I'd dreamed of, alongside a stupid blue and gold medal of honor.

The piano, played by an old friend of my parents Mr. Evans, rattled to life in the dim corner of the room and I began to sing, pushing the incendiary thoughts of my dead dream into the far back of my consciousness. As I mindlessly swayed and crooned through my first song, new, more recent memories curled inward to fill the space where I had cleared the previous from. Charlotte and her son Jake dead, her ex-husband Lester missing, and a photo with two unknown women. I wondered if this was the little amount of information Leon normally stared down a new case with.

I let my eyes pan around the room, stopping occasionally to rest on the few people who were actively watching rather than in conversation with friends or their glass of liquor. I allowed my stare to linger the longest on the men who looked most ravenous, letting my voice grow more sultry as I did, singing in the way my parents disliked. My parents weren't here tonight though, they rarely were. I could have had a comfortable life had I returned to them after losing Charles, but when I received the news he'd been killed and my housewife ambitions were torn apart, new ones took their place. I wanted freedom. Independence. Self-made stability. To forge my own life, making a living with just my talents and wits. Partly to prove I could, and maybe partly because I couldn't imagine starting over on a new dream with someone else.

The last echoing note of the song decayed into the dim room, smoke swirling around the low lights amidst a small smattering of applause. I thanked the audience, taking special care to look at a particular man as I did so. He was out of uniform, but I knew him to be a patrol officer with GPPD named Derrick Downs. I also happened to know that while drunk a few weeks ago he'd rambled to a friend about some unsavory things he'd done with a prostitute the week prior. I knew exactly the type of man he was, a type common throughout the city from the poorest slums to the wealthiest districts. He was the type I hated. The type that took whatever he could regardless of who it hurt, so long as the repercussions were never felt by him.

The piano started again and the night burned on as I finished the rest of my set in a blur of bewitching melodies and sensual stares. Afterwards, the crowd rewarded me with some applause and some money, a portion of which I carried with me to the bar and bought myself a second glass of wine for the night. Getting half the glass down and feeling its warmth, I approached the officer who had a man with him at his table that I didn't recognize. The hooks had been planted on stage; it was time to dig them in deeper. Seeing me, the officer smiled with the hideous curling grin that they always plaster onto their faces. I took a breath and smiled back; I can handle myself.

Chapter 5 - The Blue Coupe

Leon

Sept. 15th 1947
Monday
Glasspier,

I took Sunday mostly off, as I often did. Not for any religious reasons (the war had taken care of that), but because most places I wanted to look into for information on the Marlowes, such as the library or clerk's offices, were closed. So, I examined the pictures further and paid a visit to St. Gertrude's Cemetery, where I found a joint headstone for both Charlotte and her son Jake – with no sign of Lester. Now on Monday morning, I reread my journal entry from the night I took the case, over a hearty breakfast of eggs and toast. I was breaking a few of my rules in doing that: never re-read, and: keep work out of the journal. Oh well, I promised I wouldn't tell on myself. Something about this felt different from my other cases.

Leons Journal
September 13th, 1947 22:35
Entry #303

Every day I wonder what my life would have been like if not for the war. I like to think I would have followed my father and taken over the farm. I had big plans for that place; I hope her new owners respect her as much as I did. Dottie has told me before that it's not healthy for the mind to linger on the "what if's", but I'm feeling particularly sentimental tonight.

A mother and her child are dead. Shot. Many years ago. One bullet each. The scene was old, but I was able to gather some evidence in the form of two pictures and the statements of Mr. Banks next door.

I've always tried to keep my work out of my personal journal, but this case feels different somehow. Wrong. I feel as if I'm being set up for something. With Conrad showing up just moments before Ms. Baurle hiring me to find her sister... I don't think I can believe in that much coincidence. Nothing about this makes sense. If Charlotte is dead, then who sent the letter?

In the spirit of rule breaking, I read it through twice wishing I had more to go on and then tucked the journal back into its locked drawer in my room. Back in the lobby, the morning news was playing over the small static-filled radio beside the office door. The new, young mayor – Miles Wesson, appeared to be giving an address regarding the 'Foxglove Killer' we'd been discussing the other night, along with some new reported disappearance.

I'd seen Miles once, behind a podium at city hall. He'd had dark swept hair and a clean, sober face paired with a well-tailored pinstripe suit that day he'd been sworn into office. In other words – he looked like the type this city would eat alive.

"-this new victim bore the same calling card, a foxglove flower clasped between the hands. Nonetheless, I want all citizens of Glasspier to rest assured that myself and Police Chief Warren Burns and his men are taking the investigation of these 'foxglove killings' and disappearances very seriously and with utmost urgency. I have Chief of Police Burns here now with a statement in regards to these recent events."

I knew the chief too; some would say a little too well. His grizzled, sunken face came to mind as the broadcast continued.

"The modus operandi of the foxglove killings has been ruled to be poison on both accounts. Our forensics investigators suggest being wary of accepting food or drink from those whom you don't know. Be wary, but rest assured this case has our full attention and concern. That is all I can say at this time. Back to you mayor."

The gruff voice gave way, returning to the charismatic one of the mayor.

"The disappearances of major league baseball player and war-hero Henry Wakeman and his wife Barbara have not been linked to this 'foxglove killer' at this time. My heart aches too along with all those mourning the victims of these acts of violence, and for those missing Mr. and Mrs. Wakeman. I promise you, that as your mayor I am working closely with Chief Burns to ensure that this city remains safe for all its citizens, and to bring those that would wish harm upon others to justice. Citizens of Glasspier are asked to keep an eye out for the pair – Barbara is in her mid-twenties, around five foot-six, with medium length red hair and Henry, of course we all know. Should anyone have any information regarding them, or their whereabouts please get in contact with the Glasspier Police Department."

At that, the broadcast switched to a riveting discussion on the upcoming horse races and I shut it off. I fished in my pocket for the familiar silver square box and placed a cigarette between my teeth. Glasspier never seemed to change. The weather and the news always had a dreariness to them and although I'd lived here less than three years, violence and corruption seemed to be all it knew. Maybe I should have gone back to the farm, or got my own. My thumb rolled down the spark wheel and a small flame exploded beneath the end of the papery cylinder protruding from my mouth.

The farm sure had its share of bad weather too, but at least the only killing there was whenever a fox got into the chicken coop or it was time to butcher the cattle. I inhaled. Now, here I was, preparing to track a decades old murder – and on the news the cycle of violence only continued. Here, we were the cattle. I exhaled and the smoke resembled the overcast sky. It was time to get to work.

I donned my coat and hat and made for my car. I was about to pull away from the curb and head up to the clerk's office to have a look at some public records, but stopped, remembering something. I got out, going around front for the passenger door and sure enough, there it was. The card Conrad had dropped rested face down on the inner running boards, with a familiar symbol staring up at me. Well, almost familiar. It had one slight difference. Rather than a hammer and sickle it featured a hammer and wrench, but the colors were the same as the flag that had flown over the camp I'd stayed at during the end of my time in the war. Seemed memory lane had some particular bricks laid out for me today.

I was undercover with the Military Intelligence Services' Germany-Austria unit after completing training at Camp Ritchie. Got caught up in Soviet and German crossfire in a Polish town. Maybe I should have remained impartial. Maybe I should have let that German soldier kill those kids and stuck to the mission. Maybe that's why I'll never make a truly great intelligence officer, or detective for that matter. I do know that it's why I ended up with a German knife in my gut and more blood on my hands.

After being rescued from the forest by a Russian soldier, I recovered in a camp with a flag bearing a symbol very similar to the one I now held in my hands in miniature cardstock form. I released a shuddered breath I hadn't realized I'd been holding and flipped the card over to the other side. It bore the same information the one Conrad had traded me for did, with the addition of the initials 'C.C.O.M.' added at the bottom. I finally tore my eyes from the card and shoved it into my pocket, then got back behind the wheel.

I drove up Belmont and took a right turn at Alcott, deciding to take the scenic route around the outskirts of the city. Oftentimes the streets lined with their towering buildings felt claustrophobic to an old farm boy like me, so I'd take any opportunity I could to avoid the main thoroughfare. After my pleasure cruise, I arrived at the city clerk's office first. It was a plain-gray building, where I was directed to the proper section by a plain-gray secretary.

After some digging, I found names and dates matching the gravestone I'd visited yesterday. Charlotte and Jake, both listed as deceased on June 17th, 1923. I found record of Jake being born August 3rd, 1917. That would put him around six years old when he was killed for reasons that neither I, nor the newspapers from 1923 seemed to know. I tried not to think of those kids in Poland again. Or the Germans and Soviets. Or the Polish wilderness. Or the stag. Or any of it. I pushed the papers away and steadied my breathing for the second time that day. Still no sign of Lester Marlowe.

The library offered more of the same information, so I drove back the way I'd come, back to McCreary Investigations. Somewhere around the intersection of Delwood and Deauville, I became aware of a blue, late thirties coupe that had taken one too many of the same turns I had. It danced in the edge of my vision in the reflection in my rearview mirror, keeping just far enough away that I couldn't make the driver. I took a right turn as casually as I could at the next chance I got, heading more west now than I would have been for my chosen route back to the office. I drove down a less busy avenue, my eyes flickering from the road in front of me to the silver sheen of the mirror, trying to pick out a blue coupe cresting the horizon behind me.

I never saw one. Just dark gray clouds and a bobbing streetlight. I decided to burn a little more gas than I would have liked and drove far southwest in the city, parallel to the railroad that ran out west from Glasspier's harbor. I went south and crossed the tracks, eventually looping around the Glasspier Steel Mill, whose towers raked the uncertain sky. I wondered if Conrad was there now. Seeing no further sign of that dogged blue coupe, I allowed myself to relax a bit and went back home.

Pouring a double of blended malt over ice, I loosened my tie and sat beside the rotary in my office. I had one other friend in Glasspier besides Dottie and Thomas and I decided to give him a call now.

"Is this Blaine?" I asked into the receiver.

"Still is," crackled the familiar voice of Detective Blaine Cruz. "And this must be Leon, on account of being too busy to stop by and see me in person?"

"Still is. Unfortunately." I took a sip, the ice clinking against the sides of the glass.

"Oh don't tell me you're drinking without me too, while I'm tied down to this desk," he complained in what I took to be mock distress. Although maybe only partially. I knew that he disliked desk work and his days in the field were few and far between now.

"Wouldn't be, if you'd take me up on that offer to leave Trusted Eye and come out to work with me. The offer still stands, you know. And if you ask nicely enough maybe I'll even change the name to *McCreary & Associates Investigations.*"

He barked a laugh at that. "Oh yeah? I suppose that'd still be more recognition than I get around here, but I don't imagine the salary and benefits would compare…" he trailed off, still sounding mildly amused at the thought of being under my roof.

"Maybe not, but wait 'till you hear about the case that just dropped on my doorstep."

"I knew you hadn't called just to catch up. All right, out with it," he sighed, signaling me to continue.

I told him everything I could about the Jenny case, not paying too much worry about confidentiality. If I couldn't trust Blaine, I couldn't trust anyone. After all, he was who I'd worked under for a year before I'd started my own firm. After I'd relayed the important parts, I let him think on it for a couple seconds.

"Oh that's it? That's good. I was worried you were going to say you were tangled up in the foxglove murders, or the disappearance of the Wakemans."

"Trying not to be."

"You keep trying. I've heard those ones have got the buttons well and stumped. Though, sounds like this one you've got on your hands might be just as bad. At least the pay's good and nobody's died yet… save for twenty-some years ago I suppose," he amended.

"Any ideas? I'm going to start canvassing here soon if I don't turn anything up." I admitted.

"Charlotte and Jake would have been before my time. I was working as a stevedore still around then. But, do you think all these might be related? Three strange cases cropping up all at once sounds like a hell of a coincidence. And you remember what I told you about believing in coincidences."

"Not to," I grumbled. "I'll look into that angle. Thanks."

"Well, you be careful out there. These streets are twice as dodgy as they were just a couple years ago. Guess all the rowdy men came home or something."

"Something like that. And you keep your eyes out and let me know if something comes up that could be related. Who knows, I might even let you have your name in the agency title if you round up something really worth my while…" I said, reclining back in my chair with a grin.

"Take care of yourself Leon," he said with some finality, but I could hear it was through a smile.

The line clicked. I sat for a moment without moving, before placing Conrad's card on the desk in front of me and picking up the receiver again. I waited longer than for Blaine, but finally got him on the line.

I took a less friendly tone. "Conrad. Or would you prefer C.C.O.M.? It's Leon."

"Well, well. Look at you, big detective," he laughed. "I don't think our trade was exactly fair."

"No, I suppose it wasn't. *Comrade,"* I said through my teeth.

He laughed again. "Well, ya' got me. It's still in the earlier stages, but yes, I want to see a full evolution of thought on workers' rights in Glasspier," he paused. "So, you going to sic the Pinkertons on me?"

"No."

"My politics may not be popular in Glasspier, but I've got nothing to do with Jenny, or Charlotte, or any of you lot. I just showed up where the note told me to, when it told me to. Now I'm startin' to regret it."

"Whoever sent it must know you somehow, on some level. How many of those cards have you given out?" I questioned. "The ones with the special back particularly."

"Only a handful. Just to people who are looking for more than what the union provides. People who want the same as me," he stated simply.

"What kind of car do you drive?" I switched up, hoping to catch him off guard.

"I don't. I walk, or hop the train. Only really go to mass and work anyways."

"Know anyone with an older blue coupe?"

"No sir. None that I can think of."

"You keep thinking."

I hung up. I stood, finishing off my drink, which was now a bit too watered down for my taste. I spent the rest of the evening pouring more glasses and pouring through the last couple days newspapers for anything about foxglove flowers and missing baseball stars.

Chapter 6 - The Shredder

Thomas

Sept. 16th 1947
Tuesday
Glasspier,

I loitered away a couple of monotonous days at the Glasspier harbor looking for work. No big jobs had come in, so I made a pittance moving shipping containers and offloading the occasional vessel that graced the port. Leon hadn't called me yet for any further inquiry and I must admit I was a bit sour about it. At least tonight was Tuesday, which meant I had my weekly dinner with my acquaintance Stephan Lockry, who provided the jobs that really paid my bills.

I'd just wrapped up a few hours of menial shipwright duties repairing a tramp steamer, after which I rode back to my house to throw off tar and salt encrusted workwear in exchange for a white button up, a neat navy-blue vest, and black slacks. Usually, it was just Lockry at our Tuesday exchanges, but I always made an effort to present myself in the best manner possible in case other members made an appearance.

Neatness in general was a virtue, I thought, and the lack of it was the single largest complaint I had about life aboard a ship. My sitting room was clean and no nonsense – save for the occasional curio collected during my travels. It also featured a carefully curated wine rack and an equally well curated bookshelf, with titles mostly including nonfiction from my time at university, along with some literary classics. I had some time to kill beforehand, so I made myself comfortable and resumed my reading of Homer's *Odyssey.*

An hour passed quickly before I shut the book and placed it carefully back onto the dark-wood table beside me. I glanced back at the small, red and gold jewelry box atop the mantle, reminding myself what it was all for. There was a reason, I reassured myself, feeling for the smooth metallic shape in my left pocket and once satisfied that the coin was there, I threw on my riding jacket and made a heading for Lockry's place. The weather had improved since that cold, wet night at 201 Carmen, but the air still had a crispness that reflected the arrival of autumn. The sun was slipping behind the smokestacks of the steel mill and sending ochre light filtering through the sparse clouds, brushing the glass of the storefronts an orange-crimson as I cruised past.

I pulled my motorbike around the front of Lockry's house and dismounted. The house was in the suburbs, southeast of the mill and was a standard affair with no frills. A plain brown facade with black shingling and a well-kept lawn faced me as I approached the front door. The only thing out of place compared to a 'normal' house, was an aperture installed in the door similar to the one at Leons agency, which I now held a coin up to that was burnished silver and featured an embossed locust on both sides. There was only a brief moments pause and I was admitted entry, slipping the coin back into my pocket.

"Ah Thomas, punctual as always," said the tall, thin man who ushered me inside.

He had a well-kept beard and dark eyes that stared knowingly from above a hooked nose. My attention was drawn as usual to his patterned suit of choice for the evening, which featured silver-on-black flowers and vines, almost seeming to shift as I followed him. I'd never seen Stephan Lockry wear the same suit twice and was nearly convinced that they just appeared in his closet, already pressed, and each more eccentric than the last. The inside of his house was a far cry from the drab appearance outside. He had potted plants of all manner, alongside glass cabinets housing a variety of artifacts. I recognized an ornate dagger on a marble plinth from one of my expeditions that I'd sold him a year ago for a significant price. We stopped in the dining room where the table was already set and at his motion, I took a seat. A lean looking steak garnished with gremolata appeared to be Lockry's method of choice to adulate me for the night.

"Well Thomas, what do you think? Pinot noir?"

"A fine pairing," I responded and he inclined his head in agreement before disappearing briefly down to the cellar.

He returned with a bottle and poured the both of us a glass. I guessed it wasn't one of his older wines, otherwise he would have had it decanting before I'd arrived. He unbuttoned his suit jacket and sat gracefully across from me, lifting his utensils with precise care. We started with the usual small talk, before moving to business matters.

"I've got you a job I think you'll like," he started. "It's not exciting or glamorous, but The Blight is getting paid top dollar to make sure it goes smoothly. Some of that pay can be yours – if you so choose."

"What does it entail?" I asked, over the rim of my glass.

"Two shipments. One this Friday, the next at a date I won't know until sometime in the future. All you have to do is pilot the tugboat to bring the ship in, then take it back out after the cargo has been offloaded."

"Why can't the harbor's normal operators bring the ship in?" I asked, already knowing the answer.

"It's a need-to-know job and you've earned The Blights' trust these last few years. Besides, it comes in at midnight and as far as anyone is concerned it never came in at all, if you catch my drift."

"Absolutely. What's the compensation?"

"I'll get you a number once I know myself. The job was only called in recently. I can assure you it will be quite substantial," he said, cutting into his steak.

"I don't doubt it."

I let a few moments pass in silence and once being sure that topic of conversation had been exhausted, I began a new line of thought. “Any chance you know anything about a ‘Lester Marlowe’?” I questioned casually.

Lockry thought about that for a spell, nothing on his features betraying any sort of recognition. Finally, he slowed his sawing at the steak and met my eyes. “Yes, I believe I do. He worked with us,” he said, in a manner I would consider unusually tentative for him.

Lockry knew Lester? This would definitely win me some points with Leon, assuming he hadn’t already tracked him down.

“Is that so? In what capacity?” I tried not to let my excitement become evident.

“Well, I’m unsure exactly what role he filled in The Blight, I just know he worked with us. And what became of him,” he added darkly, as his knife went to work again on the steak.

My dinner lay forgotten and I held my glass of wine, but it never reached my lips. I cocked my head, signaling for him to elaborate.

“Lester Marlowe was killed over twenty years ago. Not sure why, but I was new to the organization at that time, so I wasn’t privy to its innermost workings yet.”

“Where was he killed? And by who?” I asked, the thin mask around my intrigue slipping further.

Stephan Lockry raised an eyebrow and set his utensils to the sides of his plate. “Why the interest? You must have still been in grade school during his time.”

“Just another job I’m working,” I said evenly. “Don’t worry, there’s no conflict of interest with The Blight.”

“Well, if that’s so…” he deliberated momentarily. “I don’t know *where* it was done. I do know, however, that they never found the body. I also know who did it. Silas ‘*The Shredder*’ Stevenson,” he said with some venom.

The name was lost on me. It was my turn to raise an eyebrow in questioning. Seeming to recognize my lacking knowledge, he continued:

“Back in the twenties and even before then, if someone was an enemy of The Blight, whether from the inside or out, ‘The Shredder’ took care of them. He was the most ruthless and efficient hitman who ever stalked the streets of Glasspier and didn't get a nickname like that for nothing. Big guy, big scar on his face too, nasty bloke."

"Was?"

"He retired, so to speak. Went soft. Went legitimate. He's head of Thomas Glasspier's security detail now."

I let my glass rest back upon the table. Thomas Glasspier, the unofficial king of this city, who I may share a first name with – but certainly not a tax bracket, hired the man who killed Lester. His father, Thomas Glasspier Senior established the steel industry in the port town that would one day bear his surname: *Glasspier.* Now his son, Thomas Glasspier Junior, rules over his late father's fortune and company, along with his city. He's a recluse, and squeaky clean as far as the law is concerned. The city's patron saint. Does anyone know he has an ex-murderous hired gun that was once affiliated with the largest crime syndicate in Glasspier working for him?

I marshaled my rambling thoughts. "Interesting. Anything else you can tell me about Lester, or Silas?" I asked cooly, while my subconscious buzzed with questions.

"Afraid not. Silas was already mostly the stuff of legend, a name said in hushed tones, by the time I was initiated into The Blight. If it's not obvious, I'd advise against attempting to make contact with him regarding whatever it is you're on about. A man like that doesn't stop being a killer just because his employer has changed," he warned in a low voice.

"Of course not," I said hastily. "Loud and clear."

"And remember, The Blight comes first. You may even be able to trade in that silver locust for a gold one if this job goes well."

We finished our dinner with lighter topics of discussion, after which I bid Stephan farewell and raced home. Once inside, I threw off my jacket and rushed for my phone to dial McCreary Investigations.

Chapter 7 - Pigs

Dottie

"Hey Dots, I'm the driver tonight so I need the car." My brother Angelos' voice carried from the kitchen to where I stood in front of the bathroom mirror in our small apartment.

"Then you'll have to drive me to The Gold Pig first," I called back.

"The Gold Pig?" His silhouette appeared in the doorway behind me over my shoulder in the mirror. "That's not a place likely to further the career of any self-respecting lady such as yourself," he teased.

He was on the shorter side, with slight shoulders that couldn't quite fill out the oversized black leather jacket that always graced them. He sidled up next to me in front of the mirror, leaned forward a bit, and slicked back his hair that was an even darker black than mine.

"The Gold Pig may be a little rough around the edges," I admitted, "but I make good money there and besides, that's where most of the information I've peddled to you comes from, so don't complain."

He raised his hands in mock defeat. "And The Blight is grateful to you for it."

"Well I don't want them to be."

"Fine, well maybe I'm grateful too then, but only if it pleases your highness," he grinned.

I offered no response and instead began to apply my cherry red lipstick. I'd already slipped into a low-cut, slim black dress that my previous night at The Blind Tiger had paid for. I had it on not-so-good word that Officer Downs would be at The Pig tonight and I intended to show him I meant business.

"Maybe it's time that you get some information for *me*? Surely you have plenty from all your late-night escapades with your cronies."

"And what information would you possibly be interested in, coming from the gang?" he asked, walking to the door and lifting the car keys from their hook that hung beside it.

"It's not for me. At least not fully… it's for Leon."

"Ah! I should have known," Angelo cackled a short laugh. "I suppose it's only natural, he is a suave *detective* after all."

"It's not like that," I said flatly, flushing red only slightly in annoyance. "I just want to… you know what, forget it. Just tell me if you hear anything about a Charlotte, Lester, or Jake Marlowe, okay?"

"Fine. Whatever you say." The corners of his mouth curled up into one of his annoying, lopsided grins and he twirled the keys around his finger in the entryway.

We drove south in relative silence to The Gold Pig bar. I knew that Angelo didn't want to tell me much about his work, because he thought that much of it was 'unfit for a lady' and I didn't ask, because I didn't need to worry about what crooked job The Blight had put him up to this week. Sometimes it was best just not to know. I'd accepted that whatever it was, it helped keep the lights on in our apartment and the leaser off our backs.

We arrived in front of The Gold Pig. It certainly wasn't as nice as my parents' establishment. No lighted sign shone above the entryway, just a simple board fashioned from wood featuring the name of the bar and a painted caricature of a pig. I thought it resembled some of the people I'd find inside. Angelo kept the car running as I got out.

"How will you get home? I have no idea how late I'll be…" he trailed off, concern showing in his voice despite his badgering earlier.

"I'll manage. Don't worry about me."

"I'll try to be here before midnight?" he offered weakly.

"If not, I can handle myself," I said curtly, implying that he was dismissed.

He gave a half grimace and then waved goodbye as the passenger door creaked shut and the car rattled off in a thin cloud of bluish-white smoke. I entered the bar and somewhere on that threshold, a false smile appeared on my lips and my gait changed subtlety to that of one with confidence and sway.

The bar was dingy and every surface seemed to have a film on it. A low buzz of conversation and clinking glass permeated the room, along with the smell of stale tobacco and hard luck. I heard the sharp sound of a rack being broken at the pool table atop its stained green velvet and there was a round of raucous laughter from the ragtag group of large men in the back corner near an automatic phonograph. Angelo was right, it was no place for any respectable lady. But respectable ladies rarely did anything of note, so I was determined not to be one.

I saw some familiar faces through the smoky haze, but no Officer Downs. Maybe I'd have to change my target, I thought, as I sauntered over to the microphone, a handful of lecherous eyes following me there. No piano here, the only accompaniment I'd have tonight would be my thoughts and the glass of alcohol I planned to requisition at the halfway point of my performance.

I was one song into my show, when I found myself wishing I'd acquired the second half of my accompaniment beforehand. I was receiving the usual amount of attention, but here at The Gold Pig it didn't matter how well I could sing. Here, the audience cared only about how well I could please their eyes. I could see it in theirs. Beady, and ravenous as always, but here, all pretense was gone and they didn't care to try to hide it.

Sometime during the latter half of my third song, Officer Derrick Downs entered the bar. He only knew me from the other night at The Blind Tiger, but I'd seen him in uniform once with his family at *Le Pays de Rêve*, an upscale venue in north Glasspier. I noted a flash of recognition in his face as he stared from across the room towards me. Good. He remembered.

As my voice projected through the mismatched speakers into the venue, I allowed just a hint of raspiness to come through it and started to award more of my glances to Officer Downs. He sat at a table near a grimy window after getting a drink and was in conversation with his friend, occasionally stealing a sidelong glance at me.

I finished up my last few songs in much the same manner, then got myself a glass of wine. I made small talk with the group of men who'd been standing closest to the microphone, while keeping an eye on Downs. They weren't very good conversation. Once I was sure he'd seen me chatting with them for an adequate amount of time I broke off with a smile, saying- 'Apologies, I've spotted someone I know, it would be rude of me not to say hello,' and gracefully turned away.

I took my ring necklace off and stowed it in my purse as I approached the table Officer Downs lounged at with his friend, who he was currently in deep discussion with.

"-the airfield. Yeah, hangar eight. It'll be taken care of after tomorrow night, then we'll be free to-"

Downs cut himself off and grinned a stupid grin as he saw me coming up to the table. He then exchanged a knowing look with the other man, who rose and excused himself to get another drink.

"Good evening Mr. Downs, is this seat taken?" I asked wide-eyed and innocent.

"Not at all," he replied, the ugly grin spreading wider across his ruddy face like a particularly nasty bruise.

"Wonderful." I took the seat across from him. "Remember me?" I asked playfully.

"Of course. How could I forget a voice like that?" he said, his eyes flickering briefly up and down my body.

I just smiled and pulled a cigarette from my purse, looking up expectantly at him. "Do you have a light?" I prompted.

He hesitated a second. "You really shouldn't smoke. It's unbecoming," he said, while reaching into the pocket of his checkered blazer.

"Oh? Does it make me less attractive?" I purred, leaning forward a little on the table and allowing my dress to slip slightly down my right shoulder.

"No, no of course not" he stammered just as slightly, and I feigned a laugh.

I leaned forward further with the cigarette and he obliged. I took a short draw and saw that his friend must have realized he'd been ousted and had begun chatting with a girl in a sparkly turquoise dress behind Downs. I returned my attention to Officer Downs across from me, steeled myself, and took the plunge.

"So, you're a police officer? I do love a man in uniform, shame you haven't got yours on now," I stated, as good natured as I could.

His eyes narrowed a little, and the spreading grin receded a bit. "I don't think I mentioned being with the police," he said, a cautious note surfacing in his voice.

"Oh? Silly me, I just have a good eye for them that's all. I suppose I have a type." I giggled and batted my eyes, selling the impression of a clueless dame who wanted nothing more than to be swept away by a man of authority.

His grin began to slowly return in full, ugly force.

I kept the momentum going. "You must have all sorts of fascinating stories, I can only imagine the sort of excitement you get up to these days, with everything on the news and all..."

He leaned back, basking in my faux fascination. "Yup, there's not another job like it. In fact, have you seen the news about the Wakemans' disappearance? The Sergeant's got me on that one," he bragged.

"I did see that! How dreadful... two missing – and Mr. Wakeman of all people! What was he again, a baseball player?" I feigned cluelessness.

"A baseball player? Downs scoffed. "Not just a 'baseball player', he's one of the greatest hitters the Glasspier Comets have ever had! Fifty-seven home runs just last season."

I went wide-eyed again. "Oh my, it's a good thing they've got you on the case then." I took a sip from my glass. "And what do they have you doing?"

"I'm in charge of security at the Wakeman house, making sure everything is squared away while it's cordoned off for evidence," he stated proudly.

"It's in good hands then!" I fawned. "So what is the house like? A man like Mr. Wakeman must have something nearly as nice as

Thomas Glasspier's estate? Oh, does it have a two-tone kitchen? I've always wanted one of those."

He barked a laugh. "I can't speak on the kitchen, but the house is certainly a grand Victorian," he paused. "Say, why don't you come by tomorrow night? All the evidence will be out by nine, but I'll still have keys 'till I take them back to the station… I'd love to show you around, especially the master bedroom, it's quite beautiful."

I'm sure he'd love to, I fumed internally. Quite convenient for a man with a wife and kids at home. I know he thought himself a genius for seeing that opportunity, not even having to pay for a hotel room. I wanted to plant a heel between his legs under the table, but instead I smiled and agreed.

"I'd love to!" I leaned forward and exclaimed in a whisper.

With that, he gave me the address and I took my leave, while I still retained a shred of dignity. Tomorrow, I'd take him for everything. His money, and whatever he knew that might be of use to Leon. Leon can certainly make men talk with his badge and his gun, but with just a form-fitting dress and a fawning smile I could make them *sing*.

I stepped outside for some fresh air and slumped back against the stone facade of the building, lighting a cigarette myself this time as the adrenaline and provocative veneer faded quickly from my limbs. A thin fog had begun to settle in and I shivered. I checked my watch. It was only half-past ten. There was no way I was waiting around The Gold Pig for another hour and a half on the chance that Angelo would actually come by. I knew my feet would regret it, but I decided to walk back the handful of blocks between the Pig and our apartment in those damned heels.

Glasspier's night-life was feeble on a Tuesday compared to a weekend, but there was still a decent bustle of cars and people milling about. I walked a block and the fog only seemed to grow thicker. I shivered again and thought about hailing a cab, after all, there was supposedly a killer on the loose and even in normal circumstances the streets were hardly safe at night. The apartment wasn't far though and I hadn't made much money tonight either. I'd told Angelo 'I can handle myself' and I'd meant it.

Another two blocks down and the apartment was in sight when I suddenly had the feeling of being watched. The chill of fear crept across my shoulders, deeper than the chill from the fog. I turned my head to the alleyway behind me. There, a figure in all gray stood, wide brimmed hat pulled low obscuring his face in an angular shadow. The gray trenchcoated silhouette lingered for only a moment, then slunk back into the enveloping darkness of the alleyway.

I quickened my pace and the remaining block passed by in a blur of shifting mist and city lights. Once back at the apartment complex, I double checked that no one had followed me before slipping from the dim hallway into our suite. I immediately locked the door behind me and exhaled a pent-up sigh. My finger spun the dialer to input a number that was becoming second nature to me by now on the phone that lived in the corner of our small sitting room. The line rang for McCreary Investigations.

Chapter 8 - Willow Ave.

Leon

Sept. 17th 1947
Wednesday
Glasspier,

Leons Journal
September 17th, 1947 8:40
Entry #305

Sleep doesn't come easy to me these days. I wake up every night in a cold sweat after flashes of white and red. There's blood on the snow and a golden stag. In my dreams I'm afraid, but I feel powerful despite it. I don't know how to describe it. There is something on the ground that I don't recognize and my hands are dirty. I can taste the metallic-iron tang of blood. I always wake up with a split lip. I fear I'll never understand it. Any of it.

I took calls from both Dottie and Thomas within the span of a couple hours last night (more damned coincidences), saying they both had leads. I was wary about sharing too much over the line, so I told them both to come by the afternoon of the next day to see what they had. This morning I'd tried the Glasspier police for records or for any recognition of the women in the photograph, along with the name 'Lester Marlowe', but they were cagey as usual when it came to working with a private detective. Now it was Wednesday evening around 18:00 and I was hoping by some miracle, that at least one of them had somehow beaten me at my own job and had *something* to go on. I put my journal away.

I was dressed for the field in a sharp combo: a recently ironed white button-down shirt and a recently oiled Colt M1911. Both were accompanied by a navy-blue tie and dark jacket. Thomas arrived on time – as usual, with Dottie showing up shortly after. I invited them both in and they took their usual seats. I didn't have time to offer them drinks, or ask what they'd found before Thomas started:

"Lester Marlowe is dead."

I thought about that and slowly took a seat as well. Dottie didn't look too surprised and I supposed I wasn't either. Just one more body in a city increasingly full of them. I exchanged looks with the both of them, then raised an eyebrow indicating for Thomas to continue, as Dottie and I both prepared smokes.

"I take it you already knew that then?" Thomas asked hesitantly.

"I didn't. Just not particularly surprised that the third Marlowe met the same fate as the other two," I said through a cigarette, holding a flame to its end.

"Well… not exactly the same fate." Thomas leaned forward. "Lester was murdered. By 'The Shredder'." He waited for a sign of recognition from me and I didn't give him one so he elaborated. "The Shredder was The Blight's number one man when it came to making people disappear."

That warranted a look. I was aware of The Blight, just as every citizen in Glasspier was. Vaguely, but enough to know that they were the biggest players in the world of organized crime in the city. Their involvement in this case, if true, was a concerning one.

"And how exactly did you find this out?" I questioned evenly.

"I have other friends than you two, you know."

I leaned forward and my cigarette smoldered, forgotten in my hand.

"Well, did this mysterious *friend* of yours happen to tell you anything else? Such as, when it happened? Or where it happened? Or even better- *why* it happened?"

"I'm afraid I don't have the answer to any of those," he confessed, "but I do know something else – The Shredder doesn't go by that title anymore and instead uses his real name: Silas Stevenson. He's working for Thomas Glasspier as head of his security detail as we speak." Thomas leaned back and let Dottie and I take that in.

Thomas Glasspier? This 'Shredder' that was supposedly the greatest hitman in Glasspier, was now working for the big man himself? Was he working for him, or for The Blight when he killed Lester? Was he Charlotte and Jake's killer? I didn't ask Thomas any of these questions. Instead, I wanted to know the reliability of his information.

"Just how trustworthy a source is this friend of yours? Do they have any proof?"

"I believe him. He had no reason to lie," Thomas stated simply.

Okey, so no real proof, just the good word of someone I'd never met. Dottie had been silently toying with the ring around her neck throughout Thomas' revelations and I looked to her.

"Any chance what you found will cast some light on any of this?"

She let the ring drop back against her chest. "I don't know. But I've got a date with someone who might," she said, with cryptic eyes flashing.

"A date?"

"Of sorts. More like a rendezvous. He's not really my type after all, but I'm sure his. He's a dirty cop, not sure just how dirty yet – but there's a good chance he's in bed with The Blight." She paused for a second, then grinned. "He certainly wants to be in bed with me. Particularly, in Mr. Henry Wakeman's master bed at twenty-three Willow Avenue tonight." She put the remains of her cigarette out on the tray next to her with a bit more force than usual.

"Henry Wakeman, the baseball star?" Thomas asked incredulously, beating me to the punch.

"That's the one." Dottie nodded. "As Officer Downs so helpfully informed me last night. Apparently he's acting security guard at the Wakeman house while the detectives get what evidence they can."

"And you think he might know something about the Marlowes?"

It seemed like a stretch, but I was already intrigued by the notion that the Wakeman case, the 'Foxglove Killer', and the Marlowes might all be connected somehow.

"I don't know if it's related..." Dottie admitted. "But Downs seems to be involved in the happenings at some level and maybe there's a reason this Marlowe case re-surfaced when it did, amongst all the other madness of the city as of late," she offered, echoing my thoughts.

I blew a fan of smoke and it floated above us in a jumbled gray cloud. This was the best lead I had – other than going after Silas, but I didn't need Thomas to tell me that that road likely ended up in a gutter somewhere. I sighed and put my cigarette out. Dottie waited expectantly.

"So, what happens when you go over for this... 'date' tonight?

She shrugged. "Downs either tells us everything he knows, or we ruin his life. Maybe both if he doesn't behave," she said, with a look more malicious and venomous than I'd ever seen grace her features.

I parked half a block down from the Wake house amidst a smothering fog. Dottie stepped out of the passenger's seat, adjusting yet another fitted red dress as she did so. Thomas moved to the front seat and I passed him my binoculars.

"Keep an eye on the place and if things go to hell, act in your best judgment." I said, reaching over to pull my little Mercury II handheld camera from the glove box to stow it in my overcoat. "And if any extra coppers come by, do whatever you can to alert us or keep them busy."

I'd disliked lugging around my SCR 'walkie-talkie' during the war, but found myself wishing we had a pair right about now. Dottie was already halfway up the street, swaying through the mist and approaching a figure I could barely make out, standing beneath the looming spires of the Wakeman manor. Willow Avenue was older money and surrounded us on both sides with large Victorians and lawns that looked like they were worth more than my entire agency.

Slumped low in the front seats, Thomas and I watched the officer usher Dottie inside by the waist and close the door. A dim light flicked on in the window and the curtains were pulled shut seconds later. I stepped out of the car.

“I’d wish you luck, but I know you don’t believe in it,” Thomas whispered.

“I appreciate the sentiment, considering you don’t either.”

I shut the door quietly and slunk towards the Wake house, doing my best to avoid street lamps – not that they would betray much to a casual observer through the thick shroud of fog. I noiselessly trod across the now slightly overgrown lawn and past planters with an assortment of flowers along the left side of the house. I could hear nothing from within and hoped that went both ways. Then, for the second time in less than a week I found myself at the back of a stranger’s house, poised to trespass.

The large Victorian was a pinkish color on the exterior and had a steep, sloping roof that ended on one side in a tower whose peak was lost in the fog. In the rear where I stood, there was a spiraling metal staircase that led both down to the basement and up to the second floor. Hoping that Dottie and her friend had stuck to the main level for the time being, I pulled on a thin pair of leather driving gloves and climbed upwards. I always set out with intent to work a case by the books and then just days later I’d be doing something like this. But it didn’t matter. I had to get inside for Dottie’s safety. In this city, cops kill the innocent with the same cavalier that they kill the guilty – and with the same lack of discipline. I didn’t like the idea of Dottie getting on the GPPD’s bad side.

The staircase ended in a small, glass enclosed balcony jutting off the rear facade with a door that led into the house itself. I tried it. Locked. I cursed under my breath and drew a lockpick set from the inner pocket of my coat. I’d expected this, but was still spoiled from climbing through broken windows. After a couple tense minutes of debate with the locks' tumblers, I finally got them to see my way and the door swung silently open.

Now that I was inside, I could hear the soft murmur of two voices rising up the grand, dark-wood staircase that ran from where I stood, down to the front entryway. There were three doors on each side of the staircase on the level at which I stood and I moved quickly to the first on my left. It too swung open quietly and I said a silent prayer of thanks to whichever housekeeper had kept up with its oiling. I found myself in what appeared to be a guest bedroom. It had minimal furnishings, just a simple white-sheeted bed, a dark highboy dresser, and a few potted plants for decor. I wasn't sure exactly what, if anything I was looking for, but I opened a few drawers on the highboy and found them empty.

Back in the hall I tried the next door, revealing what appeared to be a study. The room was lined on both sides with large bookshelves, chock-full. It was a good thing Thomas wasn't here, I'd never have been able to pull him away. There was a desk with a built-in lamp at the far end of the room which I walked towards, the wooden floor creaking in protest a bit louder than I would have liked it to. I glanced over the books on each side as I passed them, seeing a wide and seemingly random collection. The shelves included titles on birds, gardening, aviation, astronomy, plants, and some classics.

A black pen and two picture frames sat atop the large desk. The one on the left featured Henry Wakeman standing in flight gear in front of a small prop plane on a runway. He still had his hair undercut from his time in the services and a winning smile that I recognized, even as someone who didn't keep up with The World Series. The right, pictured him and Barbara dressed in finery on their wedding day. I picked both up and found no further information on the backsides, so I replaced them on the desk. It was around then that I heard the sound of footsteps ascending the grand staircase.

Chapter 9 - Pretense

Dottie

'Showtime,' I whispered to myself, with only a little bit of smugness. This time Thomas was the one left behind and I was in the limelight. I walked through the low-lying fog with a confidence less false than usual, ready to finally prove some worth. Sure enough, Officer Downs was posted on the front porch, this time in uniform. I emerged from the mist into the area illuminated by porch-lamp light like a crimson specter, although the way Downs looked at me made me feel more like a cut of red meat.

"Shall we?" I flashed him a warm smile and he pulled his eyes away reluctantly to unlock the large front door of the Wakeman manor.

"We shall," he said, smiling in return, the polite words sounding foreign and forced coming from his mouth.

Replacing the keys back onto his belt, Downs took me by the waist and led me across the foyer. On the way in I pretended to be in awe of the beautiful woodwork of the porch and the flowers that ran in raised beds alongside it. I made sure not to overdo it, after all, the pretense of being here to appreciate the house was a thin one at best.

Inside, a wide staircase ran up the middle to the second floor and the entryway was unadorned, save for the high ceiling and walls being gilded with floral crown-molding. As I was taking stock of the place, Downs had hung his overcoat and taken a handful of the thick, frilly curtains in the bay window of the sitting room to our right and was pulling them closed. What little light that had been coming in from the porch outside was now cut off, leaving us in the dim glow emanating from a few brass lamps scattered about the house on carved wooden end tables. The pretense slipped further.

I joined him in the sitting room and decided to take up residence on the gold-backed, red velvet chaise lounge that sat austere in the corner of the room. It only seemed right. Officer Downs remained standing and was lighting up a smoke. The now revealed service pistol on his belt caught a gleam in the light from a nearby lamp and a small lump of fear attempted to find itself caught in my throat, but I willed it away by talking.

"My, if this is how grand the sitting room is, I just can't wait to see the rest of the house. It's so nice of you to show me," I gushed.

"Yes, yes it is quite nice isn't it?" he said, somewhat absentmindedly, taking a long drag from his cigarette and exhaling it. "What's even nicer is the fact that the contents of the liquor cabinet weren't removed for evidence… suppose we could have a drink or two without Mr. Wakeman noticing?" he asked, already moving through the open doorway across from me to where I assumed the kitchen was. "If he ever even comes back *to* notice…" he added under his breath.

I said nothing. I kicked my heels off, and laid across the lounge for Downs' benefit upon his return. In doing so, I wanted to make it clear I was comfortable here for the moment in an effort to give Leon more time. I also lit a cigarette in his absence to soothe my nerves.

"There's only hard liquor I'm afraid," Downs called from the other room. "Don't see any wine… maybe there's a cellar?"

"Whisky is fine," I called back, projecting my voice as I would on stage, while keeping a drawling, airiness to it.

Downs returned with two glasses and once again glanced me up and down in a way that I'm sure he thought was discrete. "First smoking, now drinking whisky?" he tutted in disapproval, but still handed me the glass. "Someone needs to teach you how to behave like a lady."

"I think you'll find me to be plenty lady-like when it counts," I smirked in response, while internally my stomach was tying itself into a knot to rival the intricacy of the frills on the curtain beside me. I'm sure Downs didn't care what kind of alcohol I was drinking, ladylike or not, as long as it served to remove inhibitions.

"They left the whisky," I said, taking a sip to drive the statement home, "so what *did* they take for evidence?"

"Not my place to say I'm afraid."

I pouted. "Oh come on, surely there's *something* you can tell me."

He took a drink and then looked to the ceiling in thought, scratching the stubble on his chin as he did.

I continued to press him. "Well, if you can't tell me about the evidence, maybe you could tell me if you have any leads? You don't think the foxglove killer could have got them, do you?" I whispered, wide-eyed.

He met my eyes briefly, before taking another drink and turning away to pace the large sitting room. "I dunno who's responsible for the Wakemans' disappearance yet, but I know that whoever it is, we're close on their tail," he said, walking with his back towards me to peer through the small gap in the curtains. "Maybe no one is responsible. Maybe they both got sick of the weather in Glasspier and decided Florida sounded nice." He paced back in front of the lounge and didn't meet my eyes. "And if this *foxglove killer* is responsible... we'll have him soon I'm sure," he stated with some finality, picking up a small blue crystal orb from its stand on the center coffee table and studying it.

I sensed he wasn't telling the whole truth. He couldn't keep his eyes off me and now the walls and decor were suddenly fascinating? He placed the crystal back onto its bronze stand, taking another drink from his glass and smiling at me. The smile didn't seem to reach his eyes.

"That's enough about my work. I want to know more about you," he said, slowly turning to face me fully again. "For example, how about you tell me who drove you here tonight? Or, even better – why they're still sitting out there in the fog with binoculars?"

Shit "I…I don't know what you mean? I drove myself." I tried to sound confused and innocent, but the hitch in my voice didn't help me sell it. Or maybe it did. I was too shocked to tell.

His expression hardened further. "Oh, so you have two different cars then? And the man sitting in the one you drove tonight, spying on us, just got there by accident?" he snarled in a low voice.

I felt my face flush in anger at the plan going sideways and sat up to face him, dropping my guise and demeanor altogether. Maybe I could save this still with another lie.

"Look, I just wanted to know what was going on with the Wakeman case. I'm a big fan of the Comets and I was just worried about him," I explained, doing my best to sound genuine, "my friend in the car is just to make sure I stay safe."

"Maybe you should have had him come in with you then," he laughed softly, fury in his eyes, drawing his pistol and leveling it at my head.

I drew in a sharp breath, heart lurching into my throat as I stared into the barrel of a loaded revolver.

"Don't make a sound," he seethed quietly, "or I'll have to do both you and your friend out there and I don't really want to have to call my buddy in to help me get blood out of this velvet chaise."

My thoughts raced; I didn't dare scream. Something about the malevolent glint in Downs' eyes made me think he might actually pull the trigger. Staring down the glistening steel made me abandon any thoughts of coming out on top of this exchange and I thought only of self-preservation. Desperately, I tried to think of the right words to say but my head felt foggier than the streets outside those damned frilly curtains.

Downs continued, "I should have known it was too good to be true. 'Love a man in uniform'?" he laughed sourly, his features looking manic, as the gun pointed unwaveringly on. "I'm sure you do – as long as it's a baseball uniform that is." He paused and appeared to be in thought momentarily before making up his mind. "You see, I stayed here late after work to get something – and I intend to get it," his eyes gleamed, "regardless of how we go about it, I *will* get what I want." He flicked the revolver in the direction of the stairs. "Get up."

The stairs…? I thought dully, yes, the stairs! There was a chance Leon was up there. I set my teeth and hoped he hadn't searched the basement first as I rose slowly from the lounge.

I walked up the stairs numbly, with Downs behind, pushing his revolver into the small of my back. Would Leon be there? Had he even made it inside? The top of the steps came too quickly, despite my intentional slow pace and I turned my head back to look at Downs. He jerked his head to the right. I could have sworn the nose of his pistol was a thousand degrees, I could feel it burning a hole into the exposed skin of my back. We walked down the hallway to the final door.

"Open it."

I obliged, hand shaking from fear and adrenaline. Inside was the master bedroom. To my right, I was vaguely aware of a large vanity and to the left was a gold trimmed room partition near a closed door. I barely had time to take in the scenery in my haze, when Downs prodded me forward towards the massive bed fitted neatly with white and gold linens.

I turned slowly to face him, every nerve in my body screaming to fight back, but his finger wrapped around the trigger of the gun dissuaded any notion of doing so. I stood still in terror and indecision, when Downs abruptly reached forward with his free hand and shoved forcefully upon my collarbone, throwing me back onto the large bed. I curled up, turning my head to the side to stare at the wall. I couldn't bear another second of Downs' leering, grotesque face.

"Don't scream. Don't make a sound. I don't want to have to do anything drastic, but I'm afraid you've gotten in over your head."

His threat was followed up by three clicks, in quick succession. The first: his belt buckle clasp being undone. The second – moments later: a click and pop of a camera shutter. Lastly, the third and softest, but carrying the most weight: the click of the hammer on Leon McCreary's *.45* being cocked back.

"Don't scream. Don't make a sound. I don't want to have to do anything drastic," said the low and familiar voice of my friend Leon, from behind Officer Downs. He had his automatic pushed against the back of Downs' head.

I saw for the first time a small flash of fear cross Downs' face, but it was quickly replaced by hatred. "*You fucking whore!*" he seethed.

"Set the gun down slow," Leon ordered.

For a second no one moved, Downs still had his finger curled around the trigger, face screwed up in anger. Then, slowly, he bent down and placed the revolver on the floor at the foot of the bed. Leon reached forward and picked it up, slipping it into his pocket while ordering Downs to put his hands behind his head. He complied as I sat up and got off the bed, walking over to stand beside Leon. I realized I was shaking, coming down from the adrenaline, and Leon steadied me with his free arm.

"Here's what's going to happen. You're going to keep facing that way, and you're going to answer our questions as honestly as a nun at confessional. If you don't, or either of us think that you're lying – I'm sure your family and your chief would be very interested to see what develops on this camera in my pocket."

"And if I tell them that you held an officer of the law at gunpoint and set up this scene to blackmail me? Who do you think they're going to believe?" Downs retorted.

"Maybe you're right. There is another option though," Leon said, pressing the gun into Downs' ribs, "so what will it be? Your information, your career, or your life?"

I knew Leon and he wasn't a cold-hearted killer, so he had to be bluffing. The steel in his voice was doing a good job of convincing even me though, that he would not hesitate in pulling the trigger. Downs fell silent.

"Right then. Do you know the Marlowes? Lester, Charlotte or Jake?"

"Marlowes? Never heard of 'em."

He sounded genuinely confused to me, but Leon pressed on.

"So there's no connection to a Lester, Charlotte, or Jake Marlowe in regards to the Wakeman disappearance?"

“None that I know of, but I’m just in charge of security at the house. They don’t tell me much.”

I frowned. I *knew* that Downs was probably just some beat cop playing at being an oh-so-important police detective, but I had hoped he’d know *something* worthwhile for all this trouble. Then I remembered something. I spoke up, doing my best to stop my voice from shaking, “What about the airfield? What’s going on there?”

In my peripheral vision I saw Leon look sidelong at me. Downs tensed up slightly and stood in silence. I jerked my head towards Downs and motioned to Leon at his pistol. He got the idea and pushed it harder into Downs' back.

“Answer her,” Leon snarled and Downs made a pathetic whimpering sound from the iron prodding into his back.

I found myself sickly happy to hear the fear in him. I was also happy to call Leon a friend rather than an enemy. He could be surprisingly malevolent when he wanted to be and it was a side of him I wasn’t used to.

Leon clenched his free hand around the back of Downs neck and shook him a bit. “We don’t have all night! What’s going on at the airfield?”

“O-okay, okay!” he cried, and Leon let up. “The Blight paid off the force to stay away from the airfield ‘till tomorrow. I think they’re doing some kind of job there tonight and from what my buddy said, it sounds like it might have to do with the Wakeman case.”

“Hangar eight, right?” I spoke up again.

“Yes, yes, hangar eight. That’s all I know, I swear,” he pleaded.

Leon looked at me again, eyes narrowed. I stared back and the message was clear: ‘I’ll explain later’.

Leon delivered instructions to Downs, calm and smooth, “You’re going to stay here, facing away from us. We’re going to leave and you’re not going to follow. If I get wind that you’re attempting to follow, your wife and kids finding out that you’re a cheating bastard will be the least of your worries. Same goes for if you tell anyone about what happened here tonight.”

Downs nodded and Leon began to walk backwards towards the door. I followed.

“I’ll leave your weapon in the mailbox,” Leon added, as we left the room.

Downstairs, I grabbed my heels from beside the lounge, shuddering as I retraced the steps I’d taken earlier. Leon pulled a cloth from the seemingly endless pockets of his trench coat and wiped off any surface I thought I may have touched, then we were out of the house. It seemed the fog outside had gotten even thicker and I could no longer make out Leon’s car down the street. I headed in the direction I knew it to be, while I heard the metallic scrape of Leon opening the Wakeman mailbox to make a deposit.

I got into the back of the black sedan where Thomas was waiting, his binoculars having been rendered useless. Leon followed seconds later, climbing quickly behind the wheel.

“Have fun gallivanting around without me?” Thomas asked, sounding a touch bitter.

I didn’t respond and neither did Leon. Instead, he threw the car into reverse and backed down the street away from the house. “Don’t want him to see my plate if we passed by the front.” Leon grunted at Thomas’ curious stare, who seemed to finally grasp the air of tension in the car and went quiet.

Leon drove well clear of where the Wake house had disappeared into the fog, but didn’t seem to be heading the direction back to the agency. I just wanted to go home. I wanted to lock my door and tell Angelo what’d happened. I wanted to hear somebody, anybody, tell me it was going to be alright. I wanted to hear them say that I wouldn’t see Downs’ crooked, leering face waiting for me outside of some bar, ready to point another gun at me. *I had a loaded gun held to me*. A loaded gun. If Leon hadn’t been there… I shuddered again, thinking about what Downs would have done. A silent, choked sob escaped my throat and I felt tears well up in my eyes as I stared out the window, streaked with condensation. We hurtled on, beneath a blurry mosaic of streetlamps, into the unending fog.

Chapter 10 - Hangar 8

Leon

On our way through the murky streets towards the airfield, I swore we passed a parked blue coupe; similar in appearance to the one that had tailed me the other day. Though, it was hard to make out anything in the fog and maybe I was just being paranoid. The encounter with Downs had left a bad taste in my mouth. I didn't like getting that tangled up with the law and I disliked even more how much danger Dottie had been put into. I shook off the thoughts of what might've happened had something gone wrong, as the lights on the main control tower at the airfield came into view through the dense fog.

The more pressing concern now, was whether or not getting mixed up with The Blight and the Wakeman disappearance was a good idea. At the very least, after tonight I could hopefully put to rest whether or not the Wakemans were related to my case. It was with that weakly optimistic thought, that I pulled the car over a block from the fence surrounding the Glasspier Airfield and killed the engine.

"Mind filling me in as to what we're doing here?" Thomas asked.

"Our… *friend* at the house claimed that something related to the Wakeman disappearance was going on here tonight. I intend to find out what."

"So you still think the Wakemans might have something to do with your case?"

"Maybe. Regardless, it's the only real lead we've got other than Silas." I looked over at Thomas and back at Dottie, who hadn't said anything since we'd left the house and decided to remind them that neither had any obligation to me. "Now, I can't expect you two to put your lives on the line for this case any more than you already have. Downs said The Blight might be involved here, so there could be more at stake than just a trespassing charge, but if you want to come with, I'd appreciate the backup… it's up to you though. No shame in waiting in the car."

Thomas spoke up with hardly a seconds' thought, "Of course I'll come with. I can't let you go in alone, and besides, it's about time we broke into someplace together. It's been almost a week."

I nodded gravely. I appreciated Thomas' unwavering support.

A few moments later Dottie piped up from the backseat, "I-I'll come too," she said, sounding like she was gathering some resolve, then added softly, "I don't want to be alone…"

"Are you sure?"

"Yes. I'm sure." She opened her door and stepped out of the car.

Thomas and I did the same and were greeted again with the chill of the fog that laid heavy over the city. The three of us walked in the direction of the airfield, which could only be discerned by the red-flashing light atop the control tower occasionally seen amidst the gloom. Somewhere, far off, I heard a police siren wailing into the foggy night, but it sounded like it was heading east; away from us. Before long, the chain-link fence that wrapped around the airfield materialized in front of us from out of the haze.

"I'll go over first," I offered, "then Thomas, you can boost Dottie over to me and come over yourself."

I grabbed hold of the chain link and hoisted myself over easily. Then came Dottie, with Thomas providing a boost from the other side despite her protests that she didn't need any help. I lowered her down carefully to avoid her dress snagging on the sharp top part of the fence. Lastly, Thomas clambered over and the three of us stared into the murk that lay ahead. The main office building and the larger commercial hangars seemed to be nearest to us.

"The smaller, numbered hangars must be 'round the back, on the other side of the tarmac," I whispered to the others.

They offered no response and the three of us ghosted through the mist, heads low, in the direction of the control tower. From what I could see in the haze, the airfield was deserted. I wondered vaguely what time it was, but didn't dare turn on my flashlight to check my watch. I had to guess it was around 22:00. The wane moon occasionally broke between the clouds and filtered through the fog, offering a little guidance in the blackness of the airfield and eventually we made our way to the base of the control tower.

"Look," Thomas whispered, pointing, "those must be the numbered hangars."

Sure enough, on the other side of the tarmac I could make out a row of structures smaller than the main buildings behind us, but still large enough to house a light aircraft. It seemed we were across from the middle of the row, with buildings continuing in either direction to the left and right.

"Which one is hangar eight?" Dottie whispered.

Thomas made to walk forward across the tarmac. "One way to find out."

I grabbed his jacket and held him back. "Wait. Remember, The Blight could have people here. We go when the moon is fully shadowed."

"Right…"

I looked up at the crescent moon as we waited in taut anticipation and eventually its light was snuffed out by a cloud too dark to make out against the night sky. We slunk low across the airstrip under cover of fog and darkness until we reached the nearest building. Thomas was about to speak up but I hushed him, waiting with strained ears to hear any sign that we'd been seen. None came. The silence continued across the field, with only the distant sounds of downtown as a backdrop.

I couldn't make out a number on the building in the darkness, so I waited until the moon reappeared and cast its pale glow onto the face of the building.

"Hangar ten."

"Any idea which direction is higher or lower?" Thomas whispered back.

"If we think of the main control buildings as the front and read left to right, then lower numbers should run that way," I reasoned, pointing further down the strip.

"Worth a shot." Thomas shrugged.

"Either way, we're close to eight, so stay alert."

Dottie remained quiet, looking around often and holding the ring on her necklace like a protective talisman. I led the way towards the next closest building without waiting for the moon to be obscured. I figured the fog and the deep shadows between the hangars would be enough to keep eyes off us here. We reached the next building in line without any noticeable sign of discovery.

"Hangar nine," Thomas whispered.

"Let's go 'round the back," I decided, "I want to see if there's another way in besides barging through the front door on the tarmac side."

We crept along the side of hangar nine, between it and number eight. I still heard nothing from the supposed hangar of interest. Around the back of the building, I saw that we'd reached the chain link fence on the opposite side of the airfield and that there was a door for a rear entrance into number nine. The three hangars we'd seen all looked identical, so I reasoned that there would be a back entrance for number eight as well.

This time I waited for the gap in the cloud cover to close around the moon again, before we stole across the last gap between hangars. Hangar eight did have a back door, so I tried it and unsurprisingly found it locked.

"Watch my back," I said to Dottie and Thomas, pulling out my lockpicks for the second time that night and kneeling down to get to work. This lock was a bit more stubborn than the one at the Wake house, but with my prior practice earlier and another well-crafted argument, I also got this one to come around. The lock clicked and the door swung open with a soft metallic creak, revealing a pitch-dark interior. None of us breathed, we all listened intently for any sign of life inside, but heard nothing.

I stowed the lock picking kit back into my coat and drew both my flashlight and my pistol. To my surprise, Thomas also drew a handgun out from a holster concealed somewhere along his waist. I figured he had an iron or two, given his military background, but never knew he carried one. Dottie just stood behind me, watching our six o'clock.

I clicked the flashlight on. We appeared to be in a small office, walled off from the main bay of the hangar. Illuminated beyond us through the office windows with a dull gleam, was the tail of a small personal aircraft. It was silver and had faded red pinstriping along the sides. The office area had a long desk and several metal filing cabinets. Thomas had already begun carefully rifling through some of the files.

“Wipe your prints,” I urged Thomas in a low whisper, “if this isn’t a crime scene already, it sure could be by the end of the night.”

We searched the office efficiently but found nothing of real interest. Mostly just flight logs and aircraft maintenance books. I eased open the door to the main bay where the plane was. It opened silently and there was an immediate notable difference in the air quality of the hangar. I raised the crook of my arm to my mouth and nose, fearing some kind of chemical or gas leak. Dottie and Thomas seemed to notice it too and recoiled. After a moment, I realized it didn’t smell like any chemical I knew, rather, it was a scent I’d become familiar with overseas. Death. Something, or someone, was rotting.

I advanced through the doorway, forward to the left-hand side of the plane and ran a gloved finger across its wing. It had a moderate film of dust, but the ground within the hangar was dirt and even my footsteps kicked up small clouds into the stagnant air. The air within the hangar became more pungent the closer I got to the front of the plane and I braced myself for what I might find. I heard Thomas and Dottie following close behind me so I stopped to prepare them.

"I think someone, or something, has died in here," I warned, "wait here if that's not something you want to see."

Dottie was pale, but said nothing. Thomas looked defiant.

"I'll be alright," he said, resolutely, "nothing I haven't seen before."

That was new to me too. As far as I knew he'd just been stationed on a ship that'd never seen combat. That wasn't important now though, so I pushed it from my mind and focused on the details of the present. As I stepped around the wing, I began to notice a faint humming sound. Upon approaching the nose of the plane, it became clear that it was the buzzing of flies. The smell became nearly unbearable and the beam of my flashlight showed a black trail in the dirt floor that ended in a slumped mass.

A body. Face down, beneath the propeller blades of the small plane. As we got closer to stand before the corpse, I heard Dottie gag behind me and Thomas stood beside me in evident discomfort. I wasn't feeling all too comfortable myself. I felt a gnawing itch in the back of my subconscious and did my best not to scratch it, trying to force the memories of the war out of my thoughts.

"Male. Late twenties at least judging by the graying hair, probably older," I stated to nobody in particular. There was a large pool of dried blood around the victim's head and it was black now. Blackened blood on the snow, and the golden stag. No. Not now. I forced myself to be present. I looked up, mainly to avoid staring at the body any longer, but noticed the same dried substance on the planes' propeller. An accident? Or a coverup. I looked for marks in the dirt around the body. There were some. Had the body been dragged? Or had someone else visited the scene before us? I wanted to look for footprints but Thomas interrupted my thoughts.

"Should we see who it is?" he whispered in a hollow voice.

I wasn't looking forward to turning the body over. There was no evidence of damage to the back of the skull, so I imagined his face had to be in bad shape. There was no avoiding it though. Could this be Mr. Wakeman? We had to know. I braced myself and used my foot to roll the body over onto its back.

Instead of a face, a pulpy caved in mush of shattered bone, brain matter, and black dried blood stared up at me. Flies buzzed and swarmed from where the eyes should have been, angry at their feast being disturbed.

I could feel the insects. They were in my brain too. My chest tightened. 'Blood. Golden stag'. The stag. I buzzed. Flashes of white and red, a knife wound, the kids in Poland. Safe. They were safe because of me. Yes. NO. I was a killer, Leon McCreary, a killer. *Leon Bauer*, dead. Dead. The German soldier dead. Because of me. Because of me. Taste of blood, that stag… I can taste it again. It was a stag! It was a stag……… "stuck, stuck in my teeth," I said. It's stuck in my teeth. Flashes of red and white, flashes of gunfire, the flash of a knife. I had to. Antlers. They're liars, I would never. The nurse is wrong. They lie, I had to! It was a stag. so hungry. Knife in my gut. Bleeding. Soviet Forest. Golden stag in the moonlight. No choice,

The STAG
THE STAG. proud golden beast Thomas,
I had too!
THE STAG
In my teeth
white and red
Dottie-

I HAD too-
They're coming! engines –need me!

IT WAS A STAG–

Chapter 11 - Fog and Thunder

Thomas

"-Leon?"

My friend had gone stock still after revealing the mangled face on the body that lay before us.

"Th-the stag…" Leon gasped, his lips barely moving.

"Stag? What are you talking about? Are you ok?"

Dottie stepped forward from behind me and placed a hand on his shoulder. Even in the dim glow from the flashlight that hung forgotten at Leon's side I could see lines of fear scrawled across her face like a topographic map. The stench was beginning to become unbearable and over the buzzing of flies, I recognized a second humming – no, keening sound from outside of the hangar. Dottie pulled gently at Leons overcoat.

"C'mon Leon, we've got to go," she pleaded.

He didn't budge, but instead stared forward with glossy eyes and mumbled something about teeth. The same feeling of fear that'd taken me in that village in the Congo once again crept its way into my veins. I'd seen a man during my time in the Navy behave in a similar way and I knew what experience he and Leon both shared in common. Bloodshed.

While Dottie continued a more desperate attempt at getting Leon to snap out of it, I rushed around the airplane's wing, over to the door to the office we'd come from. I pulled the handle. *Shit.* It'd locked behind us. The keening of what I was now sure was an engine became louder outside as I ran back over to Dottie. My breath caught again from the stench as I neared the body, which Dottie was now slowly leading Leon away from.

She looked up at me. "We need to go. Now."

"We'll have to go out the front," I gasped through the miasma, retrieving Leon's pistol from where it'd fallen from his now limp hand. The same hand that Dottie now led him by towards the front door of the hangar.

"In my teeth…" Leon groaned in protest.

I moved in front of the pair of them and held my pistol at the ready. The hum of the engine was only getting louder and sounded to be heading our way. Dottie thankfully had the sense to take the flashlight from Leon and shut it off as I pushed the door open outwards into the fresh night air.

We spilled out of the hangar onto the tarmac, trying to be discreet, but Leon's uncooperation made it difficult. I stared down the length of the runway and saw a pair of headlights flickering through the fog like will-o'-the-wisps in some long-forgotten fen. I turned on my heel to lead an escape in the opposite direction, but another pair of headlights attached to a black sedan emerged from the fog and screeched to a stop only a handful of feet from us.

The car sat still, enshrouded by the mist swirling about its frame and dancing in the headlights like a ghost ship. Dottie was trying to pull Leon into the alleyway between hangars eight and nine, but he seemed to be content to stand on the runway and stare into the darkness across the airfield. I leveled my pistol at the windshield of the sedan.

Summoning forth as commanding a voice as I could muster: "Step out of the vehicle with your hands up!" I shouted.

"Thomas!" exclaimed Dottie from behind me, to which I turned and saw that the headlights from the other direction had split and become two. Motorcycles. They too stopped a few feet from us, their riders dismounting. I pulled Dottie close and pressed Leon's automatic into her small hands.

"In case we can't talk our way out of this," I murmured, to which she nodded white-faced and wide-eyed.

With a creak of steel, the doors on the sedan unfurled outwards, bat-like in the fog, and two men in long coats emerged. I noticed quickly the oblong shapes that each of them carried – tommy guns. I swiveled my head back and forth between where unknown figures advanced on either side and saw that the men from the motorbikes had pistols drawn.

So there we stood, illuminated between headlights, surrounded and sweltering on the tarmac despite the cool night air. I had an aversion to flying and always assumed I'd go down at sea, if age didn't catch me first. Ironic, that now it seemed I was going to die on an airstrip. But maybe there was a way out. They didn't seem to be cops and given what Leon had mentioned earlier, along with our imminent demise, I figured a gamble was worth the risk.

"I'm a friend of The Blight! Please! Stand down! I'm with The Blight!" I shouted above the idling engines, desperately digging into my pockets in search of my coin. Finally, I found its familiar, cool surface and held it before me as an aegis towards the men. I felt Dottie, who was now pressed back-to-back with me, exhale a sharp breath of surprise. Leon stood nearby and stared unwaveringly on, mumbling something that was lost to the night.

The biker on the left, who was bald and wore a loose-fitting black bomber jacket broke the silence, "Friend of The Blight huh? Well, a friend is just that. A friend. And friendships can be broken," he said, leering with a gold tooth glimmering in the light from the car across from him. He squinted at the coin, then slowly raised his pistol at my head, "Too bad ya' only 'ave got a silver one, and too bad we're on strict orders not ta' let anyone come or-"

His sentence was cut short by a sharp boom like violent thunder and died on his lips; his body lurched back equally violently and sprawled across the pavement. His pistol clattered to the ground and for a static-charged moment, no one moved. Then all at once the airstrip was a flurry of action, I raised my gun and took aim at the second biker who also took aim at me. Leon dove to the ground for cover and Dottie turned to raise Leon's pistol toward the tommy gunners. All at once the strip was electric with the crackle and pop of gunfire. Lighting in the fog. The biker and I both fired – he fell, and amidst the din I became dully aware that my shoulder was bleeding. The distinct rattle of the two tommy guns began behind me but they were snuffed out as quickly as they'd started by a second thunderous boom that I was certain was a fifty-caliber rifle and the sharper pops of what I assumed was Leon's automatic in Dottie's hands.

The concussive crackling ceased and the airfield was quiet once again, save for the idle hum of cars now without masters and the ringing in my ears. Gun-smoke melded with the fog and my left shoulder ached and dripped down my arm. Leon jumped quickly to his feet looking disoriented, while Dottie stood staring at the bodies of the two men lying beside the car.

"What the hell… how did we…" Leon rubbed his head in confusion.

"Explain later," I said, realizing that the locust coin was still clenched in my bloodied hand and pocketing it. I ripped the lower portion of my left sleeve off and tied it tightly around where the bullet had nicked my shoulder. The wound wasn't deep, but still sent rivulets of blood down my arm and threatened to become a problem if allowed to bleed unchecked. I approached Dottie and took Leon's gun gently from her hand, where she was letting it hang at her side. She tore her eyes away from the two bodies and I saw that her cheeks were tear streaked.

"Let's go. I want to go home," she said softly, turning her face away from me.

I just nodded and turned to Leon, ready to get clear from the scene before anybody else showed up, but I noticed some movement behind him. The man that had tried to shoot me, no, *did* shoot me (the pain in my shoulder reminded me so), was crawling towards his motorcycle. I walked over and placed myself between him and his bike.

"I don't think you're fit to ride my friend, so how about this: you tell me who hired you and why – and I'll do my best to make sure that you get off this airstrip alive."

The man looked up at me with desperate eyes, "I-I don't know much-" he gasped, evidently struggling to force the words out, "orders came from higher up, someone called in and wanted us to clean a crime scene… and keep the coppers away…"

Judging by the chest wound he'd sustained and the rate at which it was bleeding, I doubted getting him to a hospital would make a difference. It would also be highly difficult to explain and would tie us to the crime scene; so as much as I disliked incivility and dishonesty – the decision was easy. I reached down and pulled the key from the ignition of the bike.

"Sorry, truly am."

"No! You can't leave me here!" he coughed, flecks of blood spattering across my recently polished oxfords.

I sighed and tossed the key as far as I could into the darkness between the hangars.

Leon, who'd watched this all take place, finally seemed to be piecing together the situation and began to take charge again. "Back to the car. C'mon," he ordered and took Dottie by the arm.

The three of us stumbled back through the mist, leaving the grisly scene on the runway behind. As we passed near the control building, I heard a car roar to life and a pair of red taillights pierced through the fog at the base of the tower.

"There goes our guardian angel," I whispered, as a blue coupe roared down the airstrip and disappeared into the foggy night.

Leon grumbled, "Guardian angel? Or haunting specter?"

Once again, my head swam with more questions than I'd had before we'd set out for answers. All I knew right now was that my shoulder ached and I could use a stiff drink.

Chapter 12 - Stained Angel

Leon

Sept. 18th 1947
Thursday
Glasspier,

I completed my morning routine in a haze of faulty memories and missing time. Outside, the fog had lifted but my head hadn't seemed to have gotten the memo. What'd happened last night in hangar eight? I remembered turning over the body, then suddenly being amidst a firefight on the runway. But no, if I strained… there was something else. A stag and flashes of blood and snow. My mind drifted to the hospital I'd stayed at after the war, but I forced myself to stop thinking of such things and instead sat at the small desk in my room and stowed my thoughts away into my journal.

Leons Journal

September 18th, 1947 10:25

Entry #307

This city is grating on me. I think moving here was a mistake; the city is no place for a farmer's son. But the farmer's son is gone now. He died in that forest in Poland; hell, he died the minute he stepped foot in Europe. I may not be able to remember everything during those years, but I remember enough to know that that boy, Lionel Bauer, never made it back across the Atlantic. I came back in his place. A man. A soldier. A murderer: Leon McCreary.

I thought changing my name, changing my profession, changing where I lived would drown out the past. I know better now. I cannot forget the past. I cannot change the past. I cannot change the things I've done. I wouldn't change them.

Those kids in Poland are alive because of me. I have to remind myself of this every night.

I opened my bedside drawer to put the journal away, my hand lingering on the cover; tempted to flip to the first entry within. No. It was against the spirit of the journal. Write, flip the page, forget. Never revisit. I'd sworn that to myself the same day I'd sworn not to take another life. The journal slid smoothly back into its keeping place and the key familiarized itself with the lock once more.

Back in the sitting room I turned on the radio, both to further drown out the memories of the war, but also to see if there was anything on about last night's bloodbath. The spokesman's voice crackled into the agency and eventually the program made brief reference to the events at the airfield, but concluded saying that the police were withholding details until Mayor Wesson released an official statement regarding the shootout on the radio that night at 19:00. I made a mental note to tune in, then decided to also write a reminder in pen on my wrist given how untrustworthy my mind appeared to be lately.

I debated how best to proceed with the investigation and in the end, decided to give Jenny a call before making any further moves. I kept it vague and told her I had a potential lead but wanted to explore a few other options first. She told me she'd continue to pay as long as there was a chance at the case being solved – and that was that. After hanging up the receiver, I donned my usual attire of a white button up with tie, and slacks with braces.

I hesitated in putting my pistol into its holster. I held it in my hands, feeling the smooth blued-metallic finish of the slide, before ejecting the magazine. It was one bullet short in the mag and the chamber was empty. Two shots, one kill. Not bad. Dottie had taken one of the tommy-gunners, but who'd been up in that control tower? I was nearly certain that the blue coupe that'd pulled away from the airfield at the end of the night was the very same that had tailed me the other day. I topped off the pistol and chambered a round, the firm click of the slide focusing my thoughts the way only the weight of a loaded *.45* could.

I drove back west along Carmen Avenue as I had nearly a week ago on that fateful night of Jenny and Conrads arrival, with the picture of the three women riding shotgun this time instead of Conrad. I parked a few houses down the street from 201. The clouded sky meant that the daylight wasn't exactly broad, but the fog was no longer aiding in obscuring my movements, so I slipped between the houses of 201 and 199 as discreetly as I could. Around back, the broken window still invited me in, but the house felt less menacing than it had before. Maybe I was just getting too comfortable with breaking into places, or maybe it was the lack of rain and darkness.

Inside, things looked how I'd remembered them. It was dim outside and even more so within, but I recognized the kitchen area and sitting room all the same. I moved to the right, as we had last time, into the largest bedroom that Jason had taken up residence in. I inspected the room in the same way I had the others now that it wasn't occupied. Why was I here? Partly because the places I wanted to ask around about that picture didn't open until later, but also because I wasn't fully satisfied that there wasn't more to be found. Or maybe – I was just making up something to do to avoid going after Silas.

Moving into the smaller bedroom, I lit up a smoke and leaned against the wall, staring across at the first bullet hole I'd found. The room was still barren, save for some stray bits of garbage. I'd told Dottie and Thomas to come by the office Friday, giving them a day to recover from the airfield, but also to give myself one last full day of traditional investigation before coming to terms with the fact that Silas was the only lead left to chase. I didn't relish the idea of having to track down and confront the man that was once the most feared hitman in Glasspier, especially since we had no real evidence against him yet. Hell, we didn't even know if he was the one who killed Charlotte and Jake. I stamped the cigarette out on the dust covered wood floor of the room – and my foot nearly went through. The broken board I vaguely remembered from the other night had cracked in two and exposed a hole in the flooring of the room.

I knelt down and peered into the darkness beneath the house. Use of a flashlight revealed a dirt crawl space beneath the room that extended further than I could see in both directions. I felt the nearby boards and found that they easily popped loose and lifted up, allowing me better viewing down into the gloom below. The beam of my flashlight glinted off of some copper piping and illuminated the structural support beams of the house. Then, at the furthest reaches of my vision towards where I imagined the porch out back would be, I could faintly see something very small and dully red.

Could it be a tag denoting some water shutoff valve or electrical marker? Possibly. Could it also be the lynchpin piece of evidence that would blow this case wide open? Doubtful, but also possibly. I sighed and with my mind made up, attempted to squeeze into the crawlspace; but found the hole in the floor much too small for even an average sized adult such as myself. Standing back up, I reasoned that there must be an outside entrance to the crawl space for maintenance purposes, likely out back, but crawling around out there could draw unwanted attention. Instead, I began to work at prying more boards loose in order to widen the maw in the floor. The surrounding few were more resilient, but brute force got the job done.

I lowered myself beneath the house, where laying on my stomach, I began to follow the beam of light towards the red object. Pulling myself forward through the dirt with my elbows brought back not-so-fond memories of Camp Ritchie. Had I known then that crawling through mud beneath barbed wire in full kit was going to be one of my nicer memories from my time in the service… The thought faded as I reached the red object in question.

It wasn't a tag. It was a swatch of red flannel fabric, caught on an exposed nail-head. I brushed aside an old cobweb and carefully removed the material from the nail. It was roughly the size of the back of my hand – dusty and faded, with uneven edges. Had someone crawled beneath the porch and then through here on the night of the murder? Or was this just the remnant of some careless plumber? I tucked the cloth away into my now dirty overcoat and began the process of getting turned around in the confined space. I clawed my way back towards the hole in the floor and considered a slew of ideas regarding who may have left that red cloth behind. In the end, I decided I wanted a second opinion – and I knew where to get one. But first, I had to get out of this damned crawlspace.

I resurfaced into the Marlowe house and brushed as much dirt and spider web remnants off of myself as I could. Then, replacing the boards as close to how they were when I arrived, I made for the back window.

Back in my car, the engine roared to life, like it too had a newfound sense of purpose. Northwards, passing beneath the looming skyscrapers and into the more venerable buildings of downtown, I pulled off onto Jetter Street. There was a white building, now grayish with age that stood between an old bank with a sandstone facade and an insurance firm. The sign above the double doors in front read: *Trusted Eye Investigations.*

Although we were by all rights competitors, I had no bad blood with Trusted Eye and they had none with me. They'd even been known to sometimes pass a case my way when it wasn't something they wanted to expend the time and resources on. God knows there's enough cheating spouses and insurance fraud in Glasspier to support two private eye agencies.

Inside, the young blonde receptionist recognized me and we exchanged some banal niceties briefly before she ushered me up the stairs that ran to the left of the desk. I marched up the staircase as I had so many times before, running my hand along the worn-smooth wooden handrail as I went. Now wasn't the time to get sentimental. Before I knew it, I stood outside a door with frosted glass and a silver placard to the side that listed my old mentor and friend *P.I. Blaine Cruz* as its inhabitant. I knocked on the frosted pane.

"Well! Look who finally got off his ass and came down to see me," Cruz beamed, rising from behind his cluttered desk to clasp my hand in a firm handshake.

"Off *my* ass?" I raised an eyebrow at the desk and its many papers as Cruz took his seat again behind it.

Cruz glanced at the clutter with a sort of disdain, "Look, we don't all have the pleasure of running around playing cops and robbers every day."

"You know as well as anyone that it's not all pleasure, especially in regards to this case."

"Of course not," he amended, teasing, "just when Dottie's around."

Cruz's' antics were never much more advanced than a schoolboys' at heart, so I knew it best to just give him a sour look and move on. "How have you been keeping anyways? I hope they let you out for some fresh air every now and again," I grinned, gesturing around at the small office.

"Better than you by the looks of it," Cruz replied, staring at the dirt stains on the front of my coat.

"That's why I'm here actually."

"Hmph, not a very good detective if you ended up here instead of the laundromat."

I gave him a withering look. "I was just beneath the room, in the crawlspace, where the Marlowe kid was shot – found this." I pulled the red piece of fabric from my pocket and placed it on the desk in front of Cruz.

He reached for it. “So? Some plumber went home with a hole in his pants.”

That was one of the options I’d been thinking about, but was hoping Cruz might come to other conclusions and further validate a potential theory that I had brewing.

“Unless…” he examined the swatch a little closer, “you’re thinking someone might have gone in or out that way the night of the murder?”

“It crossed my mind.”

“Well, maybe to put the countless possibilities of what may have happened to rest you’ll just have to dig a little deeper,” he said, handing the cloth back to me.

“Dig a little deeper? I was already beneath the house.”

To that, Cruz just winked and pulled a box of Chesterfields from his suit-coat, leaning back in his chair. While he flicked on his lighter, the thought of what had to be done to put the most outlandish angle of my theory to rest dawned on me.

“If I end up finding what I’m looking for tonight, I’ll owe you a round or two at The Gold Pig once this is all over,” I said, stuffing the fabric piece back into my coat and making for the door.

“The Gold Pig?” Cruz snorted. “What do you take me for?”

“It’ll be like old times!” I called over my shoulder just before the door to his office fell shut and I jogged down the steps to the reception area and out of the agency.

Despite my eagerness to put my theory to the test, I knew I had to wait until nightfall. I decided to pass the time by visiting the aforementioned Gold Pig along with some other bars and similar establishments, to see if anyone happened to recognize the women in the photograph from the attic. A few hours later, all I had to show for it was a half empty tank of gas and the echoed words of the various patrons I’d talked to: ‘Sorry, but I don’t recognize them.’

I drove up the winding boulevard along the eastern side of Glasspier that ran by the port and overlooked the ocean. Towards the northern curve of the cities’ outskirts was a sign reading ‘Manor Dr.’ that marked a paved road that snaked through a grove of trees and out of sight. I didn't need the massive stone pillars topped by lanterns on either side of the path to deduce that this was the Glasspier estate – a large bronze sign read just that in filigreed script on the ornate archway above the road. Silas was back there. Or at least he probably was. I had a feeling that before all this was up, I'd need to find a way inside.

I glanced at my wrist and parked my car along the northern bend of Judson Boulevard. Wesson's public address would have started, so I tuned the radio beneath the low orange glow of the dashboard until I recognized the voice of the mayor.

"-broken into at the airfield. Glasspier Police detectives have confirmed that the body uncovered at the airfield was that of Mr. Henry Wakeman. Chief Burns assures me that his men are hard at work to uncover who was behind his murder, along with the shootout at the airstrip. I personally also want to assure the fine people of Glasspier something. I assure you, that corruption and crime in this great city will soon be exposed and greatly curtailed. Of course it is nearly impossible to create a completely crime free city, let alone world, but the City Commission, along with Burns and I have signed into being a taskforce and initiative to root out both corrupt police officers and politicians alike. The removal and replacement of those who have plagued Glasspier for far too long will be the first step in what we have coined 'The Dandelion Act'. I promised to you when I campaigned for this position that I would be tough on crime and tough on corruption and very soon, what has been done in the dark will be brought to the light.

The voice switched and the radio host made it clear that Miles' message was at an end. Some rich socialite was on next, talking about a masquerade party next week and what he was going to wear, so I turned the dial off and the hiss of the radio ceased. So it *was* Mr. Wakeman. Then where was *Mrs*. Wakeman? I still failed to see how these cases intersected, but the presence of the blue coupe and its driver firing overwatch for us at the airfield made me think they had to somehow. It was nearing sunset, but I wanted midnight for what I had in mind so I drove down to the Greengate Pub to pass some time.

After a drink or two, a few games of snooker, and some general loitering, I re-emerged into the now dark street a few quarters lighter but with my nerves settled. I got behind the wheel and with street lamps flashing overhead, made for my final stop of the day – St. Gertrude's Cemetery. As usual, I parked a block or two away to avoid unwanted attention and walked the rest of the distance. The crescent moon hung overhead, dripping light down into the cool, clear night like a leaky faucet. There would be no cloud cover or fog to hide me tonight. I walked the perimeter of the graveyard, hands in pockets, looking for any gap or weakness in the black wrought iron fencing that surrounded it. Along the south side I found a section of fence where the spikes on top had been blunted and bent by something. I looked around for an explanation, spotting the gnarled stump of a great old tree that had once stood outside the perimeter. Despite the blunted tops in this section, climbing safely over this fence still proved to be more difficult than the one at the airfield. After a moment silhouetted atop the wrought-iron in the pale moonlight, I landed within the cemetery grounds with a soft thud of shoes on damp grass.

I was about to head for the general area where I remembered the Marlowe graves being, then remembered another crucial step that had to be taken care of: a shovel. Something that surprisingly, I didn't own anymore. Growing up on a farm I'd just taken having them around for granted. So, I turned to my left instead and followed the roughly paved and winding road through the outermost headstones towards the 'front' of St. Gertrudes where the office building, maintenance shed, and pre-interment crypt would be.

The handful of small buildings came into view from beneath a low hanging tree branch after a rise in the pathway. Approaching the smallest of the buildings that I hoped would house groundskeeping tools, I was relieved to see that a couple of rakes and more importantly – a shovel, had been left leaning outside the shed. It looked like I'd finally caught a break. I was glad to not have to pull out the lockpick set for a third time this week. With the shovel in hand, I made for the heart of the graveyard where my answers lay, sticking to the shadows cast by trees and monoliths where I could. I stopped beneath a proud white mausoleum on a hill, the largest in the cemetery, and stood within its shadow to allow my eyes to fully adjust to the dark. While doing so, I also scanned the horizon for any signs of a night watch, but so far had seen none.

Seeing no unwelcome eyes, I began to walk up and down the rows of headstones where I was sure that the Marlowes' had rested. I wanted to avoid any use of flashlight, because despite the somewhat hilly layout and tree cover of the cemetery, a wandering beam of light at this hour would surely attract unwanted attention. I was itching for a smoke as well but decided against it for the same reasons. Finally, with eyes straining, I recognized a stone featuring a weathered angel whose wing tips had broken off. I remembered that the Marlowes' simple stone placard sat next door to it and sure enough, there they were. Charlotte and Jake Marlowe. Laid to rest in 1923, a rest that I was now poised to disturb.

"Sorry, but I have to know," I whispered to the uncaring ground. The shovel made its first cut into the six feet of grass and dirt that separated me from the dead. Then another, and another, until a pile of upturned earth began to form atop the neighboring grave beneath the faded angel. My shovel bit into the ground and what had started methodically soon turned into a frenzy as I anticipated vindication of my theory. Soon, my overcoat came off despite the cool night air and I wiped away a bead of sweat that had formed upon my brow with my gloved hand. As I worked, I thought back to the farm, glad that my hands were already calloused. I remembered the sensation of working with a shovel well – it had persisted throughout all the stages of my life so far. Digging post holes on the farm, digging graves in Poland, and now digging *up* a grave here in Glasspier… I missed when the feeling of a shovel in my hands meant I had a new fence to look forward to.

My head swiveled about every so often between loads of dirt, searching the deserted cemetery for any sign that I'd been seen. After a while of this routine, I pushed the shovel through some small roots and heard the soft collision of metal on wood. Another half hour of digging and I stood gasping and aching above two wooden caskets, one larger and one smaller, both modest and unadorned. Despite their simple appearance, they seemed sturdy and had resisted cracking or caving in. With a grimace, I pushed the blade of my shovel between the lid and the main body of the larger casket and pried upwards.

Inside, the skeletal remains of a woman lay in a faded and worn dress. No surprises there, but it was good to cover all my bases. I shut the lid and consigned Charlotte back to darkness. Now, the real reason I was here. I did the same shovel maneuver on the smaller casket, but it was more resilient, as if taunting me for my intrusion. Finally, with a small cracking sound I forced it open and saw inside. What awaited offered the pure vindication that I sought and made me certain of a larger conspiracy at play. Inside, wearing young boy's clothes and made to be roughly the shape of a child – was a wooden doll.

My head swiveled around once more to make sure no one was watching, but the only witness was the stained angel with clipped wings.

Chapter 13 - Masque

Dottie

Sept. 19th 1947
Friday
Glasspier,

I hung up the phone and returned to what I'd been doing before placing the call – loading and unloading the silver pistol I'd purchased second hand the day prior. It had the words 'Waffenfabrik Walther, Mod. PPK' engraved on the side. The man behind the counter told me that it was a good size for me and that despite our recent animosity towards the Germans, they knew how to make a reliable weapon. I had to take his word for it. He'd also been kind enough to provide me with a box of ammunition, along with showing me how to operate the surprisingly heavy little pistol. I told him I knew the basics, point and pull the trigger – it had worked at the airfield after all. I left that last part out, and the truth was, I appreciated his advice. I knew that what'd happened at the airfield was mostly luck and getting by on luck alone was not something I cared to make a habit of. Which was why I was practicing now.

My fingers were sore and beginning to blister from the repeated effort of pushing the bullets down against the tight spring of the magazine. My hand was also bleeding lightly between my thumb and first finger where I'd accidentally held the grip too high and allowed the sharp metal slide to gouge in. I didn't care, I wanted to be familiar with the gun. I just wished there was somewhere I could target practice. I'm sure Angelo would know somewhere, but I hadn't filled my brother in yet on the fact that I was there that night at the airstrip. I wasn't sure if I ever would. So for now, the gun would stay a secret, along with the fact that I had killed a man. Not just any man though, a member of The Blight. I went cold thinking again about what could have happened if Angelo had been there... and speaking of The Blight, apparently Thomas was affiliated somehow with them? That'd been one of the bigger shocks in a night chock full of them. I still hadn't decided if, or when, I would confront him, so for now I decided it was best to just let that one simmer on the backburner and hold it silently over him.

I still hadn't really come around to the idea of owning a gun. Using one to defend myself and take a life the other night had scared me, but not because I'd been shot at, although that was surely part of it. No, what scared me the most was the feeling of power when I pulled the trigger. The ease at which it killed. I'd ended someone's life. Every thought, every dream he'd ever had, spilling out onto the tarmac. Did he have family that would miss him? A wife? Kids? My vision started to go cloudy with tears, so I shoved the gun out of sight into its hiding spot at the bottom of my purse. I wanted independence, not power, but what if the two were synonymous? Maybe I should have left it all alone. No, I wanted to see it through and the phone call I'd just made was the next step in doing so.

I'd booked a show at 'The Velvet Jester' gentleman's club, a high-end establishment where the wealthy of Glasspier could get their entertainment with a side of discretion. It would be my first time performing there and was a big step up for my career, something I should have been excited about but found it hard to be. Angelo wasn't driver for the night, but he was working a job of some kind at the harbor and I couldn't even find excitement in the notion that the car was mine for the evening; knowing that Blight members had been gunned down just days prior while doing their job. Nevertheless, it was time to go – and I had to stop by Leon's first.

My car rattled to a stop outside McCreary Investigations, behind Thomas' cedar-brown motorcycle. I got out and went inside, to where Thomas was already sipping a glass of something of a similar color across from Leon. I did a double take, realizing that a third person sat beside him. Conrad O'Malley.

There were some general greetings as I hung my coat and took my usual seat across from Leon, beside Thomas. Unlike usual however, I kept my purse beside me rather than hanging it. Once I'd settled in, Leon was the first to speak.

"Conrad was just sharing with us a rather interesting encounter he had this morning. Why don't you fill Dottie in as well?"

"Got another note, like the first one, only this time it was passed to me in an envelope by a member of the union-"

"So does that mean you know who's behind the letters?" I leaned forward eagerly.

He glared with his charcoal-fire eyes and raised a hand. "Let me finish."

I sat back in deference.

"The union boy who passed me the letter was just a go-between. He said a man in a gray coat, gray suit and hat, and most interestingly – a gray mask, gave him the note to give to me."

I felt the hairs on the back of my neck rise as they had that night after The Gold Pig show, when I'd noticed myself being watched on the way home. I was sure it was the same man, after all, how many people were creeping around in all gray? I didn't voice this yet, I wanted to avoid another glare from Conrad so I let him continue.

"He gave me this sealed envelope after our union meeting." Conrad passed me a now opened envelope, "here, the others have already seen it."

I took it gently and slid out the single piece of paper within.

Get involved.
Detectives, private or otherwise, can all be bought; but I've seen your speeches and I know that you will never be silenced. You must ensure that when the truth is discovered, it comes to light. That is your role.

I handed the letter back to Conrad. “I’ve seen the gray man,” I said, in a matter-of-fact voice.

It wasn’t Conrad who responded, but Leon, “You’ve seen this masked man? And you didn’t think that was worth sharing earlier?”

“Well, I couldn’t tell he had a mask on!” I defended in a slightly raised voice, “I just thought he was some creep. He was wearing all gray and standing in the shadows of an alley watching me after my show the other night…”

The prickling chill of fear returned as I imagined the gray-masked stalker watching me. It was made worse now with the knowledge that he was wearing a mask. I hated masks, they made it impossible for me to read someone's expression or know their intentions which was something I prided myself on being able to do. Along with the fact that those who hid their face were rarely up to any good.

Thomas set his glass aside and spoke up slowly, “What if this… ‘*Gray Man*’ is on our side? Think about it. If he gave this letter to Conrad, then I’m sure he was also the mysterious benefactor who originally brought Conrad and Jenny to your doorstep. Maybe he was our guardian angel in the tower at the airfield as well, if so, it’s like he wants us to solve this mystery and he’s helping us along the way. Maybe this whole case only fell into your hands because he willed it.”

“That’s what I’m afraid of,” Leon said, sparing no gruffness in voice, “why not do it himself? Why the masks and secrecy? I can’t help feeling like we’re all being played. Also, we can’t say for certain that the letter Jenny received and the two that Conrad has are from the same source. It’s likely, yes, but not necessarily a fact.” He paused, the only sound the dull whirring of the lazy ceiling fan in his office.

I broke the brief near-silence, “So what are we supposed to do? Just play into what might be a trap? It sounds like the Gray Man wants to expose whoever is behind the killing of the Marlowes, which is also what we want to do. So our interests should be aligned right?”

“And I’m here for what? Just to drop the dime on em’ at the end?” Conrad butted in before Leon had a chance to respond. “Why can’t Leon do that? He’s the one that would present the evidence before the court anyways.”

“Because, the Gray Man seems to think that Leon could be paid off.” Thomas said, staring straight ahead solemnly, “and you know what that means? Whoever he thinks is responsible, may have enough money or power to make that happen.”

“He doesn’t though,” Leon countered fiercely, “whoever Charlotte's killer is, couldn’t pay me off. Maybe this *‘Gray Man’* doesn’t know us all as well as he thinks, because no amount of dough could sway my integrity or loyalty to my client. A private eye that allows himself to be bought off won’t be one for long.”

A hush fell over the room. I admired Leon's conviction and couldn’t help but wonder if *my* silence could be bought. I did want justice to be won for Charlotte, but at the end of the day that wasn’t really why I’d initially wanted to get involved in the case. And what about Thomas? I was almost certain he could be. He was just in it for the excitement and the pay and I knew how badly he wanted funds to travel back to the Congo. I felt a twinge of shame, maybe Conrad really was the best of us. Aside from Leon of course.

Leon tilted his head to Conrad, “What does he mean by ‘speeches’?” he asked, pointing at the word in the letter where it sat unfolded on the coffee table.

“I told you. I want to see a full evolution of thought regarding the working class in Glasspier; which means getting up on the soapbox from time to time. I’d invite you to one of my rallies, but privatized police and unions don’t exactly have the best history.”

Leon disregarded that comment and continued his questioning, “Do you ever recall seeing a man matching your friend's description at any of your events?”

"No, can't say that I do. I'd have noticed too, because I make an effort to talk to everyone individually who attends if I can. At least 'till the union busters show up."

Leon may have called him hotheaded in the past and maybe he was, but Conrad genuinely seemed to want better for his fellow man and wasn't afraid to fight for it.

Leon renewed his effort, "Can I speak with your friend from the union? I'd like to hear his first-hand account about this masked man."

"Can't imagin' he'd tell you anything he hasn't already told me – and I told you all I know." Conrad shrugged, pulling a box of Lucky Strikes from his chest pocket, "But sure, his name's Felix, and I can introduce you two sometime."

"Not sometime. Tonight. Eyewitness account is already unreliable and only gets worse with time. This is the closest contact we've had with this mystery man and I want to get as much on him as we can, while we can."

Conrad grunted. "Fine, he works late on Friday's so I'll take you down to him at the mill. All I ask is a favor in return."

Leon's eyes narrowed. "What favor?"

"Just moving a couple of boxes up to the union meeting room. There's a few of 'em and they're a little heavy, but nothing you can't handle, I'm sure." He cracked a half-smile from behind a puff of smoke.

I wanted to tag along, but the clock on the wall over Leon's shoulder told me it was nearing time to head over to The Velvet Jester.

"Well boys, I'd love to come with and see the grime of the steel mill in all its glory," I said, rising, "but I've got a glitzy nightclub full of millionaires to get to."

"Shame," Thomas grinned, "but I'll be sure to send you a postcard."

"I'd take the company of one good foreman, over a hundred of them pompous assholes any day," Conrad grumbled under his breath.

I pretended I didn't hear him, despite the fact that I agreed. I wasn't particularly looking forward to diving into the cesspool that was Glasspier's upper class, especially not in a place like The Velvet

Jester. I moved to the door and got my coat – but there was one more thing I needed.

"Oh Leon, how's the investigation on the picture with Charlotte and her friends going?" I asked innocently. I knew it likely wasn't well, given that Leon hadn't informed us that he'd found anything in that regard.

"How's it going? Not particularly anywhere so far. I've checked with the locals at various bars and restaurants, along with the police, but they weren't especially cooperative."

Conrad snorted.

I ignored him again. "Leon, these are obviously high society women that you've been looking for down in the muddy trenches of Glasspier. I play at The Velvet Jester tonight, why don't you give me the photo."

He sighed in acquiescence and rose from his chair to retrieve the picture from his office. Thomas and Conrad were silent as he did this, drinking and smoking respectively. Upon his return, he brought the frame over to where I stood near the coat rack and held it out for me. Then, surprisingly, he took my arm in a rather firm grip and leaned in close to whisper to me.

"Jake Marlowe is alive."

I tried not to let my face betray my surprise.

"Or at least there's a *very* good chance he is. You need to be careful; this case is a full-on conspiracy. Someone buried a body-double in his place. Between that, the gray man, the foxglove killer, and The Blight activity – you really need to watch out for yourself. Trust no one. There's a reason I haven't let Conrad in on this yet. The less he thinks we know the better for now, until I can figure out what his angle is."

"You take care too," I whispered back, "losing you the other night at the airfield was… well, I just don't want to see you like that again."

His face displayed a mixture of emotions that even I couldn't fully divine the nature of, mask or no mask. It lasted just a moment, then his usual look of steely resolve returned and he leaned back, his grip softening and releasing from my arm. He nodded and stepped back. I glanced over at Thomas who was swirling his drink in his glass and looking curious. My brain felt like it was swirling in a similar way. I was so lost in thought, that I didn't even make a face at him on the way out the door to rub in the fact that I knew something he didn't.

Chapter 14 - Vessels

Thomas

'What the hell was all that about?' was what I intended to say with the look I gave Leon as he donned his overcoat. '*I'll explain later,'* his grim expression returned. Conrad was looking mildly curious as well, a rare sight given his usual devil-may-care attitude. I finished the last of the dark rye and set the glass aside. It seemed our symposium was over.

"To the mill?"

"To the mill," Leon confirmed, looking expectantly over at Conrad.

He stood and grumbled as he did, "Back to the mill."

The feeble remains of the sunset were fading away, leaving an amber wash on the skyline when we arrived south of the city at the steel mill. The mill itself was a jumble of metal and concrete silhouetted against the pale sky backdrop, with '*Glasspier Steel Co.'* embossed in faded and chipped gold lettering along the side of one of the larger buildings. I killed the engine on my motorcycle and regrouped with Conrad and Leon, as the former led us inside.

It wasn't nearly as exciting as, say, some abandoned temple or remote island, but being led through the mill still piqued my interest for the simple reason that I had never been in one before. The air was stifling, with an oppressive odor that reminded me of burning motor-oil. Conrad led us across steel walkways and past an array of machines, control panels, and processes that I could only speculate the purposes of, and our tour (although it was anything but that, given the indifference of our guide) concluded near a sweltering furnace where a young man poured molten steel into a basin with the assistance of a long pole. He glanced up at us, face smeared with soot, and bobbed his head in greeting.

"Felix, this is Leon and Thomas. Leon here wants you to tell him what you told me earlier."

Leon stepped forward and shook Felix's hand while holding his overcoat in the other. I'd peeled off my own jacket upon entry to the furnace room as well and now tugged at my collar, loosening it in an attempt to allow some heat to escape. Conrad appeared unbothered.

"Well, it was a strange morning," Felix said, head bobbing up and down as he continued to work the furnace, "most days here are all the same, but our meetings add some variety to the week. I was looking forward to hearing Conrad's plan for our next rally so I was helpin' him print some stuff. That damn press put up a hell-of-a fight as usual, I swear that machine is possessed by the devil himself, I reckon-"

"Let's skip to the part where the man in the mask shows up," Leon urged, for which I was grateful. The heat in the room was beginning to become unbearable.

"Right… of course, of course." Felix let the pole rest idle for a moment and became animated, speaking with his hands, "The masked man appeared, like a bloody phantom, while Conrad was away looking for someone to help unstick the press machine. He had a gray hat, gray shirt and a gray tie, even had gray pants and shoes. I reckon if we'd of checked, he'd of had on gray socks and underpants too!" Felix cackled at that and wiped a bead of sweat from his soot-streaked forehead with the back of his hand.

"And the mask?" Leon asked.

"Gray too."

"Yes, but what did it look like beyond just being gray?" Leon spoke evenly but I could tell his patience was wearing a little thin, although I supposed mine was too in the heat of that room.

"It looked kinda like one of them masks rich folk wear to their parties, only this one covered his whole face with just cutouts for the eyes."

"A masquerade mask?" I asked, for clarification.

"Yessir, one of those. All plain, slate gray. Grayer than the hairs on Conrad's chin!" He cackled again.

"I do *not* have gray hair," Conrad snapped.

"Whatever you say old man," Felix relented, a sly grin playing across his sooty features.

Leon pressed him for more, "Is there anything else you remember about him? Eye, or hair color? Height?"

"Little taller than me, I think… don't remember his eye color. Hair, was brown… I think."

"You think?"

"I was focused mostly on the mask and all the gray. Besides, he didn't stick around long. Gave me the letter, said 'give this to Conrad' and that was that."

"Did he have gloves on?"

Felix cocked his head and frowned in thought, "Uh, yeah, I think so."

"And when did Conrad open the letter?"

"Dunno, I gave it to him when he got back. Before the meeting."

Leon seemed to think for a moment, staring into the furnace's fiery maw, then turned to Conrad. "What did you want me to help you move? Some boxes? Let's do that." Then he regarded Felix, "You've been a great help, thank you."

Felix nodded and Leon turned heel to exit the furnace room. Conrad and I followed. *What the hell?* I thought to myself for the second time that day. 'You've been a great help?' How so? Felix had told us all the same information Conrad had… minus the part about the mask looking like it was for a masquerade. Was that important somehow? Leon seemed to know a lot more than he was letting on with me, although he'd told Dottie something, so was it just something he wanted Conrad and I to be in the dark about? No, probably just Conrad I reasoned. He just told Dottie then because she was leaving. Regardless, I didn't like the feeling of being on the outside and resolved to question Leon about it if he didn't bring me into the fold the next chance he got.

Conrad had taken the lead again and soon we found ourselves in a small, grimy room with a printing press that occupied the majority of the available space. The room had a stuffy odor of paper, with metallic, yet sweet undertones. My guess was that last bit was the ink. The amalgamation of rollers, pulleys, levers and flywheels that stood before me was something I would have liked to examine more thoroughly if given the time, but Conrad directed Leon and I to a handful of cardboard boxes on the cement floor along the wall.

"I was just gonna enlist a few members to help me move these over to the union room Monday mornin', but figured might as well get 'em out of here sooner."

I stooped down and opened the top flap of the nearest box, revealing papers stacked to the brim. Pamphlets, to be more precise.

"What are they?" Leon questioned, reaching down for one, "I'm not about to become some kind of accessory just by moving these am I?"

"Just some reading material," Conrad replied, lifting a box, "you're welcome to take one and give it a look through, might even learn something! And once you've helped me move these boxes and given that a read, you'll basically be a part of the cause!" He laughed a hollow laugh that sounded overall phony in its cheerfulness.

Leon skimmed the pamphlet briefly before folding it and putting it in his pocket. I grabbed one and glanced it over as well, but it was quickly evident this would be a more in-depth read for later. The one striking feature that caught my eye however, was the insignia of a hammer crossed with a wrench in the same styling as the Soviet's hammer and sickle, that was printed at the bottom of the page near Conrads' initials. I looked up to give Conrad a questioning glare, but he was already moving out of the room with the box in hand. I shrugged, put the pamphlet in my pocket and lifted a box as well, following Conrad out of the stuffy print room.

With just two trips each, the six boxes went up the metal staircases and down the hall on the third floor to their new home in the union meeting room. The room was a hastily arranged space and had clearly been originally intended as a storage room, having since been converted to suit the needs of the union. It now featured rickety wooden chairs of various colors and a small blackboard, across from which a lone, dusty window allowed the last remnants of twilight to seep through like a nearly clogged scupper.

I slid the last box flush against the wall as Conrad addressed the two of us, "All I ask is that you have some discretion with that material. It's meant for a more… select audience."

He said it casually, but his eyes burned a warning into ours.

"Sure. And in exchange, you continue to keep my case equally discrete." Leon replied without missing a beat.

To this Conrad nodded and placed his hand on the back of a chair, leaning on it. He suddenly looked rather tired and thin standing there amongst the rows of mismatched chairs and I felt an inkling of sympathy for him. It had to be exhausting to always be fighting for something that seemed so futile.

"C'mon Thomas, we need to talk." Leon stated, turning for the door.

I followed, a new spark of excitement burgeoning within as I anticipated becoming privy to whatever it was that Leon had told Dottie. Judging by the brief look of shock that had found its way onto her features despite her proclivity for masking such things, I imagined whatever came next would mark a turning point in the Marlowe case.

'*Jake Marlowe is alive.*' That statement from Leon hadn't baffled me quite as much as I'd thought it might, but I supposed there was still time for the reality – or '*potential*' reality as Leon had put it, to set in. He did say that it was possible Jake had died on the streets, or been tracked down after the fact and killed, or even died in the war, so we couldn't be sure this new revelation had any real meaning. Although there was the matter of the body double. That aspect caught my interest more than just the potentiality of Jake's survival, after all, who would go through the effort of burying a stand-in? And why? All these things I pondered to pass the time while leaning against the rotted timbers of the dock railing in Glasspier's harbor. It was nearly midnight and nearly time to bring in the clandestine shipment I'd agreed to chauffeur for The Blight. Unconsciously, I reached for where my left arm ached dully beneath my jacket and pressed upon the wound gently, making a mental note to change the bandages once this was all through.

I pushed out from port aboard the sluggish tugboat beneath a vista of stars interspersed with wispy clouds and the waxing moon. The boat was little joy to captain, especially when compared to the small handful of sailboats I'd enjoyed over the years. It was bumbling, noisy, and stank of sulfur and diesel. Nevertheless, I was at the very least happy to be back aboard a ship of any kind – and at the helm no less. This, along with the notion of receiving 'substantial' pay for doing such a simple job, had me in good spirits despite the vessel's shortcomings.

Just five or so minutes before midnight, I sighted a small ship pulling around towards the narrow channel entry of the harbor. The lack of any lights on the approaching boat had allowed it to seemingly materialize before me out of the inky blackness of the ocean. I'd known this operation was supposed to be kept under wraps, but apparently even the chance of a bystander taking notice of the ship's entry was too high profile for whatever cargo was being delivered. I shivered in the cool night-air breeze and brought the wheel around, angling the tugboat towards the new arrival.

It was a standard affair, coaxing the ship into the harbor with the tugboat, and one that I still couldn't believe I was getting paid top dollar for. As I brought the larger vessel into port, I tried to gauge the make of the ship or the point of origin of its crew, but the small amount of chatter on deck was drowned out by the gentle splashing of water against the hull. I docked the ship to my starboard side along the pier and realized that in the brief time I'd been out, a small caravan of cars had arrived along the shore, but more notably – so too had a boxcar bearing train from the Somerset Line. The lights from the train crested above the large steel containers littering the shipping yard, behind the row of four parked cars that now stood between my mooring and the city.

I stood upon the deck of the tugboat and stared across the wide pier to where the men from the cars met with the men disembarking from the ship. I was certain the men from shore were Blight members, although I didn't recognize any of them in particular. But who were these foreigners? For that was what I was now convinced they were, having heard not a bit of English from them so far. They lacked a distinctly 'western' appearance as well and I found myself scanning the ship and their dark clothes as they unloaded their cargo for any kind of markings or writing that would give context to their nationality.

I saw none, but soon became curious about something else altogether: their cargo itself. The men from the ship and the men I'd assumed to be Blight members, worked together quickly with little exchanged in the way of words, to unload the shipment. Whatever it was, came in the form of two very large wooden crates, which were deposited nearby the shipping yard. I heard an order barked from someone nearby the row of parked cars and the men began moving the cargo from those wooden crates into one of the steel containers. I strained to see what was being transferred, but from the few glimpses I got, I only saw something large, semi-rectangular, and non-uniformly shaped, beneath a sheet covering.

That was when I saw him. Another order was given and I sighted, standing amongst the parked cars, who had issued it. The Gray Man. He was partially veiled by the headlights of the car to which he stood to the left of, but it was unmistakably him. All gray trench coat and hat, beneath which a gray mask dully reflected the light issued from the car beside him.

"*Son of a bitch,*" I cursed under my breath. Here he was, the man seemingly behind it all and I couldn't do anything about it. Even if I'd been ashore rather than waiting aboard the boat, what would I have said? '*Hello, I believe you're the one who's orchestrated the whole case my detective friend is working, care to weigh in on that?*' The men in the shipyard seemed to be wrapping up their task, and the foreign men were already walking silently up the pier to board their ship once more. I started the process of backing the tugboat into the harbor behind the mysterious ship, watching helplessly as the gray man on shore faded out of my sight.

The trip back out to sea with the mystery ship was uneventful, but I was preoccupied with other thoughts anyways. I knew now that the Gray Man was affiliated with The Blight in some way, but was he working for them? Or paying them to work for him? Regardless of which it was, Leon would want to know, but could I tell him? Lockry had made it clear that as far as anyone was concerned, this little exchange had never happened. To go against the wishes of The Blight once trusted by them, could mean excommunication or even death. I didn't want to end up like old Lester Marlowe, especially after Lockry had hinted at the notion I might be nearing my entry to the inner circle if this job went smoothly. And telling Leon about any of it definitely had the potential to make it *not* go smoothly the next time. Maybe I could tell him that I'd found out some other way that the Gray Man was involved with The Blight? But how? He would be suspicious and I was already lucky enough that he seemed to not remember the incident at the airstrip where I'd announced that I was 'a friend of The Blight'. But surely Dottie remembered? Had she not told him? I was surprised not to have been confronted by either of them on that matter… I cursed under my breath once again, frustrated with what I'd originally intended as a fundraiser for my return trip to the Congo turning into such a dilemma.

The larger ship slunk away into the horizon where the sky met the water in murky communion and I wheeled the tugboat back around towards the bay, hoping to take a closer look at the goings-on of the shipyard. By the time the tugboat groaned to a stop beside the pier once more, the shipyard was desolate. Both the large shipping container that had housed the cargo and the train – were gone.

Chapter 15 - The Velvet Jester

Dottie

The nervousness that usually accompanied a show was absent. Something about breaking into an airfield, finding a dead body, and then being in a shootout seemed to take the edge off from performing in front of a crowd. Nonetheless, I found the comforting metallic smoothness of the ring-necklace between my fingers and sighed, letting it drop against my chest. What would Charles think of me now? Would he be proud of me, swaying and singing beneath the twinkling lights of The Velvet Jester; a high society establishment that would put the old Blind Tiger to shame? Would he be proud that I'd kept myself alive, even if it meant I'd become a killer? No. I wasn't a killer, I reminded myself. I'd killed, yes, to stay alive, but that wasn't the same as being a killer. Had he been forced to do the same?

Crooning the last refrain of my final song for the evening, I realized my knuckles had gone white around the shined-chrome microphone. I took a staggered step back, releasing it, to the sound of applause and the last clinking notes of the sleek grand piano. I looked out into the crowd, half expecting to see Down's horrible face but was relieved to see only a bunch of unfamiliar fat, rich, old men. Probably the first time I'd ever been relieved by that sight.

I curtsied in the afterglow of a successful performance and did my usual batty-eyed routine with the men closest to the stage. As the bustle of conversation began to crescendo once more, I parted with a last few longing glances and retired backstage. The warmth gleaned from the glass of complementary wine I'd quickly downed upon entry to the gaudy venue had long since faded and I looked forward to a top off before intermingling with The Jesters patrons.

"You were fantastic out there! Truly sublime!" the eccentric talent host babbled in a high voice and shook my hand, leading me backstage.

He was a short, pudgy man with a tall black bowler hat that didn't match his red and tan suit. The green room he led me to was fairly simple compared to the elaborate front-of-house where the dancers performed. It was fitted with a handful of modest couches and chairs sat between large vanities for preparing makeup and hair, so many of which, that it made the room feel larger due to the reflections. It was mostly empty now, with the majority of the girls out performing.

"Thank you sir." I smiled. "And about that house fee?"

"Yes of course, of course! You've earned it!" he beamed, shoving his short, stubby fingers into the pockets of his suit coat. He produced a wad of bills which he carefully counted, a deep v creasing his sweaty forehead in concentration as he did so.

"Fifty even!" he finally exclaimed, "and I promise more the *next* time so long as you keep pulling crowds like that! I told 'em we should take a gamble on you, I did," he said, head bobbing and sweat glistening. "I could tell there was something about you, even on the phone…"

I accepted the money graciously, not concerned at the moment with the fact that he could have certainly paid me more *this* time. It was a good price, great even, compared to the rates I normally made. So with a promise to come back and another handshake I broke away towards the bar cart and he turned heel to provide a young girl seated in front of one of the vanities with some makeup advice; advice that I was certain wasn't asked for, nor needed.

I re-entered the venue proper from a door to the right of the stage, purse in one hand and a fresh glass of pale-gold chardonnay in the other. More so than usual, I noticed the weight of my handbag as I prepared to dive once again into the mud and roll around with the city's swine. It was laden with the weight of both the gun and the picture frame, along with the responsibility and purpose that came with each. I surveyed the glitzy room as a coyote might assess a pig pen, determining that the pigs here were older and fatter than the usual prey – and wealthier too. Through the dim haze of the smoky club, I spotted flashes of silver bands with oyster shell dials wrapped tightly around bulging plump wrists, finely pressed suits with gaudy ties encircling corpulent necks, pudgy fingers adorned with clunky gold and silver rings, and the occasional raised glass of expensive champagne. Amidst the lounging men, scantily dressed young women performed 'exotic' dances and careened to and fro to earn favor with the loathsome crowd, and in turn, money. A phonograph started up behind me in lieu of live music and added to the din of the room.

With a long swallow of wine and an inward bracing, I approached a laughing group of the glittering-eyed higher society. My aim tonight was simple: blend and assimilate.

Chapter 16 - Three of a Kind

Leon

Sept. 20th 1947
Saturday
Glasspier,

<u>The Mobilization of the Masses Starts Now</u>

For far too long the people of Glasspier have been disenfranchised, cast to the side as a menial workforce to increase the ever-gloated riches of a wealthy few. And to this, I say no more! All individuals are equal whether by the law of God or man and for far too long it has not been this way in our fair city. We, the people, built this city of steel and concrete and the Glasspier family and their cronies have reaped all the benefits from our labor.

Thomas Glasspier hosts his lavish parties for the wealthy elite, parading their fine food and drink around the halls of his extravagant mansion without a thought for those whose backs were broken to allow them to be able to afford

such luxuries. The lives of our children, fathers, brothers, friends, and comrades sacrificed in Europe and the Pacific has allowed the politicians and the affluent to recline on their velvet thrones wearing silk and jewelry worth more than our entire yearly earnings. No more. Friends, comrades - change cannot be made by the few. If we wish to improve our lives we must unite as one against those who would keep us down beneath them.

And this, my dear brothers and sisters, is why on this day we are announcing the *People's Party of Glasspier*. A political organization that shall work for the people and be run by the people. Along with being a rallying point for our cause, the party shall also publish a newspaper called *The People's Spark* in which news of the masses and ideologies will be shared throughout the city - and no more will the media be controlled by those in the pockets of the wealthy few! We must stand together, for a chain made of a thousand links cannot be broken by the strongest hammer of oppression. The furnace fires of Glasspier are alive and well, all we must do comrades, is get them roaring with a little spark. Workers of Glasspier, unite!

-C.C.O.M.

"Goddammit," I sighed and rubbed my temple, picturing Conrad preaching his message on a soapbox with a flyer just like this one clenched in hand.

I'd read Conrads' manifesto over late last night after the steel mill, and reading it now a second time this morning I'd still hoped somehow that it would say something different. I set the pamphlet aside and sipped my coffee, eventually placing the mug beside it on the table. It wasn't that I disliked his position. I didn't know much about all that political nonsense in general and usually tried to keep my nose out of it altogether – but I certainly wasn't the biggest fan of the extremely wealthy either. No, what had me on edge was the timing of it all. Why right now? Why now, amidst all the other bullshit going on in the city at the moment, had Conrad decided to stage his communist revolution? More coincidence? I thought about what detective Cruz would say along that line and came to a decision – the masquerade party was the place to go for answers.

The other day, sitting in my car with the radio on, someone had been on the air talking about a masquerade after the briefing on the airfield shootout. Then, the Gray Man who seemed to be intrinsically involved in this case, Felix had described as wearing a 'masquerade style mask'. And now, lastly, Conrad specifically mentioned the Glasspier estates lavish parties in his manifesto. All roads seemed to be pointing to the mansion – and to Silas. Silas *'The Shredder'* was still suspect number one as far as I was concerned. He'd killed Lester so there were good odds he'd done the whole family… but Charlottes' neighbor had claimed that Lester was long gone before her murder… why wait so long to finish the job if it was him? And why'd he even do it in the first place? The motive seemed even more elusive.

Regardless, in lieu of another suspect, Silas was number one for now. I rose slowly from my chair in the lounge, lifting the coffee mug from the table. It was cold. I thought about reheating it, then opted instead to reach inside my inner breast pocket. I'd started carrying again. Not my gun, I'd never stopped that, no – carrying a flask. I poured a healthy splash into the mug and stepped out of the agency for the Sunday paper. Outside, the feeble autumn sun attempted to show here and there through a blanket of clouds, making for a day less gloomy than usual. I stooped down for the paper on my step and unrolled it.

Foxglove Killer Claims Third Victim!

A few days ago, a headline like that would have spiked my heart rate a little and set me to wondering, but now after what I'd seen and done in the past week I simply stepped back inside and laid the paper out on the table. Besides, there was no clear connection whatsoever between the foxglove murders to my case at all. It stated (with no shortage of fear mongering) that a third man had been found dead in his hotel room at the Pullman Hotel in north Glasspier, bearing all the signature signs of a foxglove murder: flowers clasped between the hands and poisoned.

Staring at the page and thinking about the previous killings, I was struck with a notion. I slid the paper to the right, folding it under itself so just the article about the foxglove killer was visible. Then, from the rack sitting to the left of the front door against the wall, I dug through and retrieved the paper from the day Jenny and Conrad had appeared – the day after the second foxglove murder. I kept old newspapers for about a month past, a fact that Dottie had chastised me about before due to the 'unsightly stack of them' at the front of the lounge. The unsightly stack came in handy now though and I was able to find the paper that featured the killer's first victim on September 9th, before they'd been dubbed with the '*Foxglove Killer*' moniker. I laid them both beside the most recent on my coffee table, smoothing them with the backside of my hand.

The facts were these:

On September 9th the killer had taken their first victim, or at least their first with the foxglove flower calling card. Bradley Stafford, dead – poisoned in his home, survived by his wife Melissa and three-year-old daughter Mary. I remembered reading this paper with mild interest before chalking it up to the usual depravity and shelving it.

On September 12th, the day before Jenny and Conrads arrival, the murderer now bearing the title '*Foxglove Killer*' claimed their second victim. Stanley Rourke, also found dead in his home, in the master bed – same as the first victim. He too left a wife, Anna, but no children.

And most recently, yesterday on September 19th, Clark Dorson was poisoned in a hotel room at the Pullman, leaving his wife Molly and two kids Shelly and Nathan behind.

All men, all married. Three of a kind. But what I found most curious about all this, was the fact that the Dorson's were Glasspier citizens. Why would someone who lives in Glasspier need a hotel room? I took a drink of my cold coffee and thought about that. There was an obvious answer, but I wanted to give Mr. Dorson the benefit of the doubt. Maybe he was there for a business meeting that ran late? Or maybe he had other business in north Glasspier that made it convenient for him to put up at the Pullman? I read further down the article and found the segment on Clark Dorson's' life. A railroad switchman on the Somerset Line. That likely ruled out a business meeting, leaving only one other easy explanation. Infidelity.

If I were working the case, I'd probably start by interviewing the widows, I'd find out where they were on the nights of the killing and if they were suspicious at all of their husbands cheating. I sat back on my chair and peered outside through the venetian blinds to see the sun losing its battle with the dark gray clouds. I wasn't working this case though. I'd seen no correlation so far between it and mine and I was sure that the police had noticed the same patterns I had. Hell, I was sure that after today even a relatively dull, but observant paperboy could notice the similarities in the victims.

I folded the papers back up, finished the last of my coffee, lit a cigarette, and stepped outside again for a drive. My objectives were threefold and listed in my head in order of difficulty: figure out when the masquerade was, find somewhere to get masks made last minute, and devise a way to get into the party despite certainly *not* being invited.

Sliding behind the wheel, I shifted out of park and drove north to downtown; dreaming of masquerades, foxglove flowers, and blue coupes.

Chapter 17 - Sapphire

Thomas

It had been a lazy Saturday. I slept until nearly noon in recovery from my late-night rendezvous at the harbor and had spent the majority of the day thus far absentmindedly cooking an elaborate breakfast of poached eggs with Cumberland sausage. The sizzle and pop in the pan was drowned out with the echoes of hushed foreign voices on the wind and the lapping of water against a ship's hull. The peppered herb aroma of the sausage too was dulled with the vivid memory of sulfur and brine aboard the tugboat. *They had to have been Russians right?* It was the only language I could think of that matched the brief snippets of dialogue I'd heard, and their clothes, although nondescript, would fit that mold as well…

Beyond chores and housework, I didn't have anything planned for the day. So, while working on refitting the loose trim around the kitchen countertop, the speculative musings continued. It was early evening when my phone rang, jarring me back to the present. I left the trim where it was and went to my sitting room, raising the receiver from its hook.

"Thomas, it's Leon," crackled the familiar voice on the line.

A brief wave of anxiety washed over me as my dilemma regarding whether or not to inform him about the happenings at the harbor was reopened. However, the moment was just that – brief. I chastised myself for being so nervous with Leon who was, after all, a friend.

I'd decided anyway to keep the hush job hush for now until I could see any real benefit that would outweigh the potentially grievous downsides of letting the secret out. I responded evenly with a simple greeting and Leon got to the point.

"I've decided that the best course of action with the case is to get in close. We've danced around for too long chasing weak leads and muddling with business unrelated to the real matter at hand. Dottie is still working on tracking down the women in the picture, which I still believe to be important, but I've got a new task for you if you're up to it."

"I'm all ears."

There was a pause, then Leon continued, "We need to get into the Glasspier estate masquerade."

He fell silent again to let that sink in. I let it, intrigued and somewhat excited at the prospect, after all, I'd never be one to deny that I had expensive tastes and interests.

"All roads seem to be pointing to the masquerade," Leon elaborated, "the Gray Man's mask, the fact that our prime suspect is there, and now Conrad's flier which I'm sure you've read."

I had read it; late last night, while changing the bandages on my arm. "And what would you like me to do?"

"Find a way in. Or at least help me come up with one. Right now my best idea is to see about getting hired on as additional security for the event, but it's risky. With Silas as head of security, I'm worried that we could show our hand pretty quickly just by applying. And someone like Thomas Glasspier probably already had everything planned out and ready months ago. I also want Dottie in there with us, which won't work if we're security."

"I agree, it's a good thought, but I don't think that's the way to go. Too conspicuous."

"Yes. Which is why I called you – and I'll be calling Dottie right after. I did find out pretty easily that the party is on the twenty-sixth of this month, seems to be public knowledge, so we have less than a week to figure this out."

I hesitated, not wanting to over promise, but decided it was probably feasible. "I've got an idea… but I won't be able to confirm it immediately. Give me a couple days at most and I'll get back to you about it. And definitely still see what Dottie can drum up, I know she has her ways."

"Affirmative. And if you do find a way in, I've got a lead on a place to get costumes but we'd need to give her at least a couple days to make them."

"Time is of the essence then, understood."

"All goes well, and we'll be rubbing elbows with high society before we know it!" Leon barked a laugh.

"Looking forward to it." I grinned back and returned the curved ivory handle to its cradle.

I sat for a moment beside the phone, staring out the room's small bay window. Outside, it looked as though it might rain at any moment but the sky hadn't quite decided yet. I spun the rotary and the line rang just once before being picked up.

"Hello."

"It's Thomas."

"Ah Thomas, what can I do for you on this dreary Saturday? I trust that all went smoothly?" Lockry's voice oozed through the speaker like well refined honey.

"Yes, it did."

"Wonderful."

"I'm calling to see if we could move our usual meeting up any earlier. Perhaps Monday, or even tomorrow night? I've got something I'd like to discuss and it's time sensitive."

"Of course. Tomorrow night, the usual time."

"Yes. That works."

"Good. See you then," he confirmed and the line went dead.

That evening, I finished the repairs on my countertop and afterwards made myself comfortable in my preferred armchair with a somewhat mediocre glass of wine and my copy of *The Odyssey.* It was a re-read, but even still, the going was slow. As the dusk set in and with it, the rain, I realized that I'd often read the same paragraph multiple times without a single word sinking in. The Greek heroes kept giving way to mental wanderings involving foreigners, masked men, and opulent parties. I finished my glass and was intent on at least reaching the end of the section on 'returning to Ithaca', when a new distraction came forth in the form of a knock on the door.

I put the book aside and rose from the armchair, creeping as softly as I could to my bedroom where I retrieved my pistol from the bedside stand. I wasn't expecting any guests and I didn't have the luxury of an aperture on the door. Something that I should remedy, I bemoaned internally, especially as I got closer to being a fully privileged member of The Blight. With the gun in my right hand behind my back and the doorknob in the left, I turned the knob and carefully peered through the crack between the door and the jamb. Standing beneath a small black umbrella, from which rivulets of rainwater dripped down upon the stone of the front step, was Dottie. I quickly placed the pistol out of sight within the curved buffet cabinet in the foyer and opened the door fully.

"Hello Thomas, care for some company?" she asked with a shyness I wasn't familiar with in her.

I was a little taken aback and strained to recall how she even knew where I lived, as she'd never paid me a visit before. Just about all of our socializing was done at Leons and yet here she was, dressed noticeably more casually than usual and looking a bit forlorn.

"Of course," I said, and motioned for her to come in.

She lowered the umbrella and shook the water out of it before stepping inside. She glanced around the foyer and into the sitting room while leaning the umbrella beside the cabinet. Why was she here? Was she finally going to confront me about the airfield? That question lingered while I walked across the sitting room and directed her to a mahogany chair across from, and identical to, the one I had until recently resided in.

"Can I get you something to drink?"

"That would be swell," she replied, sitting down with legs crossed.

I approached the wine rack in the kitchen, "More sweet, or more dry?"

"More alcoholic," she laughed, "you choose."

I selected a bottle that I'd been saving for no specific occasion; one more refined than what I had been drinking earlier. It was rare that I entertained company, so I figured there was no better time for it than now. Dottie waited in patient silence as I uncorked the bottle, gathered two smaller glasses and brought them to the sitting room.

"Aw Thomas, I said *more* alcohol," Dottie mock pouted, eyeing the shorter glasses I'd set down on the table between us.

"This is Port," I explained, carefully pouring us each a glass, "it's fortified, so trust me, you'll get what you wished for." I set the bottle down and Dottie reached for her glass, taking an experimental sip. I did the same.

"Now, not that I mind the company, but is there a particular reason for the visit? Did Leon become a shut-in? Or by some miracle, suddenly develop a social life?"

"He has, actually," Dottie smirked, "I caught him halfway out the door; said something about owing a 'detective Cruz' a drink."

"Hm, I didn't know Leon had friends. Besides us, of course."

She responded with a short, airy laugh. "So yes, I apologize for not calling ahead, but I was already out and just wanted to be out of this dreadful weather… and I wanted somebody to talk too," she added, sounding a bit more serious.

I took a nervous sip from my glass. Heart-to-hearts weren't exactly my strong suit, but Dottie was a good friend, so I braced myself and prepared to do my best.

"Oh? What about?"

"Just… everything. There has just been so *much* lately and I don't know what to think of it all. I mean, we both shot people," she whispered in a scared voice, "I've been trying to come to terms with it, but…" she trailed off and held the glass up to her lips, taking a deep drink.

I frowned and strained for a good reply but nothing came to me, so I decided to do what I was familiar with: telling stories.

"I first killed in the Navy. It wasn't some glorious battle inspiring patriotism or anything of that sort. A couple fellow servicemen and I were drinking at some run-down bar in a port town overseas. Things got heated between one of the locals and one of us, can't even remember what it was about – something not worth dying over I'm sure. The local was a big guy and was beating on a buddy of mine pretty bad. I tried to pull him off and got a black eye for my efforts. Next thing I knew I was clenching a smoking gun and there was a pool of blood forming beneath the both of them there on the ground." I paused there, looking warily at Dottie for any sign of disgust or fear but found neither. She just looked sad.

"Then what happened?" she asked from behind the rim of her glass, holding her ring necklace that she always had on.

"We covered it up, well enough for a night at least, then quietly shipped out the next day. I probably saved my friend's life, but sure didn't feel like a hero. And the other night at the airfield, another life – another stranger. I've found it's too easy, shooting strangers." I took a long drink from my own glass. "Maybe I've just got so much else on my mind that it's hard to have their deaths there as well, or maybe I'm just heartless," I said, not meeting Dottie's eyes and instead examining the carpet through the fishbowl effect of my wine glass.

"I don't think you're heartless."

I didn't reply, but tore my eyes away from the floor.

She continued, "I'm sick to death of putting on a farce every night to win the favor of *truly* heartless, vulgar men. I came here because I wanted to talk to somebody honest for once, someone who doesn't humor me just because of my looks."

"And how do you know that I don't?" I joked weakly, but was half curious as to what made her so certain that I didn't.

"You had someone too, didn't you," she said softly, holding the silver ring necklace out in her palm, showing it to me, "I can tell by the way you always look at my ring. Most men's eyes skip over it and continue downwards, but not yours."

She was quite perceptive. I stood slowly from my chair, almost trance-like, leaving my glass forgotten on the table beside me. The small red and gold box was lifted from its place atop the mantle and I held it near-reverently before placing it with utmost care upon the coffee table before Dottie. Her expression was hard to read as she stared at the box, but when I made no further movement she glanced up at me, asking permission. I must have done well enough in conveying it, because she gently lifted the lid with her crimson nailed hands, revealing the gold banded ring inset with a brilliant sapphire. A work of art that I'd only had the chance to see my fiancé wear on her deathbed.

Dottie looked up at me with watery eyes. "What was her name?"

"Maria," I whispered, like a prayer. The syllables felt foreign on my tongue, like a word from another time, from another life. I realized dully that I hadn't spoken her name aloud since the funeral. I gestured to one of the curio cabinets in the room. "All these artifacts that I collect and expeditions that I go on – it wasn't my passion. It has *become* my passion, because it was hers."

Dottie nodded, with gentle eyes and seeming to understand.

"Charles," she too whispered, with a hand clenched upon the silver ring around her neck and eyes staring off into the past, "his name was Charles and he never came back from France."

I nodded back.

And so we drank, and told stories of dreams new and lost, the sapphire glowing in the lamplight between us. Outside the rain continued to fall and for once, I didn't mind.

Chapter 18 - In Color

Dottie

Ever since the night with Officer Downs, the game felt different now, more dangerous; but I was prepared to go all in on another round with my newest prospect – Jon Barry. Mr. Barry, I gathered, was a man of extraordinary wealth, judging by the manner in which he threw his weight and his money around the Velvet Jester. Most of The Jester's patronage behaved in a similar way, ordering serving girls around and making flashy shows of wealth; but Jon Barry was different in one way and it was the only way that mattered to me. He recognized the girls in the photo.

I'd received a call from the eccentric talent coordinator that morning, asking me back for a show; which I accepted against my personal wishes to never step foot into The Jester again. Despite my reluctance to mingle once more within the ranks of Glasspier's most vile, I knew it was where I was most likely to find someone who recognized the women alongside Charlotte in the dusty color photograph. On Friday, and now today, I'd shown the picture to a small handful of rich men under various guises in reasoning. I told some they were my long-lost family, to others I claimed that I wanted to meet with them because they were mildly famous singers from the decade past. Tonight though was the first real bite, with the affluent Mr. Barry claiming to have known all three of them. The Jester was its usual cesspool of twinkling lights, noxious perfumes mixed with tobacco, and hungry eyes, as I showed Mr. Barry the photograph.

"I would just love to have a photo done like that," I drawled, "a professional photoshoot would do wonders for my singing career… I've had that picture for a long time and always envisioned myself with them on that settee in autochrome."

Mr. Barry tapped the photograph in thought. His dark eyes had flashed the briefest inkling of confusion when I'd first handed him the picture, just after they'd given me one good assessment head to toe. At the very least he seemed to be more in control of their wandering than the rest of the men I was used to here, because after his first initial glance his gaze remained fixed stoically upon my face and the picture frame.

The ghost of a smile touched the corners of his lips. "Well my dear, it appears it's your lucky day. I was there when this picture was taken."

He handed the frame back to me across the table and with my mind alight from the gravity of that claim, I couldn't help but to not feel particularly lucky. There was something cold and calculating about Mr. Barry that snuffed out most of the excitement found in finally making such a breakthrough with the picture from the Marlowe attic. His steel gray hair, firm jaw, and unwavering stare seemed to cut through my moxie and go straight to the bone; but I continued to play the part. I continued to pretend to be enamored with both him and the idea of having a professional photoshoot.

I set the frame on my lap and giggled. "Oh my, that *is* really lucky! Did you do the picture? Do you know who the girls are?" I let the questions spill out in girlish fashion. They *were* genuine questions I had; it was just the *delivery* of them that I falsified.

"I knew them, yes. Can't say that I do anymore… that was quite some time ago. A long enough time ago and an acquaintance short enough that I'm afraid I don't recall their names. A friend of mine took the pictures and she has a far better memory than me – we had a business arrangement and still do actually, but I haven't employed her services in some time."

I cocked my head slightly to question why.

"Lack of new talent and lack of necessity." He waved a hand dismissively. "I've been in the business long enough that there are few who interest me enough to bother with it and besides, I've made enough in investments since then to not *need* to bother with it."

"What would it take for you to bother with it again?"

A creased expression came across his face and his eyes gleamed with a new interest. "A girl with exceptional... *talent,*" he said, with a sly grin that made my skin crawl. I made sure that my discomfort was buried beneath a winning smile.

"You wouldn't happen to know such a girl, would you?" I twirled my hair through my fingers for the full effect.

"I might."

I turned and lowered my head coyly as Mr. Barry reached into the inner pocket of his suit jacket and produced a white card alongside a sleek black and gold pen. He scrawled a quick note upon the back of the card and returned the pen to his jacket before standing up and passing the note to me.

"Goodnight, Ms. McFarlane."

He left his glass on the table and threw a wad of bills beside it, then turned to make his way through the crowd. A small sigh of relief escaped me as he exited the venue. The act set to take the stage after mine, a saxophone piano duet, flared to life with a slow crescendo of improvisation in E minor as I held the card up in the low light to read what Jon Barry had written.

'*Bronze Crown. 6pm tomorrow. Look your best.*'

I intended to.

Chapter 19 - The Blood of Jupiter

Thomas

The red and gold box sat again in its place atop the mantle and the rain had abated outside, its departure made known in the form of steam rising from the street as the dawn broke over the city. The empty chair across from where I took my morning coffee and newspaper, too felt a vacancy that ached a bit more than I'd expected it would. Sometime between Dottie's arrival at dusk and her departure many hours later, I realized that I'd missed having someone intelligent and understanding to talk to into the small hours. With coffee drained and newspaper read, I put the both of them down and sighed. It was best not to dwell on it, I decided. Save that for the memoirs. And besides, there was work to do.

With the necessary home repairs taken care of yesterday, today I set to work on some of the routine maintenance on my motorbike that I'd been putting off for want of better weather. And better weather it was, I could hardly remember the last time I'd seen the sun stand so proudly above the Glasspier skyline. I busied myself in my front driveway with cleaning carburetor jets and replacing spark plugs as the day trudged on in anticipation of my meeting with Lockry. Sometime in the mid-evening, I put the tools away and wiped the excess oil off the freshly lubricated chain before going inside to freshen up and change into something more becoming of a dinner party.

By two minutes to six I was leaning my motorcycle on its stand outside the residences of Stephen Lockry, where he too was just now arriving in a gloss black Mercedes sedan. Punctuality was something we both held in high value I knew, so I was surprised by how closely he was cutting it. All previous times, I'd been met at the door with a serious smile and led to an already prepared table; although we had never met on a Sunday. So much for resting on the Sabbath I thought, as I approached the front door while Lockry stowed his car in the attached garage park. I only stood on the step for a few seconds with my coin held to the aperture before hearing a click followed by the door opening before me.

"Thomas," Lockry's solemn voice resonated in acknowledgement. He was wearing today an ensemble much less flashy than usual: a plain (but expensive looking) black jacket with matching slacks and a maroon necktie in a simple knot. I noted despite all of this, that a rather extravagant maroon-dialed watch peeked out from beneath his right cuff, as his hand held the door open. It was good to see that the usual Lockry flair was still there somewhere albeit in a reduced fashion. I stepped inside. He turned as usual for me to follow, dark eyes delivering a small wrinkle of apology before doing so.

"I'm afraid I was caught up in some business affairs just prior to our meeting that became much more involved than I was anticipating," he intoned, as we entered the sitting room, "so I'm sorry to say there will be no proper meal to garnish our discussion tonight."

"Unfortunate, but I know how things go," I responded politely. I didn't really mind; I was here to ask a favor anyways.

Lockry motioned me towards a chair near a curio cabinet housing some valuable necklaces from the Caribbean isles. "I do, however, have some good news to assuage this disappointment."

I took the directed seat.

"Your payment is in," he said, before disappearing through the door to the kitchen and presumably down into the wine cellar. I waited as patiently as I could in the sitting room, marveling as I did every time I visited, at some of the artifacts and oddities on display. There was a broach inset with a large ruby that I was unfamiliar with, beside a jade statue of an elephant that I'd personally acquired and sold some years back. I began to recall fondly the gentry estate and its sprawling emerald fields in Tuscany where I'd bartered for the small figurine. Before I was able to tread too far down memory lane, Lockry returned holding two glasses filled with a red wine in one hand and a black briefcase with silver latches in the other. He set the briefcase on the table between us and held out the wine glasses for me to take the closest of, before sitting down.

I raised the glass, swirling it. "What is it?"

"You tell me," he said, gesturing for me to drink.

I did. It was savory, with a slightly peppery finish that plunged me back into my earlier wandering memories of the Italian countryside.

"*Sangiovese*. The Blood of Jupiter." I smiled inwardly, at the happenstance in his choice of drink, glancing sidelong at the jade elephant once more.

"Correct. We'll make you a sommelier yet. Now, about this." He pushed the briefcase towards me and motioned for me to open it. I obliged. The smooth silver clasps came undone with a satisfying click and pop as I lifted the case open, revealing its contents. Inside, were ten clasps of crisp twenty-dollar bills laid out in grooves inset into the case. Reaching slowly for the leftmost clip I counted five twenties. The other nine clips looked to be identical.

"A thousand," Lockry confirmed, leaning back in his chair.

Damn. Easily enough for me to get to the Congo and back and finally put that curiosity to rest. It was my ticket to leave my mark on the world with a significant anthropological discovery. But Leon needs a way into the party, I reminded myself. Was I really going to give this up for that? I placed the clasp of money back within the case and shut the lid before pushing it back a couple inches towards Lockry.

“Thanks, but I can’t accept it. Not yet at least.” I was here for a reason. More money would come once I was a full member of The Blights upper circle and then I could take all the trips I wanted.

“Because the job’s not done?” he questioned, “you've done half and we trust that you’ll pull through for the final shipment.”

“No, it’s not that. I intend to complete the final shipment, no worries there, but *there is* something else. It’s why I called you to meet sooner than our usual night.”

He drank his wine and waved his palm, gesturing for me to continue.

“I need to get myself and two others – actually, make it three others, if possible, into the Glasspier estate party this weekend.” I had a feeling Leon would think it important to have Conrad there as well.

Lockry didn’t look surprised but I knew he could be thinking just about anything under his mask of formality and his features would never betray it.

“That’s this Friday, is it not?” he asked mildly.

“Yes. The twenty-sixth.”

“Good, because the final shipment is the twenty-seventh. So there will be no conflict of dates, nor interests.”

“Correct. Midnight again?”

“Yes.”

“I’ll be there.”

He nodded. “Then I will do everything I can to make sure you can be at the party. But it’s not going to be cheap. I know that invites are *very* hard to come by.”

“I figured as much. Use however much of my cut is necessary to make it happen,” I said, pushing the briefcase towards him once again. This time he picked it up and placed it on the ground beside his chair.

“You are quite the enigma. I hope this party is everything you hope it to be.”

“So do I.” I took another sip of the Italian countryside and stole a last longing glance at the briefcase filled with potential closure.

So do I.

Chapter 20 - Entr'acte

Leon

Sept. 22nd 1947
Monday
Glasspier,

Leons Journal
September 22nd, 1947 13:30
Entry #309

When I was young, I was accident prone. You can't expect much more from a boy growing up on a farm who hadn't grown into his feet yet. Every time I'd skin a knee or break a finger, my father would tend to it and tell me to go easy on myself. I said I would, but never listened. It was just the two of us; I could never leave all of the work to him. "Healing isn't always linear", he would say when I inevitably re-injured myself.

We found Henry Wakeman in the hangar five days ago now.
I remember the sleek silver airplane in the gloom before finding the body. Then I couldn't feel my feet or my fingers and there was a metallic taste in my mouth. The world turned white and I could hear something in the distance; some kind of screaming.

I was back in those woods, starving, and there was a golden stag in front of me... taunting me. My Ka-bar heavy in my hand and I knew in that moment as I always did – that it was him or me. So I chased him. I chased him until the sun went below the horizon and the world turned to darkness, the moonlight just barely seeping through the canopy. And there he was. And then he was dead and I could feel my hands again. They were dripping with blood, the blood of the stag, darker than the shadows that lurk in the back alleys of Berlin. But I wasn't there, I was on the tarmac with Dottie and Thomas. I probably owe them my life.

'Healing isn't always linear'. I thought about that sentiment from my father while locking the journal away. I'd hoped that writing down my thoughts would somehow draw out the darkest of them, like bloodletting to cure a disease. Was it helping? Possibly, although at times I felt it only served to ensure my hands remained stained a dark crimson.

I held a smoldering cigarette in my office; small bits of ash tumbling carelessly onto my black slacks and making a contrast as stark as the rakish shadows that bisected the room through the venetian blinds. I was thinking about Jenny and our business arrangement. She'd promised me thirty a day plus expenses and so far, she'd delivered on her end. It was nearing time that I returned in kind. I thought about calling her to tell about the notion of Jake possibly being alive, just to deliver something, but then I remembered how she'd handled the news the night of her first appearance and decided against it. I was beginning to question if thirty a day plus expenses was really worth it, now that I was starting to understand the scope of the case.

I took a final drag and brushed the flecks of ash from my lap. It didn't matter if it was worth it. I'd made a deal and set my price – more than most get to do. I planned to honor it.

Chapter 21 - The Crown & the Orchid

Dottie

Following a day of delicate autumn sunshine was a damp Monday. I leaned against a street lamp with a cigarette in a hand slightly shaking before the shining facade of the Bronze Crown. On the street, cars rumbled by, their tires splashing in the leftover puddles from an overnight rain. I knew the Bronze Crown had a reputation as the most expensive restaurant in Glasspier and it'd been a dream of mine to perform there on its grand stage for its stuffy patrons and their deep pockets. But that dream seemed hazy and far off now in light of recent events. Still, there was a spark of excitement buried somewhere deep beneath a surface of anxiety as I waited for Mr. Jon Barry.

The clock tower down the bustling street read two minutes to six and I wondered how I would recognize Mr. Barry amongst all the other socialites emerging from expensive cars to hand their keys to valet drivers in their spotless white gloves. My wondering was answered for me when the clock tower struck six and a glossy white car exuding luxury rolled around the corner beneath it and hummed to a stop in front of the Bronze Crown. I put out what was left of the cigarette under my shoe and stood up straight, smoothing the front of my sleek rosebud colored gown as I did so. Mr. Barry, in an ensemble of all black, white, and silver, stepped out from the rear doors of the flashy car and his driver pulled away, merging back into the rest of the traffic. So, Mr. Barry was in a wealth bracket above the use of valet services. Good to know, I thought, while making a conscious effort to unset my jaw as I pictured briefly the battered old sedan my brother and I shared. Mr. Barry greeted me with a smile of perfect white teeth that mirrored the finish on the car he'd arrived in, then took my arm and led me into the Bronze Crown.

The extravagant meal was multi-course and delivered by silent tuxedoed stewards who careened gracefully between the venues elaborate table settings. After seeing the rococo-style burnished bronze crown molding that crawled all the way up the domed ceiling like ivy, I had a guess as to where the restaurant had gotten its name. Conversation was sparse between Mr. Barry and I, instead, it was more of a monologue. We did talk briefly about my singing career, during which I mentioned that I'd always dreamed of performing here. Following that, he bragged at length about his career, his numerous properties, and his vacations to various exotic locales. Thankfully for my sake, he was often interrupted by associates that he knew. Throughout the evening, I came to realize that his true design in dining with me here was to show me off amongst his rich colleagues, many of whom also had beautiful girls half their age clinging to their arms.

The meal wasn't particularly filling, prioritizing aesthetics and 'refined taste' over substance. Such seemed to be the theme with Mr. Barry and his many peers. As the final covered dish was placed before us, (poached pears in a red cream) I was looking forward to getting this whole portion of the evening over with so that I could meet the supposed photographer. However, none of my words, actions, or expressions throughout the whole experience would have led anyone to believe I was anything but enamored with the charming Mr. Jon Barry.

By the time we stepped back out into the petrol laden air and I was escorted to the open door of Mr. Barry's car, the sun was already sinking low behind the skyscrapers of downtown. While taking my seat in the plush upholstery of what I could now tell was a brand-new Rolls Royce, I shivered in both excited anticipation and fear of what was to come at our next stop. Mr. Barry sat beside me in the back and the driver pulled away once again from the Bronze Crown. The car rode smoothly and silently through the streets of Glasspier and Mr. Barry and I, too, were silent. There, in the privacy of his fancy car, was the first time that he seemed a bit withdrawn compared to his usual self-assuredness. I made a few half-hearted attempts to ease the tension by remarking about certain buildings or by recalling the finer points of my first foray into the Bronze Crown; but his one-word answers and placating nods led me to give in and allow him to continue staring out the window in silence.

My speculation about the shift in his demeanor was cut short when we arrived outside an upper-class hotel and the car came to a smooth stop beneath its lighted awning. The calligraphed script on the placard above us read: '*LeClaire Orchid Hotel & Suites*' and the text was encircled by yellow light bulbs. The nervous hitch returned to my stomach en force, only slightly assuaged by feeling the dense weight in my purse as I lifted it exiting the car. Why were we at a hotel? Was this really where such photoshoots took place? I resisted the urge to take the picture out and look it over again for signs of it being staged at the LeClaire. The hotel was fancy enough that it was plausible, but I couldn't help but have some misgivings.

Mr. Barry seemed to take notice of this, or maybe he was just making conversation, while we walked through the front doors. "Don't worry, Katie is a lovely girl. You'll like her."

I mustered an easy-going face and took in the grand lobby of the hotel. There was white and gold covering every inch of the room save for the potted ferns standing vigil along the dark navy-blue pathway leading to the front desk; which Mr. Barry and I now approached.

"Here for Katie Garcia, she should be expecting me," Mr. Barry said, leaning with one arm on the counter, behind which a girl around my age sat dressed professionally but looking bored.

"She is. Room 383."

Without a word of thanks Mr. Barry straightened up and offered me his arm. I took it and he ushered me into an elevator with golden doors.

Room 383 was a glamorous contrast to anywhere I'd ever stayed, permanently or otherwise. Everything in the room seemed as though it had its place and the decorations and furnishings were all matching. There was a color scheme of bronze, dark woods, and red velvet running throughout the room, with books and magazines placed here and there for a sophisticated effect. Despite all of this, the room felt hollow. It didn't feel like a place anyone actually lived, but was rather more like a movie or theater set. A stage. The camera setup on a tall tripod facing the chaise lounge to our right rounded out this effect. *God, not another chaise lounge*. If the room was a stage, entering scene left was an eccentric looking woman in a flowing forest-green dress with bobbed white hair and a round face. She appeared only slightly younger than Mr. Barry and her presence was enhanced and made larger than life by a long, eastern looking scarf encircled around her neck and trailing behind her as she approached.

She embraced Mr. Barry briefly before extending a dainty downturned hand for me.

"Charmed to meet you my dear," she drawled with a French accent, "Jon sure does have an eye for high art… and it's been far too long." That last sentiment seemed to be directed at nobody in particular.

Regardless, meeting Katie set my nerves at ease. Or at least as 'at ease' as they could be. She had an aloof but kind nature about her that made any sort of situation like the one with Officer Downs seem like an impossibility here. She waved a hand, beckoning me over to the camera. Mr. Barry remained quiet and I was vaguely aware of him taking the chair across from the lounge seat.

Katie adjusted some of the dials on the camera, looking at me expectantly as though she assumed I had already been told what to do by Mr. Barry earlier. All he'd told me was how his trip to London last month had been 'exceptional' and how his vacation home was in need of a renovation on its swimming pool. Rather than posing on the lounge as I imagined I was supposed to, I set my purse down beside the seat, taking from it the photograph of the three women.

"Is this your work?" I asked, pushing the picture frame towards Katie. She seemed unphased as she held it and simply replied 'yes' with a gentle smile. I pushed a bit further, "Do you remember their names? I've had this photo for a long time and as a young girl I always wondered who they were…"

Katie flipped the frame over with a serene expression, like she was divining the answer from a card reading or some other form of mystic insight.

"Alyssa, Charlotte…" She read the two names on the back before flipping the frame around once more and staring hard at the girl with dark hair on the right. My eyes briefly flickered towards Mr. Barry despite myself and he was sitting stock still, doing his best to look mildly interested. But I could sense something was troubling him.

"...Jasmine. Yes, that was her name," Katie finally decided. She passed the photograph back to me which I took reluctantly, hoping for more.

I smiled appreciatively, "What a pretty name, do you remember their last names?"

"No."

Well. That was an abrupt and decisive 'no'. Mr. Barry had a look of satisfaction on his face that stayed affixed there for the rest of the evening. I placed the photo on the small table near the camera, hoping that Katie might consider it further as the night went on and then took my place as directed by her upon the chaise lounge. She took her place behind the camera and we began.

The photoshoot was relatively painless. I modeled a few poses at Katie's direction while she operated the camera, moving it occasionally for different angles.

"So, Jon tells me you're the newest up-and-coming star in the entertainment world of Glasspier?" she asked, between the brilliant flashes of the bulb above the camera.

"One can only hope," I laughed, dazed from the popping of the flashbulb. "I've always dreamed of-"

"-move your left hand back a little and rest it on your thigh."

I followed her suggestion and adjusted my posture accordingly. "-always dreamed of singing in the Bronze Crown and seeing myself on the cover of a magazine or in the papers."

"Well, you've made a good acquaintance in Jon then, *-tilt your head back just a bit, good-* he's brought up a few stars in his day." The camera popped and flashed once more.

We took a few more on the lounge and then she turned the camera to the left and had me stand beside a marble plinth with a bronze vase perched on top, vines spilling out and creeping down towards the base. After a couple more dazzling pops and flashes from the camera, Mr. Barry, who'd been a silent observer until this point, rose from his chair.

"Okay Katie, now a couple for me," he said in a low voice. Katie looked from me to Mr. Barry expectantly.

"Must we do more? You're welcome to any of those." I pointed to the camera's reels, feigning exhaustion.

"I appreciate that, but those aren't quite as… *revealing* as I would like for my personal collection," he said through a hungry grin with those perfect white teeth. I caught Katies eyes with mine. It was only a second, but she seemed to sense my apprehension and get the message.

"I thought you two had an agreement prior to coming here," she stated firmly, looking back and forth between Mr. Barry and I, with her now hardened expression settling on the former. "She's an aspiring singer and obviously not some common whore from The Den like the rest," she hissed at Mr. Barry under her breath and I noticed her eyes dart down to the picture of the three women beside her on the table.

The grin slid from Mr. Barry's face and morphed into a scowl, but even he seemed mollified by the indignant Katie and her coiling scarves. The picture, The Den, Katies wayward glance – *common whores.* Could it be? I knew The Den, well actually I knew *of* it.

"Are you satisfied with the photos we've got dear?" Katie asked, turning her back to the still scowling Mr. Barry. I resisted the instinct to throw another nervous glance his way.

"Yes, quite." I offered a smile and my hand in thanks.

"Good. I'll have these ready in a few days, I'm sure they'll turn out wonderfully," she said, addressing the both of us. She then had me write my address down for her, a step I'd nearly forgotten. I'd already gained what I'd hoped to from coming here; Katies admonishment of Mr. Barry and her glance at the picture had given me more than enough. Actually getting the developed photos was a somewhat trivial detail to me now.

The tension between Mr. Barry and I was such that I waited, hoping that Katie would offer a ride home but she just made herself busy with taking down the camera after bidding us both '*adieu*'.

If I'd thought that the mostly silent ride *to* The Orchid hotel had been awkward, it was nothing compared to the return trip. The silence before had been a simple rift between two people with little in common, but now it felt more like an uncrossable chasm of tensely simmering animosity. Walking to a payphone and calling for a ride was something I considered, but Mr. Barry seemed content to exist in tenuous silence with me, so I didn't bring the notion up. I did, however, ride the whole way back with my purse in my lap.

It was twilight now and slowly, agonizingly slowly, the Rolls Royce coasted smoothly to a stop alongside the curb in front of the Bronze Crown. I got out of the car as quickly as I could without it being offensively so, and to my surprise Mr. Barry did the same on the other side. He came around the rear of the car.

"I'm sorry."

I waited, not daring to make a cynical face at his uncharacteristic apology.

"I'm sorry," he repeated, "I didn't mean, but with the Jester and all… I assumed…" It all sounded strange, to hear him being genuine, or at least trying to be. I wasn't sure how to respond. I opened my mouth, hoping that the right words would come out, but he spoke first. "Goodnight Ms. McFarlane."

Then he was back in the car, its deep glossy surface colored with the orange tinted glow of sunset as it slid away into the coming night. There, beneath the streetlamp again, a cigarette found its way to my lips – and this time the hand that held it there was still.

Chapter 22 - The Red Dress

Leon

Sept. 23rd 1947
Tuesday
Glasspier,

The sign outside the small boutique store on Harlow Street had a crimson painted ribbon weaving between the letters of: '*The Red Dress - Alterations and Custom Pieces*'. Not my usual type of venue, but I walked inside with a confidence like it was. I'd pulled out my best suit, combed my hair and shaved my face like I was going to a wedding – or maybe a funeral, I corrected myself, seeing the black clad reflection in the glass of the door on the way in. Everything to give the impression that I was someone who belonged at the same table with the Glasspiers. My canvassing the day prior had come up with a few shops, but The Red Dress seemed to be the best option to get something quality enough for the Glasspier estate while still being a degree under the radar.

Inside, an assortment of clothes hung on racks and stood rigid on mannequins alongside rows of neatly polished dress shoes and heels.

The majority of the clothes seemed to cater towards women, however there were some smaller sections devoted to suits. They all looked to be far out of my usual price range but I didn't plan to let anyone here know that.

Visual survey passing muster, I approached the plump woman at the front desk who was in the process of mending a tear on an old military green overcoat. She looked about the same age as the coat and twice as worn. Glancing up above an oversized pair of horn-rimmed glasses before returning her focus to her work, she asked: "What can I do for you?" in a voice so soft I thought her words might blow away before they reached me.

"Good evening madam," I said, doing my best to imitate the talking manner of dignified gentry, "I am here to inquire about having outfits fashioned for the Glasspier estate masquerade this weekend."

She looked up slowly again with renewed interest, but I wasn't sure if she'd fully bought my performance. It'd felt a bit heavy handed and I silently wished I'd rehearsed my act a little beforehand.

"Cutting it a bit close aren't we?"

I laughed. "That I am, however, I would ensure that you're properly compensated for your time and the rush, you have my word on that."

"It'll take more than your word," she said, setting the needle and thread down on top of the old coat, "and did you say *outfits?* Plural?"

"I did, yes. Myself and two associates have found ourselves lucky enough to be considered in the Glasspier's last round of invitations. It will be a first for all of us, so I apologize for the delayed notice but I only just recently became aware myself! Some of my other associates recommended your services in high regard for our masks and formalwear, so, here I am." I worried that I'd gone too far with that last part and hoped that she wouldn't ask for names of those fabricated colleagues. Luckily, it seemed to do the trick and she didn't ask for any further detail, instead, she stood and motioned me over to a bare patch of floor between the counter and a nearby mannequin wearing a thick fur coat. Somewhere between the front desk and the designated spot, a tailor's tape measure had found its way to her hand and she quickly put it to use.

“Since they’re not with you, do you have your associates’ measurements?” she asked, while looping the tape around my midsection and making a note of the number on some loose paper.

Damn, I didn’t. Some forethought there, I thought bitterly. “I don’t actually,” I forced a laugh. “I can call you though? Just after this, I’ll get their measurements and call you. I’ll put the money down now of course.”

The mention of money down seemed to win her over and she smiled. “No problem.” She rolled the tape back up, seemingly satisfied with the notes she’d taken down. “Now, tell me what it is that you’re looking for.”

“Just a nice suit and a mask to go with it.”

She cocked her head at me with lips downturned in playful disapproval, finally speaking with some vigor, “Oh come on, have some imagination! It’s a masquerade! Just about everyone will be sporting some color and most will have masks displaying animals or monsters of some kind. What would your associates like? Maybe we can start there.”

I thought for a moment, straining to think what Thomas and Dottie would like, but I was no fashion designer. I decided to go with my gut.

“For my friend Thomas, let's go with something smart and sharp. No nonsense. Blues and blacks.” I was spitballing here.

“Wonderful.” She wrote some more. “And for the other?”

Dottie was a bit trickier to pin down an idea for. I couldn't help but feel particularly unqualified to come up with an outfit for a lady. What would Dottie want? I knew the answer, reluctant as I was to admit it. Something innocently suggestive, something that she could use to her advantage. Not overtly sensual, but something that could be playfully so, with the right wearer.

I described that general idea in simpler terms to the seamstress, whose name I realized I didn’t even know, and she made a few more notes. I told her to defer to her best judgment when it came to the dress and its stylings. Then it was time to pick mine. But before that, I was compelled to make an additional request.

"Do you think you could throw in an additional mask? Nothing complicated, just a simple red one. It wouldn't need a suit to go with it." I didn't intend to pay Conrad's whole way, but couldn't shake that continual feeling that he should be there.

The seamstress squinted behind her glasses, but didn't otherwise question the additional guest. "It's no problem, just will bring the cost up slightly. I may even have one already made around here somewhere that could work if it doesn't need to be personalized."

"Thank you." I feared what the final price was going to be, but couldn't let on to that here. As far as 'The Red Dress' was concerned, I was capable of buying the entire shop if I so choosed. Jenny *did* agree to 'plus expenses' after all.

"And for your mask?" She held her pen poised above the note paper, ready to mark down my choice.

"How about a golden stag?"

Chapter 23 - Disguise

Dottie

"First the Jester, now The Den?" Angelo bemoaned, "are you *trying* to destroy your career? And any respect I've got for you..."

"Oh c'mon, I know that you know where I can find it, or that your cronies do," I replied, brushing off his comment.

"They're not my 'cronies'."

"Fine... your *compatriots.* Either way, I'm not destroying my career, I'll only be there for a night – and not for work. I just need information."

Angelo rolled his eyes, finally taking off his jacket and sitting down across from me in one of our uncomfortable and creaky wooden chairs that we kept in the entryway. I did feel a little bad about bombarding him with questions the second he arrived back at the apartment, but only a little.

"For Leon I assume?" he asked, but it wasn't really a question.

"Yes, for Leon."

"Can't imagine he'd want you traipsing around in places like The Den either."

"He does. Because unlike you he knows that I can handle myself." I'd crossed my arms unconsciously, but wasn't backing down now.

Angelo sighed. "It's not that I don't think you're capable... it's just... it's not a good look for Glasspier's supposed rising star to be seen going down there."

"So you *do* know where it is then."

He ran his fingers through his dark hair, slicking it to the back. "Yes, I do."

"Now I'm the one losing respect," I said, suppressing a smirk. Didn't want to agitate him too much, he still needed to spill about the location.

"Not… like that. I don't partake, but I've dropped Lenny and Bill off there a few times."

"Great, so my car has probably already been seen there, wherever *there* is. I'll fit right in."

"*Our* car," Angelo reminded me, "and I make sure it's not seen. The venue is inconspicuous anyways."

"Do tell?"

He sighed again, deeply this time and shook his head. "Fine, *fine*. But you owe me a favor."

"Sure." He knew I was good for it, we had nothing if not each other's word.

Angelo pushed his hair back again. "It moves around sometimes to keep the law off the scent, the few lawmen that care at least, but right now it's in an old converted speakeasy on Curwin street behind a clothing shop called 'The Red Dress'. Well more like beneath it actually." The humor of that was not lost on me. "You have to go down these shady looking steps to a door that leads into its basement. It'll look dingy on the outside, but it's very different inside. Or so I've heard."

The Red Dress. The name sounded familiar; I was sure I'd passed it by at some point. I'd lived here all my life but it seemed this city still had some secrets left for me.

The phone behind me rang. "Or so you've heard." I winked knowingly and rose from my chair which creaked in protest.

Angelo spoke over the sound of the phone's ringing, "You know Dots, some would say a 'thank you' could be in order. That's some 'in-the-know' info I just gave you. At the very least, I want the car this Saturday. That's my favor. Got a job at the port again that night…"

I waved a hand dismissively, agreeing to let him use the car Saturday and only half listening as I picked up the receiver and held it to my ear. It was Leon.

It had been easy to convince Angelo to let me have the car for the evening since he'd already claimed it for the upcoming weekend. It rolled now to a creaking halt in front of McCreary Investigations, about an hour after Leon's call. Catching a last glimpse of myself in the grimy rearview mirror, I stepped out of the car and grimaced at how well my current appearance matched the ripped-up seats and faded paint of the vehicle. It'd been easy to convince Angelo to let me use the car for the evening, but less so in convincing him to help me alter my appearance in such a way.

He'd found me a tattered old dress while I applied some heavy makeup, which I purposefully smeared a little just below my eyes. Messing up my hair and slipping into some worn shoes completed my disheveled appearance. My disguise. Now, here at the agency, lingering on its front step, I felt a twinge of embarrassment over letting anyone I knew see me like this. But no. I shouldn't. Leon and Thomas were both smart enough to understand the necessity of my guise. Or they would be, once I explained it. So with that thought, I pulled the door handle and made my grand entrance.

"Dottie? What the hell happened?" Leon was on his feet in an instant and rushing over to me in the entryway. Thomas too had risen from his usual chair with a concerned expression quickly replacing the smile from whatever he and Leon had been laughing about when I came in.

"Please, it's nothing. I'm okay, I did this," I explained, raising my hands to fend off their concern, but the statement only seemed to add confusion to their worry.

"Why? I know you said you had something big to share when we talked on the phone… this have something to do with it?"

"It does. Now let's all sit, so I can explain why I'm the greatest damn sleuth in all of Glasspier," I joked, hoping to further alleviate their concern. "No offense to you of course Leon."

The beginnings of a grin touched the corners of Leons mouth and he and Thomas relaxed a little, returning to their seats. I joined them. Once the drinks had been poured and they were both satisfied in my good state of being, Thomas waved a hand good naturedly saying, "All right, we've all been held in suspense long enough, out with it."

I made a big show of taking a long drink from my glass of wine, to which I received eyerolls and exasperated sighs. Then, sure that I had their undivided attention, I finally relented.

"Our dear, supposedly rich and highborn Mrs. Charlotte Marlowe… was a prostitute."

Leons jaw stuck out and his eyes narrowed in confusion. "What?"

"You know, like… a whore. A harlot. A woman of the night, a baw-," Leon's serious expression made me cut myself off. "Look, the point is, I met two individuals who actually knew her and although they didn't outright say she was, it was heavily implied."

"So you don't know for sure? And who were these individuals?" Leon questioned.

The cool stem of my wine glass rolled between my fingers. "Well… no, not with a hundred percent certainty, but I intend to prove it, which is why I'm done up like this. And the two individuals in question are Mr. Jon Barry, a *very* wealthy businessman and his photographer associate Katie. She took that picture you found at the Marlowe house, at Mr. Barry's direction."

Leon's expression was skeptical at first, but soon the crinkles beside his eyes smoothed into a tentative understanding as he toyed with the idea. "Charlotte Marlowe, a prostitute… why didn't I think of that – it would give reason to why someone would want her bumped off and also make it possible that Jake Marlowe, if he survived, may not be a Marlowe at all!" A familiar gleam had found its way into Leon's eyes and I was sure all the possible timelines of events were turning over in his head.

"A bastard?" Thomas mumbled, looking lost in thought.

Leon stood again, pacing behind the armchairs. "I know what you're thinking," he stated plainly, looking down at my tattered dress, "and it's a good idea, but risky and unnecessary."

"Unnecessary how? It's our best shot at finding out what happened that night. She had to have friends in the business," I retorted, looking at Thomas for support but he'd adopted a rather blank expression.

"Unnecessary because I haven't even talked to this 'Mr. Barry' or his photographer yet. Are you sure they told you everything they know? We may not need for you to go this far…" his words faded at the end, making his rebuttal sound flat and I could tell the allure of hearing it straight from the source of someone who *really* knew Charlotte was beginning to take hold.

"I'm not sure I could even contact them again if I wanted to. Katie is supposed to get a hold of me sometime to get my pictures to me, but I'm quite confident she doesn't know much more. Mr. Barry seemed to be keeping her in the dark on a lot of things, even regarding me."

"So we talk to Mr. Barry then."

"He contacted me," I explained, "wouldn't know how to reach him again beyond just getting lucky and running into him."

"Fine… fine," he said weakly, before finally ceasing his pacing about the room and slumping back into his chair.

Thomas finally voiced his thoughts, "So just to be clear and to make sure I'm up to speed, you're talking about posing as a prostitute somewhere in the hopes that you run into some other prostitute that knew Charlotte? Seems like a shot in the dark."

A smile crossed my face in anticipation for my second reveal of the night and I explained:

"It's not, because I've got a good idea of the place that she likely operated at. It's called '*The Den*'. And I've already taken the liberty of finding out where it's located."

Leon sat more upright from his previous defeated position and Thomas drank quietly with a face creased in worry. The two of them eyed each other and nodded, after seeming to come to some kind of unspoken agreement.

"What's the plan then?" Leon asked, finally.

"Nothing that you two need to worry yourselves about. This time, I go in alone. I handled myself just fine with Mr. Barry and Officer Downs and this should be a walk in the park in comparison."

Leon frowned at that. "I seem to remember you being held at gunpoint during the Downs fiasco. Don't know if I'd call that just fine."

"Well I seem to recall that that wouldn't have happened if Downs hadn't taken notice that I was being watched over."

"She has a point," Thomas interjected, before Leon could raise a counter argument, "Dottie can tread rather safely in places that we cannot and us being there may just jeopardize the whole ruse again."

Leon sighed and finished off his glass, placing it on the table in resignation. "So what, we just hang around here and hope you're not getting shot and dumped into a gutter somewhere?" The empty glass had barely made itself at home on the table before he reached for a smoke.

I'll admit, I felt bad that my friends would be worrying so much for me in my absence tonight and I didn't relish the idea of not having any backup. But I was also glad that I had friends that cared enough to be worried about me in the first place. So, emboldened by that thought, I rose and set my wine glass on the table next to Leon's tumbler.

"Yes. Precisely that. Stay near your telephone and don't be surprised if I'm not back until early morning."

Leon had lighted his cigarette and took a long drag from it before nodding assent. "Be careful. I trust you. But be careful."

Chapter 24 - Disguises

Dottie

Curwin Street was mostly dark when I arrived, with sporadic street lamps making pin pricks here and there in the gloam. Taking a leaf out of Angelos book, I parked the car down the way from the rear of the place, in a darker section of the street and waited. To my best knowledge, the entrance to The Den was in an alleyway across the street to my left some fifty feet further down the road. Although there were plenty of people walking about and loitering near the alleyway entrance, I couldn’t tell if anyone was descending down into The Den. What was I waiting for exactly? I wasn't sure. The confidence I’d had earlier was beginning to wane with the light, so maybe I was just waiting for my nerves to settle. It was just another act, nothing more, I chastised myself while lighting a cigarette and throwing my purse over my shoulder. The car door opened with a pop and squeak.

I was across the street as soon as there was a gap in the traffic, eyes kept down, only flashing upwards enough to ensure I didn’t collide with any of the people milling about the sidewalk. Not long after, following a quick glance up and down Curwin Street and being satisfied enough of no one watching, I slunk casually into the space between buildings. The engulfing darkness of the alley between the rear of The Red Dress and the neighboring office suites enveloped me without anyone on Curwin being the wiser.

The backstreet was even dimmer than the main road, with just a lone reddish orange bulb hanging in a metal casing above a rough-hewn staircase going below the clothing shop. The only other glow came from the street behind me and from the end of my cigarette. Despite having rehearsed in my head a hundred times already since that morning, I ran my lines over in my head one last time in a further attempt to quell the nerves that surfaced before a performance. The temperature noticeably dropped a couple degrees descending the stone steps to where a sturdy looking metal door sat recessed into the wall.

Not knowing what else to do, I knocked. I waited, exhaling smoke into the air while rolling the cigarette to the tips of my fingers and then letting it hang at my side. My other hand reached unconsciously for my ring necklace, but I'd left it at home to complete the disguise. I didn't like how naked I felt without it. Maybe that was what had me so on-edge. I let the cigarette fall from my fingertips and land onto the cracked bottom step, the burning end face-up like a less proud smokestack from the steel mill. Finally, the heavy door grated open.

"Please, I have nowhere else to go," I pleaded, to the largest man I'd ever seen. Stooped over in the doorway due to not fitting beneath it, stood a giant of a human standing well over two heads taller than me, his own looking like it'd been chiseled crudely from a sandstone block. He had shoulders like a billboard that barred me from seeing past him and was wearing a suit that I assumed had to have been custom made. A bit taken aback, I hoped that my opening line had landed as I planned for it to but then decided that the added shock as I delivered it could only really have enhanced the effect I was going for. The massive man didn't make any indication he'd heard me, but simply stepped back out the way into the underground room and allowed me entry.

Crossing the threshold tentatively, partly out of genuinely being rattled by the appearance of the hulking figure and partly as necessitated by my act, I was greeted by warm lighting and the strong smell of lavender perfume. The room, despite being a basement, was actually quite inviting. Around me, it was all ruddy brick walls, ornamented with amber light bulbs that cast shadows off the celluloid plastic plants ornamenting the room. Directly across from me was a floor-pillow lounge occupied by three women around my age, each wearing rather revealing color-matched gowns and undergarments. To my right, a large wooden bar absent of any alcohol and now seeming to serve as a receptionist desk of sorts, stood partitioning off that wall, and the doors behind it, from the rest of the room. A few empty decorative bottles on a shelf mounted to the wall seemed to be all that remained of the bar counters' former life in the speakeasy. Between the counter and the decorative bottle racks, was a woman with blonde hair who looked quite a lot older than the others and was dressed only marginally more modestly in a gown of purple silk.

With big eyes, I approached the counter and the lady behind it. She leaned over onto the bar with a face already softening at seeing my condition. I kept my voice on the edge of tears and let my disheveled appearance do the rest. "M-my name's Alice," I trembled, "I have nowhere else to go. My husband… h-he…" I let my words break off into a sob. The woman in purple nodded emphatically and I could see movement in the periphery of my teary vision as the other girls rose from the lounge to comfort me. I let them. Then, after some consoling, I thanked them and made a show of getting my emotions in check. The short woman wearing yellow was the first to introduce herself.

"I'm Daffodil Rae, this is Lavender," she waved her hand towards the girl in pink, "and this is Natalie Scarlet. She's our newest, other than you of course." Natalie was, naturally, wearing red to match her red hair.

"Are those your-"

"Real names?" Daffodil laughed, "no they're not. And I suggest you think about what you might want to go by and what color looks good on you if you're going to stick around." The other two hid small smiles and finally the older woman in purple behind the counter introduced herself as 'Madame Violet'. She suggested that Daffodil show me around, to which the cheery girl happily agreed.

I followed her lead down the dim hallway that departed the main lounge opposite the front desk. The hallway was lit by more reddish bulbs and had five closed doors lining the length of it. Daffodil was explaining the usage of the rooms, but I was only half paying attention. My thoughts were otherwise occupied, trying to see a solution to the newest layer of complication. The girls used *stage names*. None of them went by Alyssa or Jasmine, although I suppose both of those could be real names or fake ones. Regardless it didn't matter, the only one old enough to possibly be from the picture was Violet and she wasn't a match in name or appearance. There was the girl with red hair and there *was* something familiar about her, but she was far too young to be Alyssa. Maybe she was related? *Damn,* I was going to have to dig deeper than I'd hoped, but I guess walking in and running into exactly who I was looking for was a lot to ask.

Back through the dim hallway, Daffodil brought me into the main lobby once more. The large man still stood stoically beside the door and I found myself glad that it appeared to be Madame Violet who was calling the shots around The Den and not him. I had a feeling that he would have been much less sympathetic. In the lounge, only Lavender was still present, which further vexed me since Natalie was the one I couldn't shake the feeling I needed to get closer to. There was something gnawing at the back of mind with her, a familiarity that I couldn't place. Did she look at all like the red-haired girl from the photograph? I strained to picture them side-by-side, itching to take the frame from my purse and refresh my memory. I fought back the desire to do so.

Daffodil brought me around the counter and reached for the sturdy door behind it. It opened, revealing another poorly lit hallway, albeit a much shorter one. She talked while we walked shoulder-to-shoulder down it. "The money isn't bad, although I doubt that as much of it reaches us as it should. Violet keeps a bigger share of course for keeping things in order, but I suspect she's under someone's thumb as well… regardless, it's good enough money that you can live on it – if you can live with the work that is. Most girls make enough to have their own places, although a few stay here full time."

We reached the end of the short hall and went through another door, into a room just as large as the main one, but sectioned off with red curtains. There was a main walkway up the center of the space with 'rooms' formed by the curtains on each side. City light seeped feebly into the area from a ground-level window high up the basement wall at the end of the lane. I followed Daffodil in the direction of that window between the curtain rooms until we reached the second row from the end. Most of the ones that we passed were drawn closed, but of the few that were open I could see single beds, vanities with large mirrors, and hanging racks for clothes.

"This is where we get ready, take our breaks, and oftentimes stay the night. Some of the ladies live here full time. You'll get your own eventually if you stick around long enough." She beamed at the thought. "For now though you can share with Jasmine, she enjoys taking the new girls under her wing."

Jasmine? Could it be? Hearing that name had me far more excited than the idea of having my own curtain room. Maybe I'd finally had a stroke of luck, lord knows I was due for it. Daffodil announced her presence and then pulled the curtain aside without waiting for a response. It revealed a little room like the others before it and she ushered me in. A woman with dark hair sat half clothed on a padded stool in front of a vanity set mirror, seemingly in heavy concentration as she applied mascara. "This is Alice!" Daffodil enthused, "she's new here, so you can show her the ropes."

Jasmine leaned closer to the mirror with the brush and didn't acknowledge the intrusion apart from thanking Daffodil in a monotone voice, to which the friendly girl flashed me one last smile and pattered away back through the rows of curtains. I waited until her footsteps faded to nothing before I made any sort of move or said anything. Jasmine didn't seem to be in a hurry either. She glanced up and caught my eye in the reflection of the mirror briefly while placing the brush back into its red container. It was her. I was sure of it. The resemblance to the picture was near exact and I marveled at how little she seemed to have aged since it was taken.

I struggled with how best to lead into my questions, but a faintly musty and acidic smell coming from the curtain-room next door was making it difficult to think. I broke the silence and the stuffiness with a cough and with the mascara kit back in its case on the vanity, Jasmine turned finally to face me, seeming to size me up as she did.

"Did you know Charlotte Marlowe?" I asked in a quick, low whisper. I don't know what came over me asking her outright, but it seemed like the right thing to do, given that I was certain she was *the* Jasmine I was looking for. No use in beating around the bush and keeping up the charade of looking for shelter here longer than I had to.

Jasmine's ambivalent face darkened, turning grave and aging ten years in the second those words left my lips. “No, I’ve no idea who that is,” she said sternly, regaining some composure.

“You don’t…?” I faltered, and my thoughts piled into one another trying to make sense of why she would deny such a basic question with what I *knew* was a lie.

“No. I don’t.” The statement was final and her lips pressed together into a thin creased line that told me that there was to be no more discussion down that subject of questioning. Why such forceful denial? I lifted my purse for the photograph, a motion that made Jasmine come quickly to her feet with a portrait of fear painted onto her face. I paused, and in that moment of tension between the two of us it dawned on me the nature of her adamant denial. *She had been shut up.* Paid off, or otherwise threatened by someone to keep silent. Leon was right – this whole thing ran deep.

“It’s okay. I’m not here to force you to say or do anything, but I *know* that you knew Charlotte. I’m part of a group looking to bring the truth to light. To make things right,” I said, with equal parts gentleness and assured confidence. Seeing Jasmine's tensed posture relax a little, I continued my reach into my purse drawing out the photograph. Holding the frame out before her, the air was completely quiet and still, broken only by the occasional car headlight from the street outside filtering through the lone window into the gloom below. That subtle acrid stuffiness from the curtain-room next door made the dim basement feel twice as smothering.

With trembling hand outstretched for the picture, the darkness rolled off of Jasmine’s face in a wave and was surmounted by an air of profound sadness. She held the photo, staring at the frozen image of her past with a distance in her eyes suggesting a heartache that ran its throughline straight from 1923 to the present. A single tear streaked its own throughline in her sparkling dark-green mascara so recently applied, but she only looked up and whispered: “He made me swear not to tell…. anyone. Ever. Or bad things would happen to me and the other girls." She was shaking now, like the subtle vibrations of a plucked string. It was now or never.

"I'm working with an investigator, he's a good man. You can trust me that it will stay between us and him until we're ready to blow this thing open. And we're so close, but we need you. We need what you know, to bring justice for Charlotte and her son." The pale light reflecting in Jasmine's watery eyes was beginning to show something through the sorrow: an inkling of hope. Seeing her in such a state, some long-dormant fire was kindling within me too. A fire fed with the desire to see those who mistreat the vulnerable and the weak brought low and exposed. A desire to see their lies and corruption and games at an end – all being stoked and fanned to life by the evidence of broken lives left in their wakes. Lives like Jasmine's.

"I don't… know if I can-"

"You can," I spoke with a newfound intensity, "you have to. Whoever did this will continue to do it, unless someone is brave enough to stand up to them. I've dealt with hundreds of these types of men, on both sides of the law, who all think that they can take and do whatever they want in this city. It's time that we remind them that we have a voice – a voice that speaks the truth in the face of whatever intimidation they try to keep us down with. Truth that will tear through their false sense of invulnerability and vindicate Charlotte's memory." I stopped for a breath and Jasmine had ceased her trembling. "We need to know who was responsible. So will you please tell that truth?"

At first, she didn't reply. She clutched the picture frame hard in her hands and stepped forward towards me. A moment of indecision born from years of silence seemed to plague her, but she surmounted it and slowly spoke a name:

"...Thomas. Thomas *Glasspier*." She spat the last name. The magnitude of what she was claiming refused to set in for a moment and we both stood staring at each other in stricken silence. Then, all at once the severity of it crashed down like the final accented note of a symphony, lingering with you long after the piece had concluded. In its cacophonous wake I could only muster one word:

"*Why*?"

Jasmine turned, propped the picture frame up against the vanity mirror, and then sat down to tell me exactly why the patron saint of the city had come down from on high to murder her best friend.

Chapter 25 - Revelations

Leon

Hours had passed since Dottie had climbed into her beat up two-door and made a heading for The Den. In her absence, Thomas and I took to drinking to pass the time. It seemed to have worked a little too well though, because my watch dial now read 23:30 and I'd admittedly had a bit more than I was planning on. I'd planned to stay sharp in case Dottie called in the cavalry, but after a story or two from Thomas and a glass or two of whisky, I was feeling a little fuzzy around the edges. As the laughter faded away from what I think was his second or third re-telling (that'd I'd been present for at least) of the story about the portly steward from Puerto Rico, I slowed down on the idle chatter and the booze, instead taking out a smoke. Thomas too, fell silent and nursed his glass of whisky while staring out into Belmont Street through the gaps in the blinds.

The silence lingered, so I rose and retrieved my journal and a pen. Thomas didn't seem to mind that, and he drew some small pocket book from the inside of his jacket. Leaning back in my chair, with the cigarette softly smoking on the edge of the metal ashtray beside me – I thought, and I wrote.

Leons Journal
September 23rd, 1947 23:40
Entry #310

I'm worried about Dottie. Although I've still managed to avoid doing so, she's had to get blood on her hands already for this case. I hope she's doing alright with everything that comes with that. She's been a hell of a lot more invested in this case than I'd expected her to be. Even more than Thomas somehow, who has a knack and an interest for this sort of stuff. I'm glad for her help – it's been invaluable really. In fact, I'd say she's damn near running the investigation at this point, while Thomas and I sit around drinking and joking. I wish there was more I could do right now, but we all have our part to play... even Conrad, somehow. It's been some time since I've checked in on him, I think I'll give him a call tomorrow. With the masquerade looming on the horizon, I want to have all my ducks in a row – or at least as many of them as I can. And Conrad is still a potential unaccounted-for duck.

I still can't help but think we're being set up, like cattle led into a slaughterhouse. All the masks and secrecy and mysterious messages. It's enough to mak

-the sound of gravel crunching beneath tires out front of the agency tore my attention from my writing. Thomas lowered his book too and we both turned expectantly towards the sound. The headlight glow through the frosted pane on the door snuffed out and I heard the familiar mechanical wheezes and sighs that usually preceded Dottie's arrival. Just seconds later, the doorway admitted her still disguised self, thankfully looking no worse-for-wear. She hung her purse on the rack while we stared, eager for something. Anything.

"Pour me a glass." She approached where we were drinking casually, but her wide eyes told me that she was just burning to tell us something. Could tonight finally bring all the closure we'd need?

Maybe the masquerade wouldn't be something I'd have to endure – although I recognized that was some forced optimism. I came to my feet to grab a bottle of wine. "That's fine," she said, motioning to the half-empty fifth next to me. I shrugged and retrieved a glass, pouring her a modest portion.

"What did you find?" Thomas asked, giving in once again to her dramatic withholding of information.

It seemed that even she couldn't bear to go any longer without telling all. Face alight, she jumped into a hurried stream of information. "*Glasspier is behind everything*. Thomas Glasspier. He killed Charlotte – well *he* didn't, but he ordered someone to. Probably Silas? Anyway, he had Charlotte killed to protect his reputation and because he was tired of sending money to keep her quiet. But her two best friends knew, because they were with her when Charlotte first met him!"

My head spun with that bombshell, although it could have also been the whisky. *Goddammit.* We were so far in over our heads that I couldn't even see the shovel throwing the dirt onto us anymore. I'm sure my face was screwed up as I put the pieces together through the haze and Thomas too had an intense, yet cloudy expression in the wake of Dottie's revelations.

There were two things that needed clearing up, other than my head. I started by asking the first one: "Wait, so where did Charlotte and the other two meet the high-and-mighty Glasspier anyways if they were lowly prostitutes? Can't imagine a man like him could frequent The Den, or really anywhere without being recognized."

"At one of his famous estate parties of course, just like the one coming up in a few days."

Damn, that masquerade was still at the center of it all.

Dottie continued, "Jasmine, who's the one I talked to tonight by the way if you care, told me that the three of them had managed to sneak in. They were in search of high paying clientele, along with having personal socialite aspirations."

Thomas directed a question at Dottie, one that I realized I had too. "Hold on, if Thomas Glasspier is supposedly behind it all, why would he send Jenny and Conrad to us, to dig it all up? I thought you said he was paying people to keep quiet, and killing them if they didn't? Seems counterintuitive to have people digging around into it again."

Dottie frowned slightly, "That's something I'm not quite sure about yet, maybe there's a third party involved that wants someone to cast some light on Glasspier's dirty past?"

"The Gray Man." I said it like a statement of fact. Something I was damn-near sure of. What I wasn't sure of though, was his stake in it. It seemed logical that he was the one pulling the strings that'd led to us finding out what we had so far – against Thomas Glasspier's' best wishes.

I felt we'd skirted around my second question long enough so I put it out there, although the moment it left my mouth I knew the answer. "Why did Glasspier suddenly feel the need to kill Charlotte *and* her son, if they'd been keeping things hush?" The question lingered on the air between the three of us like a cloud of smoke exhaled after a long final drag.

"I think you know why," Dottie responded gravely, dissipating the haze. It was clear to all of us, though unspoken, exactly why. *Jake Marlowe wasn't a Marlowe. He was the bastard son of Thomas Glasspier!*

Chapter 26 - Garden Hesperides

Thomas

I knew what we were all thinking in that moment. Jake Marlowe was likely actually Jake Glasspier, in which case, *where was he*? Someone, at the order of Thomas Glasspier, had attempted to kill him and in failing to do so, faked his death. Before, his whereabouts had been purely an interest in getting Jenny reconnected with her nephew, but now the potential of him being alive and well was a matter of some serious weight. If Glasspier was known to have been unfaithful to his wife Elizabeth, with a surviving bastard heir out in the world somewhere… it would have potentially disastrous implications for the entire Glasspier estate. Not to mention if we could prove his involvement in Charlotte's murder.

Maybe fame and fortune in the form of anthropological discovery just wasn't in the cards for me and I'd have to settle for being known for my part in blowing open the biggest scandal in the history of the city. Though, wasn't that what Conrad was supposedly involved for? Whoever sent us down this trail wanted him to ensure the evidence came to light, in the event the rest of us got paid off for our silence like the girls had been. Smart really, other than for the fact we'd kept Conrad at a bit of a distance. Knowing his politics, he'd love to see the Glasspiers brought low more than he'd love any sum of money.

He did work for the steel company though, so would he really want to take the chance of his livelihood being destabilized? So many unknowns… the one certainty that remained was that we needed to get into that masquerade. We needed to find some kind of hard proof. I hoped that Lockry would pull through with those tickets.

"This might be outside our line of duty," Leon said, cutting off the long quiet of our individual speculations.

Dottie narrowed her eyes, suddenly burning with intensity at that statement. "What do you mean? We have to get the truth out. Thomas Glasspier has to pay!"

I was surprised by her sudden outburst; I didn't think she had that much skin in this game.

"Look, I want to see people get their dues just as much as the next guy, but this is the most powerful man in the city we're talking about. Possibly one of the most powerful in the world. Maybe we should think about how much this is all worth to each of us. I don't want to endanger my life, or yours, or Thomas' any more than I already have if we don't need to. Jenny might not even want this case taken that far."

I tended to agree with Leon. Although it would be nice to see Glasspier get his comeuppance for what was surely a heinous act, was it worth the risk for what was essentially just a job?

Dottie continued her impassioned argument, "Don't you dare tell me that the Gray Man was right. That you could be scared, or paid off." Her bottom lip was quivering and she rose to her feet in indignation. "I thought you had an honor bound duty to your client. I thought you cared. You've seen Charlotte's grave; you've seen the aftermath of what he's done. If only you'd seen Jasmin and how scared she was…" she broke off in a sob and Leon stared at the floor.

"Perhaps Leon has a point Dottie," I spoke gently, "the litigation alone could take *years* and that's *if* we can even find hard evidence without getting ourselves killed."

"*Christ*, not you too! If you're both able to work up the spine to do the right thing, call me. Otherwise, I'll be out finding justice on my own for Jasmine, Charlotte, Alyssa, and whoever else's lives Glasspier's ruined in the last twenty years, thinking himself untouchable." And with that, she stormed out. Her car roared to life, sounding surer of itself than I'd ever heard it, and she was gone.

Sept. 24th 1947
Wednesday
Glasspier,

Leon told me he'd make a few calls and then let me know what was happening regarding the investigation tomorrow. That was last night, after Dottie's tirade and dramatic exit. With the masquerade being the day-after-next, I hoped he'd come to a decision quickly. Although regardless, I'm sure it would be too late to call off having The Blight produce tickets for the event should Leon decide that attending wasn't necessary. Perhaps I'd just go myself anyway… I must admit I was looking forward to the occasion, despite the now even more present looming threat associated with it. I had a feeling that Leon, like me, wouldn't be able to resist seeing it through to the end and would be calling me any moment with such a verdict.

So, I planned for a stay-at-home day beside the phone, with wine and classic literature in hand. It was my second favorite kind of day, closely after one on the open water with fair winds and billowing sails. The time passed quickly and after some hours the phone rang, jarring me from the world of Greek heroes and monsters. I lifted the receiver, expecting Leon's voice but instead was greeted by the smooth syllables of Stephan Lockry's. We exchanged greetings and he got to the point of the call.

"I'll keep this brief. You should be hearing a knock on your door before this call has run its course. Before the top of the hour." I glanced at my watch, which showed two minutes to four. I didn't question how Lockry knew where I lived, at least not out loud. He continued. "Inside a package left on the step, will be what you requested. I will stay on the line until you verify you've received it and that they are satisfactory."

"Alright, so I'll just-" I heard a heavy knock on the front door. Right on schedule. "I'll be right back." Leaving the receiver beside the dialer on the table, I went for the door. Outside, there was no sign anyone had been there, save for a thin brown envelope placed neatly on the step. I brought the unmarked package inside, and using a letter opener, carefully broke the sealing tape on its end. Inside, were four identical metallic black and gold tickets, embossed with a vermillion wax seal depicting a masquerade mask. There was a machine-typed note included with them:

One of these tickets is genuine. The other three are forged. This is what we were able to come up with on such a rapidly approaching deadline. Our specialist is good at what he does and I would put the fakes up to even the highest level of scrutiny without qualms. We were unable to determine whether or not a guests list is being implemented at the party; however, it is a masquerade where anonymity is the intent, so we must hope that the tickets are sufficient for entry.

This time, after you've taken the ship back out, I want you to personally oversee the delivery of the shipment to its destination at the mill. The personnel we had in charge of it last time will be making preparations elsewhere.

Burn this note after reading.

-SL

Picking up the tickets again, I held all four up to the light and strained hard to see any difference in them knowing now that only one was real. There wasn't any. At least not as far as I could tell. Satisfied in the craftsmanship of the fakes, I returned them to the envelope and lifted the receiver back to my ear. 'They look good, thank you' was all I said.

"I'm glad to hear. We'll speak again at our usual meeting time next week and celebrate a completed job… and perhaps the first steps to a promotion as well."

"Looking forward to it." I hung up the receiver, tucked the tickets safely away into the envelope, and began to get a fire going in the hearth. With some coaxing, flames soon licked at the edges of the paper which curled inwards and crumbled to ash in the fledgling fire. I'd had enough waiting. With one hand clutching the envelope and the other operating the rotary, I dialed McCreary Investigations.

Chapter 27 - Preparations

Leon

Sept. 25th 1947
Thursday
Glasspier,

Yesterday I'd spent so much time on the phone that the handset was starting to feel like a growth on the crook of my neck. First, I was informed by Thomas that he had a way to get four people into the estate party tomorrow; although he didn't get into specifics. I told him I'd call Jenny, see what her disposition was, and then get back to him with a plan of action. Or lack of one. Though at that point, even before I'd called Jenny, I was pretty certain I was going to go through with it. I'd promised her that we'd get to the bottom of whoever was behind it and 'make them pay', even if I wasn't looking forward to getting all gussied up and waltzing around with the city's elite.

Next I called Jenny and kept the information minimal. Although I believed she really did care about her sister, I was worried she might call the whole thing off if she knew there was no family fortune. Besides, telling a lady that her sister was a prostitute didn't rank too highly on the list of things I wanted to do that day. I did tell her there was a good chance at a sizable settlement in court if everything panned out and that seemed to keep the fire going. She promised another payment on Monday of next week and I promised that I was nearing the end of the investigation – something I only half believed.

With Jenny still bought-in, I called The Red Dress to check in on the clothes and masks that I probably couldn't afford. The seamstress who's name I didn't know, but who's frail voice I recognized, told me everything was 'coming along nicely' and would be ready for pick up the morning of the event. Funding, tickets, and getup were in order, so all that remained was to get the word out. I lit my second cigarette within that half-hour and dialed Thomas first. Surprisingly, he didn't have all that much to say, but expressed his excitement and assured me he'd be 'round my place well before the masquerade to get ready.

Dottie was next. She said she was 'glad I'd finally come to my senses' when I told her how I hadn't been thinking clearly and had just been shocked by the scope of what we were getting into. That seemed to satisfy her and she too planned to be at the agency plenty early to prepare.

So with that, I finally hung the handset up for the night and poured myself a double. There was one final call I needed to make, but decided it could wait until tomorrow. And well – it was now tomorrow. Or today. Whichever. The evening before the masquerade to be precise and that was all that mattered. My head still throbbed dully as a result of my choice in nerve settling the night prior and I braced to further my headache via a conversation with Conrad. The dialer was ringing now.

"Hullo, this is Conrad."

"It's Leon."

I heard a sigh from the other end of the line. "What do ya want?"

"You want to get to the bottom of this right? Put it behind us? Because that's what I want. And I think I finally see where you fit into the puzzle." There was silence from him which I took as permission to elaborate. "I don't want to say too much, we're playing this real close to the chest you see, but come by tomorrow around nightfall and I'll explain more."

“No can do. I’ll be busy then. Party business.”

“Party business? You mean, Glasspier estate party business?” What the hell could Conrad already have going on involving the estate?

“Well, yes. Technically. Party business in both senses of the word ‘party’ I suppose. *My* party will be protesting at the gates of *the* party. I’m all set to give a speech and everything.”

“Goddammit Conrad this is important.”

“And fighting for equality isn’t?”

Of course Conrad would be the one to make things difficult. Hearing that he’d be rabble-rousing outside the estate all but made up my mind to not tell him about Thomas Glasspier’s involvement in the case. I didn’t need him spouting Glasspier’s sins on the front lawn of his home while we were still trying to keep the case under wraps. I tried to work a new angle with him. “How about this? What if we could get you inside to talk to Thomas Glasspier himself directly?”

There was a pause, then Conrad laughed. “Well, now that could be fun. Party crashing and a chance to give Glasspier a piece of my mind… but why do you want me in there so badly anyways?”

“The gray man in the mask has been helping us uncover something big and he seems to think that you’re an important part of it. He might only talk to you.”

“Didn’t know we were trusting masked strangers now, but yeah I suppose I could break away from the protest for a little while.”

“Ok, we’ll grab you on our way in.”

Conrad grunted an affirmative and the line clicked dead. I leaned back in the waning light, soon noticing that another cigarette and a tumbler of whisky had found their way into my hands. Along with them, was my journal. The three, when combined with a pen – served to clear my head and organize my thoughts. And so, streaking black ink onto the page, I began that evening's bloodletting with a single line:

Leons Journal
September 25th, 1947 17:35
Entry #312

Tomorrow, I'll be face to face with the richest man in the world.

Chapter 28 - In Cauda Venenum

Thomas

Sept. 26th 1947
Friday
Glasspier,

The golden hour of twilight washed through the agency's blinds and from beneath an equally golden crown of antlers, Leon briefed us on the masquerade. “We’re looking for anything that could serve as hard evidence against Glasspier. Anything that could pin Charlotte's murder on him. Even just proof of the affair would be plenty to call his character into question and get the ball rolling.”

I nodded my understanding, but had to admit that I was only paying half attention to what was being said. It was jarring to see Leon so garishly dressed, especially with such bold color. He’d chosen a pale gold-and-black color scheme for his suit, crowned with a half-mask of branching antlers. For my no-nonsense friend who was usually hard pressed to feature any color at all beyond a dark navy blue, it was quite a sight.

Talking around a cigarette, he continued, “One possible weak link could be his wife, Elizabeth. We don’t know if she’s aware of her husband's infidelity; but whether she is or isn’t – she’d have the most reason to be upset about it. Just might take some convincing to get her on board." He eyed Dottie while he said that and she pursed her lips, all of us understanding what Leon was asking.

Dottie looked much more at home in her costume than Leon. Hers featured a half-mask with a glossy porcelain sheen that swooped up in silvery accent lines to a pair of rabbit-esque ears. Amazingly, that finely crafted mask wasn't the focal point of the ensemble; for, draped loosely around her shoulders, fell an elegant multilayered ball gown that appeared to quite literally glow in the light of the low sun as its rays passed through the silvery-white waves of fabric. The end result was radiant, making my simple black mask feel mundane in comparison. Wherever Leon had sourced them from had perhaps done too good of a job and I worried we might draw more attention than we'd hoped to.

From my motorcycle jacket that was draped over the back of one of the chairs, I retrieved the brown envelope containing our way in. "Only one of these is real," I explained, while distributing the tickets to Leon and Dottie, giving an extra to Leon. "For Conrad."

He slid both into his inner jacket. "We'll grab him on the way in."

Dottie eyed me knowingly while tucking her ticket into the top of her dress. "So, if only one of these is real… then the others are-"

"Forged, yes." I said, returning her knowing glare and realizing that was the closest she'd come to acknowledging my Blight-related outburst on the airstrip. "They look identical, they'll get us in," I assured the group, but my palms were clammy. I really hoped that there wasn't a guest list.

"Shall we then?" Leon said, putting a posh accent overtop his usual gravelly voice and extending his arm to the door in mock formality.

Dottie laughed and returned in kind, "We shall."

To spare my neatly combed hair and newly pressed suit from the wind, I'd decided to forego the bike; leaving it on the curb in front of the agency and climbing instead into the passenger seat of Dottie's car. We were to be posing as a couple for the evening, with Leon driving separately and being in charge of picking up Conrad. The car was as rough around the edges inside as it was out – and Dottie fought with the ignition for a moment before getting it to sputter to life.

"I could fix that for you, you know. Sounds like a bad starter. Pick up a new one and bring it over next week in the evening sometime if you'd like."

"I'd appreciate that. Just not on Tuesday night, right?" she said, shooting me a knowing grin.

"No, not on Tuesday," I agreed. Then, with the engine warmed, we pulled away from McCreary Investigations behind Leon's black sedan and drove north.

The city was a whirl of streetlights and flashing signs; even more so than usual because the outer reaches of my vision were hazy as a result of pocketing my glasses to accommodate the mask. As we rounded onto Judson boulevard, I was only a little bitter that my experience at the masquerade would be a somewhat blurry one. Next time, I'd personally oversee the creation of my mask to ensure that glasses fit comfortably beneath it. And there *were* good chances of there being a next time, once I entered The Blight's more trusted ranks.

We drew closer to the north bend of the boulevard and Glasspier Police were directing traffic on Judson the best they could; a barricade of flashing lights dividing the line between regular traffic and those of high society. Leon pulled off underneath a fancy bronze sign that read 'Glasspier Estate' and Dottie steered the car off the boulevard and down the winding road right behind him. As we rumbled across the threshold of Judson Boulevard and Manor Drive, a congregation of men in grubby workwear bearing red signs on stakes caught my attention. They were posted up just off of what must be considered estate property and on a raised platform their leader waved his hands and shouted in impassioned bravado. Conrad. A small sea of bobbing signs and raised fists before him gave the appearance of a frenzied clergy; howling for justice in a city blind to the concept.

I wished Leon would just leave him out of it. As it was, I was conscious of a sleek car pulling down the drive behind us that was worth easily twice as much as all of our vehicles combined. If being affiliated with Conrad didn't give us away, being spotted in this car certainly would. Luckily, as we rolled through the alley of painstakingly hedged trees, Leon pulled off the paved drive to the left into a guest lot halfway between the boulevard and the manor itself. I could see the mansion for the first time in the distance as Dottie wheeled the car around into the lot; albeit it being a little fuzzy. Other, more esteemed guests were stepping out of limousines directly in front of the pillared entryway.

"Park as far away from the others as you can," I advised, but she was already doing just that and taking advantage of some trees in concrete planters to put as much visual barrier as possible between ourselves and the other attendees. Leon did the same and we all stepped out, walking quickly in the direction of the party to put as much distance between us and the evidence of our real social standing as we could. Glancing nervously around, I only saw one or two people even paying any sort of attention to us. The few others in the copse of trees that formed the parking square were too busy fiddling with their masks and straightening their ties to take much notice. Dottie passed me the keys to hold, due to her lack of pockets.

"What happened to grabbing Conrad on the way in?" I whispered to Leon while we strode onto the walkway running parallel to the drive; attempting to look as dignified as we could.

"Change of plans. Way too high profile for the opposition leader to be seen hopping into my car on the way in, so he'll just have to take a walk. I'll circle back and grab him, then meet you two inside."

"Sure you don't want us to wait for you?"

"Nah, they're your shady tickets. You can have the first crack at it." He grinned and clapped me on the back. "Best of luck!" And with that he turned heel, casting a long, antlered shadow down the drive in the crimson sunset.

Dottie and I continued on, past marble fountains and immaculate hedgerows to the front step of the looming estate. It was grand. There was no other way to describe it. Situated in front of expansive parkland, the three-and-a-half story baroque structure was aglow with lights in each of the front windows; of which there were nearly three score. Four large columns supported a massive arch-pediment awning that jutted out around the double doors; opening and closing periodically to admit partygoers. On the front step beneath that grand overhang, stood a member of Thomas Glasspier's security detail. Could it be Silas? No, he was far too young. The moment of worry passed quickly, but it'd been enough to set my nerves on edge. They stayed there, taut as a fiddle string, as I handed over my ticket to the man whose silver name badge read 'Fletcher'. He looked only briefly at the ticket before passing it back to me, my slick palm struggling to return it to my jacket pocket as I waited for Dottie's to pass inspection.

"Enjoy the party," the guard said with little emotion, before turning to receive the guests queued behind us. With the sound of faint strings emanating from inside, I offered Dottie my arm and together we entered the masquerade.

Inside, the scene was equally grand. Perhaps even more so, due to the art which adorned the stone walls of the massive entryway. Oil paintings of beautiful vistas and stately men hung proud throughout the chamber and above the double doors before us was the largest of all: a portrait that I recognized to be Thomas Glasspier Senior. The man who raised the skyscrapers from the soil and established the greatest steel industry in the world; the man whose blood ran in the veins of every automobile, every boat, every airplane, and every building of this metropolis.

"Well, are we going in?" Dottie asked, with arms crossed. Enamored with the history and beauty of the place, I hadn't even realized she'd dropped my arm.

"Oh… yes." She meant into the masquerade proper, for there weren't many people lingering in the entryway and the chatter of voices was coming from beyond the doors beneath Glasspier's watchful eye. With renewed confidence, I stepped through the doors into the grand ballroom.

Chapter 29 - Entrance

Dottie

The ballroom was certainly a sight, even for one without any particular interest in grandeur of that sort. To say the large, rectangular room was high-vaulted would be an understatement; the ceiling rose more than three floors high above us. It seemed that the ballroom ran crossways through the center of the whole building with storied wings flanking on either side. More expensive decor hung here and there on the marbled walls, or sat in the form of busts on carved plinths along the edges of the room. The patronage of the party reminded me of that of The Velvet Jester, although a certain degree more prim and proper. Flashes of wealth surrounded Thomas and I, as we made our way around the ballroom in a cursory tour to get a sense of the place. Gaudy watches hung from the wrists of the men, and gaudy jewelry from the necks of the women, and everyone was drinking wine and champagne lifted from trays careening to and fro in the arms of tuxedoed stewards.

Then there were the masks. Leon had done well and we definitely fit right in, but our masks were tame in comparison to some of the more extravagant ones I spotted. There was a man with a golden dragon's head, one with a jet-black panther, and laughing heartily in front of the string quartet was a man in a lion mask; fashioned with what I was convinced was real mane hair. Most of the women wore classic designs of full or half-face masks; bedecked with feathers and jewels and elaborate gold filigree. All of that wasn't to say there weren't masks simpler than ours. Some of the more serious people appeared to have thrown on a monocolored half-mask that matched their tie and called it a day.

Everyone, save for the busboys and security, was wearing some kind of face covering. So to put it simply: it was a nightmare. I hated masks. I say hate, because I wouldn't call it a phobia. Phobia implies that it was irrational in some way, but I felt very justified in being leery of anyone who felt the need to hide their face. Sure, here it was the current social expectation, but that didn't stop them from making it near impossible to get a read on someone's expression – along with just being downright creepy. The only masked person I was sort-of hoping to see was the Gray Man and he was nowhere to be found.

Thomas and I completed our tour around the ballroom, during which we'd both acquired glasses of red wine and champagne respectively, then took up residence beside a standing table.

"See that older man with the tuxedo and satin black Colombina mask?" Thomas asked, pointing to a man matching that description at the center of the room. "That's–"

"Glasspier," I whispered, knowing instantly who it was despite the mask. The large, heavily muscled man beside him was a giveaway. The man beside Glasspier had a significant scar across his left cheek and wore a security uniform identical to the one the door greeter had been wearing; but looked about twice his age – and twice as mean. Glasspier's wife was absent at the moment.

"Within the next half hour or so, I'll try to distract him and Silas so that you and Leon can look around the house. Until then, we should mingle and try to get an idea of who knows who."

"You're going to distract him? Doesn't that role usually fall to me while you and Leon get up to trouble?"

"Usually yes, but I did my research before coming here. I've got a plan."

"You'll hear no complaint from me. The further I can stay from him and his guard dog the better." I took a sip from the champagne while casually watching the pair of them. "And speaking of which, how do you know that's Silas?"

"Like I said, I did my research. It's the scar mainly, but it also makes sense that Glasspier would want his top man beside him."

If it *was* Silas, even more reason for wanting to avoid him. He was still suspect number one in the murder of Charlotte. I didn't reply, forcing myself not to stare at the two men responsible for all the suffering that we'd uncovered and instead, took to scanning the room for any sign of Leon and Conrad having made a successful entry. My attention was captured by a woman with red hair in a scarlet red dress and matching Venetian mask making her way through the crowd. She stopped, leaning over a standing table on the outskirts of the room beneath an ornately framed still life of flowers and peacock feathers. In the same way I'd instantly recognized Glasspier – I too knew this woman. Scarlet. Natalie Scarlet, from my night at The Den. What was she doing here? At the moment, she was talking closely with Conrad of all people, who was wearing the red mask from Leon. I couldn't let her recognize me, not after I'd disappeared that night after making claims that I'd run out on my two-timing abusive husband and 'had nowhere else to go'. Having also seen someone in a silver wolf-esque mask earlier that I was fairly certain was Jon Barry – the list of people I was avoiding continued to grow.

"Well, Thomas," I said, taking a final sip of my champagne and leaving the half empty glass on the table, "let's get to know these fine gentlemen and ladies."

Chapter 30 - Burgundy

Thomas

Abandoning her still half-full glass and offering a quick 'good luck', Dottie cut a path through the crowd for the opposite side of the ballroom. I glanced around the crowded room, both to see what could have possibly made Dottie suddenly so skittish and to see if I could spot Leon or Conrad anywhere. Through the flashy crowd, a couple clad in red and black caught my eye in the opposite direction Dottie had gone. Was that Conrad? I had half a mind to take my mask off briefly in favor of my glasses, just to confirm it was him, but his stature and impassioned mannerisms gave him away soon enough. But who was he with?

I turned back to Glasspier, who was just breaking away from the group of older men he'd been conversing with. If Conrad was inside, Leon must be as well, and Glasspier was currently unoccupied. Now was my chance. Bringing my glass with me and running my opening lines over again in my head, I approached the city's wealthiest man.

"Ah, just who I was looking for!" I said, raising my glass, "I was hoping you might be able to confirm for me whether this fine Bordeaux is that of the nineteen-twenty-eight or nineteen-twenty-nine vintage?"

His eyes crinkled behind his mask for a half-second, before a faint smile replaced the shadow of uncertainty. “Should be the nineteen-twenty-*nine* if the stewards got it right. I keep some of each good vintage you see. Decided to serve the twenty-nine tonight because–”

“You’ve found that the twenty-eight keeps better?”

He was practically beaming now. “My dear man, have we met before? I apologize if we have, but it is a masquerade after all so you’ll have to forgive me.”

“I don’t believe we have. Thomas.” I extended my hand, which Glasspier clasped firmly with his own.

“A man of great taste and a great name!” We both laughed politely and I took that opportunity to have another sample of the wine I was holding.

“A good year to be sure,” I confirmed, nodding. But I’d imagine it’s nothing compared to what resides within your cellar here. I believe I remember reading somewhere that your estate houses the largest collection of pre-phylloxera wine in the States?”

“That it does!” Have you had a chance to try such a vintage?”

“One of the finest I’ve ever had the pleasure of trying was an eighteen-fifty-eight Romanèe-Conti during a stay in Burgundy.” That was a complete and utter lie of course. Such a wine was so far out of my current affordability that it was laughable. Glasspier seemed well enough convinced though, nodding approvingly and then glancing around the ballroom, perhaps seeing if anything needed his immediate attention before making his next statement:

“Well, let's see if we can do better then shall we? A true welcome to the estate. As long as you keep it between us,” he said, surveying the ballroom again, “Thomas to Thomas.”

“Of course.” I replied demurely, trying not to sound too eager. If my efforts in distracting the host happened to have other benefits, who was I to complain?

Glasspier and I walked side-by-side through the crowd towards the far end of the room, opposite the doors I’d entered the party via. Silas, who had been and still continued to be a silent observer, followed in tow behind us. We passed by Leon and Dottie, who appeared to have finally met up and were in casual conversation. I caught the eyes behind the golden stag mask for just a second with my own, and then we were out of the ballroom. There were still a few stray party goers in the back hallway, coming and going from a pair of lavatory doors on the left-hand side of the corridor.

The hall was dimmer than the ballroom, lighted only by old fashioned gas lamp sconces spaced sporadically along the walls between more oil paintings. The clatter of voices and strings from the main venue receded in the background and soon we reached a 'T' in the hallway where another security guard stood watch, preventing people from wandering too far into the rest of the manor I presumed. Glasspier paid him no heed and took a left. I continued to follow him further and further into the labyrinth that was the Glasspier estate, making small talk about my fictionalized experiences with expensive wines that I'd only read about. Before long, we arrived at a door no different than the multitude we'd passed since leaving the ballroom.

Through the door, the click of dress shoes on stone echoed down into the subterranean space. To me, the word 'cellar' evokes ideas of rough-hewn basements lined with stone or brick. Basically, a much larger version of Stephan Lockry's home wine cellar was more or less the image I had in mind when thinking of what the Glasspier collection might look like. Seeing the cellar now, I was obviously mistaken. Rows upon rows of bottles lined the edges of the square room, behind which, beautifully cut mahogany paneling encased the entire space. There was a wine bar set up in the center of the cellar beneath hanging lights with amber bulbs, the glow from which reflected off crystal decanters and silver corkscrews. There also appeared to be instruments for heating and cutting glass, to be used for very old bottles. Glasspier approached the table.

"The ballroom is grand, but this is my favorite room in the estate," he stated with an air of pride, lifting the only decanter currently housing any liquid, "and truth be told, I was looking for an excuse to take a respite from the frivolity upstairs."

I voiced my agreement, understanding completely, while he retrieved two glasses from beneath the bar table.

“I poured this earlier, to enjoy and unwind after the event tonight, but it’s not often that you meet a fellow connoisseur such as yourself.” He lifted the decanter gently to examine its reddish contents. “A rare vintage: eighteen-seventy, Burgundy Thorins.”

“Start of the Franco-Prussian war.”

“Ah, a historian too? Yes, around the time of the battle of Nuits-St-Georges. But that’s not what makes this year so rare.”

I strained to remember the growing conditions of 1870 east-central France. “No… it was the drought. Some say it was the frost that spring, but it was really the drought that followed. It allowed only for a small harvest in late September – the best since eighteen-sixty-five though I believe. They say harsh growing conditions can create the best, most complex wines.”

Making two generous pours of the reddish-brown Thorins, Glasspier laughed and replied: “They say that about men too.” He passed me a glass. “Well, now that I can be sure you have an appreciation for the vintage, let's drink.” He inclined his glass slightly and I followed suit, all the while Silas stood silent at the foot of the steps watching over. “To complex wine and complex company.”

I made a sound in the affirmative and we drank. Despite the experience of excellent wine, my thoughts drifted to Leon, Dottie, and Conrad upstairs. Complex didn’t even begin to describe it.

Chapter 31 - Marble Streets & Dead Ends

Leon

I was acutely aware of the weight of my *.45* in its holster beneath my arm as we approached the security guard in the hallway. I'd taken a gamble on getting it in and the lack of a weapon check at the door made it feel almost *too* easy. Maybe after all these years Glasspier really had begun to feel untouchable; although the high number of security guards, such as the one that stood before us now, was a counter to that theory. I put on the face of a concerned husband as Dottie launched into her performance.

"Hello? Sir?" she stammered and clasped her hands together over her chest, "there's a quarrel in the restroom down the hall and it gave me a dreadful fright. I fear they'll soon come to blows! Please, could you do something?"

The man stood a bit taller, setting his mouth into a hard line. "Show me," he grunted, and followed Dottie's lead back down the hall the way we'd come. I made to follow, but once the guard's back was turned to me my pace slowed, eventually coming to a complete stop. I waited just a moment more to see the man step into the restroom, before turning heel completely and continuing down the corridor past where the guard had been posted.

The problem with this case was a unique one: the crucial events had taken place over twenty years ago. Anything tangible tying Glasspier to the murder was surely long gone by now and even if there *were* financial records being kept in the building, I highly doubted a man like Glasspier would be stupid enough to keep any detailing underhand blackmail money laying around. Hence why I'd brought my gun. I had a feeling I'd need to initiate some conversation with it before the night was through.

I made my way deeper into the manor while portraits of dead rich men sneered down at the intrusion of a farm boy into their elegant halls. Once I felt well clear of the party and its guards, I made quick progress at doing what I did best: going into places I wasn't supposed to. I was hoping to find the security guards quarters, to maybe find something on Silas. Any door that could be opened – was. Any cabinet or drawer that could be rifled through received a shakedown. I didn't linger too long in any one room, staying moving and staying alert. If I ran into anybody, I wanted to get the drop on them.

I quickly determined that there were too many rooms to give each a thorough searching. I found a billiards room, a few different libraries, a handful of guest rooms and studies, and some rooms that were completely empty. Must be nice having so much space that you can't even use it all, I thought bitterly while observing another marble countertop in a space that seemed to serve as an auxiliary dining quarter. Much like how we repurposed things on the farm, I imagined how the resources in this whole gaudy statement of wealth could be put to use in the city. Maybe not streets paved with gold, but I reckoned there was enough marble in here to repave all of Glasspier into some kind of nineteenth-century bastardized version of heaven. It'd be an improvement on the pothole riddled asphalt at least. Staring at the white marbled surface made a dull ache start to pulse behind my eyes so I retreated back into the hallway.

How long had it been? Long enough to hope that Dottie was turning up something better than my dead ends. At the end of the hall, I came to a grand marble stairway with velvet runners and gold on the trim. I sighed and climbed silently to the second floor.

Chapter 32 - Behind Closed Doors

Dottie

As I ushered the security guard towards the supposed disturbance, I took note of something odd. A younger man with dark, swept back hair flowing out from above a simple black mask similar to Glasspier's and Thomas', passed behind me and continued further on into the mansion. He was escorted by the guard with the name tag 'Fletcher' who'd checked our tickets on the way in.

"Thank you! I'm sure you've got a handle on things here; I'm going to reunite with my drink!" I called, voice echoing into the restroom after the guard. My drink had been long abandoned and I had no intent of re-entering the sea of masked strangers in the ballroom. Instead, I turned to follow the two wayward men, taking as soft of steps as I could in my heels. At the fork in the hall where security had until recently been posted, the pair veered right. I waited, wanting to allow for a little more distance between myself and them. The footsteps stopped and the jangling of a key ring echoed brightly down the corridor, followed by the dull metallic scrape of a key slotting into a doorknob. I peered around the corner in time to see the two men slip quietly into one of the many doorways in the corridor, shutting it behind them with a click.

Rounding the corner, I kept my eyes trained on the door that they'd disappeared into. Why was security escorting this particular guest to a random room within the estate? He didn't appear to be being detained, and there was something strangely familiar about him. If only I could have gotten a real look at him. God, how I hated masks. At the door, I pressed my ear carefully to the doorjamb, hoping to gauge whether the two were on the other side, or if they'd continued on further into the manor from whatever room lay behind the door.

A muffled voice, low and monotone, was resonating from inside, "-to plan… yes… got it here…" I strained, only picking up bits and pieces of what he was saying. The other voice was more vibrant, allowing me to catch most of his words. His voice was almost familiar somehow, but from where?

"Good, once that's taken care of, we should be well set for that half. Then there's the second shipment tomorrow for the more… physical side of things. Everything on schedule? Have you been in contact with the Russians to confirm?"

Russians and a second shipment? What the hell? This could be big, if Glasspier was involved in under the table deals involving importing things from Russia, it could solidify the case against him. But were these two acting under orders from Glasspier? Or on their own? The lower voice started to respond and I once again strained to hear.

'... no need… is set… be here… harbor onto… then train,' was all I could pick up.

"Then tomorrow, begins the fall," replied the louder voice. "Cheers."

There was a silence from the other side following that, then the click of dress shoes on wood flooring made my heart skip a beat. *Shit.* I peeled myself from the door and made a hasty retreat down the hallway, towards the ballroom. Re-entering the faceless crowd to the crescendo of Schubert's Quartet in D minor, I took slow, cyclical breaths and grabbed a drink to further steady myself – and to help me blend in. I took in the masquerade again, searching for a sign of whether or not Thomas was back from his rendezvous with Glasspier. I couldn't pick him out of the bustling crowd, but there was Conrad, standing alone and staring unwaveringly forward. Following his gaze, it was clear what had his attention: Thomas Glasspier.

With the glass I'd claimed from a passing server meeting my lips, a red this time, I noticed with a subtle glance out of the corner of my eye that only the man in the black mask had returned to the ballroom from the hallway. Where was the security guard Fletcher? Questions and theories formed in all manners and tangents, but the one detail that had me the most concerned was this: Angelo had mentioned he needed the car tomorrow for a job at the port. The men behind the door mentioned the 'harbor' and 'tomorrow'. What was happening at the waterfront tomorrow night? Was Angelo in danger? I could feel my palms growing slick around the stem of the wine glass and forced myself to think positively. This could be a good thing. Angelo could tell me what's going on. Maybe he'd had the missing information we needed to put a wrap on this case all along! That is, if I could get him to come clean about The Blights activities…

My rambling musings were whisked away in an instant, seeing Conrad shove his hands into his pockets and stride resolutely towards Thomas Glasspier. I made a start to intercept him, but decided against it. As far as I was concerned, Conrad could say or do whatever he wanted to Glasspier, as long as it didn't pertain to our investigation – and I knew he wasn't dumb enough to cross Leon like that. So instead, I leaned back against another standing table to watch the show.

Chapter 33 - Manifesto

Conrad

Massive mansion for two. Priceless oil paintings. My brother's life. Marble carved fountain outside. Marble lined bathrooms. Ridiculously expensive wine. My brother's life. A wristwatch worth more than my house. Hired security. Hired servants. Acres of property for two. Gilded ceilings. My brother's life.

The sins of Thomas Glasspier piled up and tumbled over each other in my head. My fists balled in my pockets. My tongue pressed against my teeth, preparing its scathing manifesto – one it'd been itching to deliver for years. The woman in red wanted me to get thrown out of the party. Said it would be worth my while. I didn't need her encouragement to give Glasspier a piece of my mind. It was the only reason I'd put on this ridiculous suit and mask in the first place. Now, there was nothing in the ballroom besides me, Glasspier, and the shrinking distance between the two of us.

"Do you know who I am?" I cut his conversation off with the fat man beside him.

He looked surprised, but answered cordially. "No? I'm afraid I don't. Apologies. Kind of the point though, isn't it?" He gestured around at the other masked guests. I didn't follow his hand, instead continuing to stare him in the face.

"My brother lost his life in your machine."

"My machine? And what machine would that be?"

"The machine in which capital exploits wage labor. The Capitalist machine," I spat, "but more specifically, a conveyor in *your* steel mill. Glasspier Steel Co. is yours – owned and overseen by you right?"

"It is. But I'm afraid I'm not sure what you're talking about. Everything in the mill is held to a high degree-"

"Bullshit!" He flinched and his hired muscle beside him stepped forward, but Glasspier held out his arm, keeping him at bay. "That's bullshit." My nails dug into my palms. "I submitted a statement, a statement saying that machine was unsafe. The damn thing nearly ripped my arm off a few times." I removed my hands from my pockets and rolled up my sleeves to reveal the scars on them and along my arms. "But no. You know what your management board told me in response? That it would cost too much to replace the machine, and it would cost too much to make the current one safer. Too much for their budget that fiscal year. Too much?" I laughed. "You could have sold one fucking painting from your estate, or opted for a nineteen-*thirty-four* Rolls Royce instead of a nineteen-*thirty-five* and that would have been more than enough. And my brother would still be alive…"

Glasspier made a placating gesture. "Look, I'm sorry if your… brother-"

"Callum. His name was Callum. Though nobody would ever know that, because you and your team swept it all nicely under the rug didn't you?" I became animated, pointing my finger beneath his masked nose. "And do you know what the biggest bullshit of all is? After it was all hushed up? A shiny new machine replaced the old one the next week. You had the money after all didn't you? How convenient. Just didn't want to spend it on worker safety when you could be spending it on a new car or a new suit."

Thomas Glasspier's jaw hardened and he leaned in, whispering, "What's the point of this? Just wanted to blow off some steam? Use me as a punching bag for the fallout from a decision made by an entire board of people? Accidents happen. What's done is done. Get off your fucking high horse."

“The point is,” I seethed, “is that *I* organized the protest happening on your front lawn tonight. The point is, there are people who agree with me and are rallying behind the idea. The idea that the people carrying this city, this country, on their backs should be treated like human beings instead of expendable labor to prop up the very ones who laid the weight of their burdens upon them!” I stopped for a breath, finally turning my head to his peers in the vicinity of my tirade and seeing that most had shied away, but a few were watching and listening with faces hidden behind expressionless masks.

Thomas Glasspier flashed me a patronizing smile. “Is that it? Anything else to say?” I didn’t respond immediately, so he continued with a question: “Why do you still fight? America doesn’t want a revolution; we just won a war. People are celebrating, they’re happy to have their sons and fathers home. I’ve seen your flyers, read your newspaper. They’ll never get on board with your anti-American ideology. Just give it up and settle down, start a family, and enjoy the American dream I made for you.” He turned his head to the man beside him. “Silas, get him off my property.”

Silas moved quicker than I expected for his size and his age, and in an instant had my arm in his iron grip. “Come on, don’t make this difficult” he grunted, in a voice thick with tobacco tar.

I’d already been difficult enough for one day I figured, and I liked the way my arm was in its socket, so I didn’t resist. Being escorted out, I finally found the answer to his question and called out behind me:

“I don’t fight because I think I'll win. I fight to be able to look back one day after the dust clears and say ‘I fought’! And the dust will clear! One day, all this finery and wealth will come crashing down, maybe not upon you, maybe not upon your sons or their sons, but it will. And when it does, I'll be there saying ‘I fought!’" I shouted across the ballroom at the man that I held responsible for Callum's death. What a privilege and a joy it was to be thrown from his majesty's hallowed halls for saying something so true. And as I was dragged from the room for speaking the truth, there she was, that woman in red; winding through the crowd towards Glasspier.

Chapter 34 - Specters and Killers

Leon

The second floor held more of the same. Empty rooms and wealth beyond the dreams of a farm boy like me. I'd wasted enough time sightseeing Glasspier's labyrinth with no sign of anything to show for it. Were the guard's quarters even in the house? I stood at the top of the stairs, preparing to make a subtle re-entry back into the midst of the party, when the faint echo of a door shutting down the hall stopped me. It was the first sign of anyone else within the back half of the manor. I moved to investigate.

Nearing the halfway mark down the dim hall, I became aware of a second sound. The steady clack of dress shoes on marble steps. I tried the nearest door and it relented, ushering me into a dark guest room. Wiping a bead of sweat that'd formed at the top edges of my mask with one hand, I held the doorknob in the other and turned it, producing a small gap between the door and its frame. With one eye, I kept vigil on the corridor.

A figure with no face appeared at the top of the stairs, turning to stride down the hall the same way I'd come. At first, he was difficult to make out in the low light, with the only features I could make out being broad shoulders and a masquerade mask. That was, before he passed beneath one of the gas lamps. The light revealed no color, just slate gray from head to toe. Our ghost. *Dammit, it was now or never.* I burst from the room, my gun finding its way into my palm as it had so many times before in one fluid motion.

"Explain." The command carried its own force, with the additional weight of the automatic backing it up. I aimed it true and steady at center mass.

The Gray Man made a small start, before slowly raising his hands. "We're on the same side," rumbled his baritone voice, showing little concern over the threat of the gun. "You're a hard man to find. I intended for this conversation to happen over drinks in the main hall. Nonetheless, I've got something for you. It's tucked into the inner chest of my coat, on the left-hand side."

How convenient. That's where a pistol would sit in a shoulder holster like mine. But much of what we'd found so far could be attributed to him and if he'd wanted to, he could have gunned us down at the airfield like the rest of the gangsters there. Assuming that *was* him up in the tower.

"Reach for it slow," I said, finger tense around the cold trigger.

"I'm going to, and you're welcome to splatter my head across these beautiful chestnut floors if I make too sudden a move." His gray gloved hand reached slowly down and across his chest, then slid its way into his trench coat. Would I really fire if he drew a gun? No, I couldn't. I swore I wouldn't. Never again. The pistol was just a tool – not a weapon to be used to take life. A tool to get people to talk, to give me the power in a bad situation. But if it was him or me? Could I? My hands were slick with anticipation on the gunmetal; the bead of sweat had re-formed above my brow. Don't draw. Don't-

"Here." The Gray Man extended a thin manila folder towards me. Slowly, I stepped forward, automatic still trained on his chest, and received the document. "You got this from a security guard at the party. One who wanted his identity to remain anonymous. Got it?" he said.

I flipped the folder open. What was I looking at? Medical records? There was a blood test on one, the page behind it outlining something called a 'serological protein test'. Proof of paternity. All topped off with a signed agreement between two parties: Thomas Glasspier and

Jake Marlowe. At the back, there was a new death certificate for Jake, listing him deceased in 1944. A wartime casualty. Everything was there, everything I needed. It was good, too good.

"I hate to even ask, but what's the catch? Why give me this on a silver platter?"

"Same reason anyone does anything. I was paid to."

"Who are you? And why me?" I asked, my gun lowering to my side.

He shoved his hands into the outer pockets of his coat and turned away. "Anonymous, remember? All that matters is that people have seen you here and that a turncoat security guard giving up the goods is a believable story. And you? Always getting into things and places you shouldn't. Willing to bend the rules to get what you need. A war hero. I imagine that's why he chose you to put the pieces together-" A distant crash from behind me punctuated his statement and I spun to stare down the murky hall.

"Stay out of it," the Gray Man grumbled, "you need to keep your image clean." He then turned his back to me fully and disappeared down the staircase. I tucked the folder into my own jacket, torn between quitting while I was ahead – or going all in. I had what I needed, I could get the others and get out. But there was something going on here, something that the Gray Man knew about… like hell I was going to turn my back on it. My mind made itself up in an instant and my body followed suit, careening down the hall towards the sound. Wasn't that what he'd said anyway? About why I'd been chosen? Whoever was paying him chose me for my skill at getting into things I shouldn't. Why stop now?

It was the big set of double doors I'd seen on my first pass of the second floor. It'd been locked before, but now there was movement within. Pistol at the ready, I shouldered open the right-hand side and swept the room with the muzzle. The master bedroom. The nose of my automatic passed over a four-poster bed with a figure sprawled upon it and landed on a woman dressed in scarlet standing beside it; placing a flower into the grasp of the dead man: Thomas Glasspier.

Foxglove. Without it being a conscious decision, I raised my voice. There wasn't time for a polite discussion. "Don't move!" I shouted, "put your hands on the back of your head." She straightened up, quickly and coolly doing as I ordered. I needed to double down. "You're gonna start talking and you're gonna answer every question I ask, or Glasspier's servants are going to be scrubbing your blood out of these sheets for the next week!" I snarled. Would I really shoot her? No, but it was important that she thought I might. I never claimed the *.45* made for polite conversations.

She was shaking now, trying to play calm, but I could see her arms trembling behind her head. "You're not a cop… are you? No, cops can't say stuff like that. Please, this is a horrible man. He deserves everything he got and more."

"I can say whatever the hell I want – and who are you to decide what he deserves?"

"He was unfaithful to his wife and was prepared to be again. That's all the evidence I need," she cried. The room was dark, lit only by candles, but even as my eyes were in the early stages of adjusting to the dimness I could tell: she had red hair. Killing cheating men? Something slotted into place in the back of my mind.

"Take your mask off."

"Wha-?"

"Off!" I ordered, taking another step forward and brandishing the pistol in the gloom. Her hands were already behind her head, but now they worked to undo the ribbon holding her crimson mask in place. She let it fall on the bed beside Glasspier's motionless body. The wedding day picture from Willow Avenue flashed in my memory. Barbara Wakeman. I was certain of it. "You killed your husband, Henry," I accused, "but not like the others. He was the first, wasn't he? The one that started you down this path."

"Why do you care? You're not a cop, or you would have arrested me by now. So either shoot me, or let me go."

"I care, because I was building a case against the man you just poisoned. So tell me: who put you up to this?"

"Put me up to it? No one put me up to it." She stepped forward and I could see her eyes longing for the door, to flee into the hall.

"Tell the truth!" I growled, and she shrank away, curling in on herself like burning paper.

"I just overheard it!"

Overheard it? How was that possible? This was something that'd been kept under wraps for a long time, under threat of violence even. Jasmine had only told Dottie because… wait, that was it. "Let me guess, at The Den?"

"How-?" she began to ask, eyes wide.

I lowered my gun. "It was Jasmine, wasn't it? And you've been camping out there, disguised as one of them in their prostitution ring. Easy access to prey." I looked over at Thomas Glasspier. "Speaking of – how long does he have?"

"I-I don't-"

There was a thud on the door behind me as it was shoved open. I spun and the candlelit room moved in slow motion. The large man with the scar who'd been at Glasspier's heel all night was silhouetted against the brighter lights of the hall. I raised my gun – he drew his. Two gunshots rang out in the room full of killers.

Chapter 35 - Candlelight

Thomas

Where was Leon? I hadn't seen him since I left with Glasspier for his wine cellar tour.

"Yessir, I have a lot riding on ol' *Vicar*," the portly man in the copper, wolfish looking mask stated boisterously. His compatriots in the semi-circle around me nodded in approval. Having no stake in the upcoming horse races, my attention was focused on Thomas Glasspier and the woman in red, who some odd minutes ago, had disappeared into the very same hallway he'd led me down. Who was this red woman? Dottie had seemed to want to avoid her, and she'd been talking closely with Conrad earlier. Making a swift decision, I politely took my leave of the group of men discussing the races. They didn't seem to take much notice of my abrupt departure.

I set my glass of wine on a nearby raised table with a sad moment's hesitation; for although it wasn't anything like what Glasspier had shown me in his cellar, it was still quite good compared to the usual swill I subjected myself to. Parting with it, I navigated through the crowded ballroom towards the rear hallway where I'd seen them disappear. Moving past the restrooms and turning round a corner, I was surprised to find myself alone for the first time, with only the dull sounds of chattering aristocrats and the soft playing of strings in the background from where I'd come. Where were the security guards? No matter, I'd take the small victories when I can. The first-floor hallway was deserted, so I ascended the stairs to the second level.

At the top of the stairs, the path split, and I paused in torn hesitation. I didn't have to wait long, before my decision regarding which way to proceed was made for me – by the muffled crack of what sounded like the report of a firearm. Twice. It came from the way to my right. And was that a woman's scream? Throwing caution and regard for my finely pressed suit to the wind, I broke into a sprint down the passageway toward the sound, gas lamps casting gaunt shadows of my passing through the corridors. A room with a rather large wooden double door caught my eye, because unlike the rest, it was cracked open. The master bedroom?

It was poorly lit in both the grand suite and the hall preceding it, but I could make out a torso sprawled within the room in front of the open door, accompanied by the sound of heavy breathing. My chest grew tight. I pushed the left door inwards for a better view into the darkness beyond and what I saw briefly rivaled the terror I'd felt in that mountaintop village of the Congo. Before me stood Leon, with gun in outstretched hand. No, not Leon, but rather a proud pagan god bathed in flickering candlelight, with antlers casting gnarled shadows upon the gasping form he loomed above. There, for the first time since I'd known him, I was afraid. The amalgamated form of my friend and fearsome stag lowered its gun, the eyes behind the mask losing their intensity as it did so. Once again I recognized the man I knew before me, but in those first perilous seconds he had been something else entirely to me.

I drew a shaky breath, looking past Leon to the bed. "Is that-"

"Glasspier," Leon confirmed, holstering his pistol beneath his jacket and tearing his eyes from the gasping man on the ground before us.

What the hell had happened? It was a lot to take in. The woman in red was here, standing beside the bed housing the motionless form of the man who I'd just recently shared a drink with. Then there was Silas, bleeding out on the ground. Two ragged tears in his chest were spilling blood into a growing pool around his prone form and he was struggling for breath.

Silas tilted his scarred head forward. "Morris…" he croaked, holding his chest, his hands coming away slick and dark. "It's Morris…" Leon kneeled down beside him.

"Morris? Morris who? What did he do?" Leon questioned.

Was that name supposed to be familiar? I tried to remember, but so much had happened; so much was happening – *and were those footsteps down the hall?*

"...Fletcher… Morris Fletcher," Silas gurgled through a mouthful of blood, "...he knows… I trusted him… told too much… was drunk… plan- planning something… going to ruin everything…"

Fletcher! I pictured the name on the rectangular silver badge. He'd taken our tickets on the way in, I was sure of it. The footsteps grew louder and I looked back to Leon. "We need to go-"

Two men in Glasspier Security uniforms stared into the master suite. Leon and I stared back and for a moment no one moved. A flurry of action broke the tension; the two reached for their sidearms as we rushed them. I was closest the doors and swung a clenched fist at the guard on the left, while Leon charged a shoulder into the one on the right. Knuckles connected with jawbone in a sharp crack, downing the man in an instant. The guard that Leon had slammed reeled back into the hall, gasping for wind.

"Find Morris! Don't let him get away! I'll deal with this," Leon shouted, swinging a fist towards the second guard, who'd seemed to have gotten his feet back under him and dodged the blow. The one that I'd floored had rolled over and was struggling to rise. I gave him a sharp kick to the ribs, sending him sprawling again onto his back, before breaking away from the brawl and sprinting back down the corridor. Back to the ballroom.

Chapter 36 - Exit

Dottie

Conrad had gotten himself thrown out, Leon was god knows where, and Thomas had disappeared now as well, following behind Glasspier and Natalie Scarlet. I'm not sure what Natalie's goals were, but I could think of a few ways that getting in bed with the richest man in the city could be beneficial. And a few ways it could come back to bite you. Given what I'd learned on my undercover excursion to The Den, I had a bad feeling of history repeating itself and that poor Ms. Scarlet would be among the next to be silenced by both money and force. Just another reason to hate him.

I looked around, at a loss for what more I could do. Finding Mrs. Elizabeth Glasspier was still something that could be useful, but it seemed that she was either very incognito in her costume – or squirreled away somewhere. Maybe the best-

"Attention! Attention please!" blared the tinny echo of a bullhorn. The strings cut off mid crescendo and the crowd babble hushed to an uneasy whisper. Standing above the crowd on a makeshift soapbox at the far end of the ballroom was a man wearing one of Glasspier's security uniforms. He raised the megaphone again. "Due to some unforeseen circumstances, I am very sorry to announce that this year's masquerade must come to an early end. Please remain calm and exit the building in an orderly fashion. Thank you." The whispering of the crowd instantly rose into a frenzied babble of questions and protests and I noted a congregating of guards into the room, forming a united front to herd the masked guests out of the manor.

Whatever was going on, I was sure we were involved. I should get to Leon and Thomas; they might be in trouble. Standing my ground against the flow of partygoers vying for the door, I searched for a gap in the crowd and a gap in the guards that I might be able to slip through. There, on the right-hand side of the room where the quartet was packing up, a guard was distracted; arguing with a couple in matching blue and bronze attire. Leaving my drink yet again, I jostled through the crowd against the flow of traffic with eyes on the gap that would lead me back into the rest of the mansion. Almost there… I glanced side to side, preparing to slip through when no one was paying attention – but it seemed someone else had the same idea. He was coming the other direction, from the back halls of the estate. I recognized the jet-black mask instantly as we came face to face between the ever-shrinking sea of people and the disjointed wall of security guards.

"Thomas? What's going on-"

"Explain later, we need to go," he panted, and I realized he'd been sprinting. "Where is Morris Fletcher?" I must have looked confused, because he started to elaborate. "The security guard that took our-"

"Tickets, yes," I finished his sentence, starting to regather my bearings. "I knew there was something up with him! He was talking with someone and he escorted them into a room in the back. I overhead-"

"Yes, yes, we can debrief later – where'd he go?"

He sounded urgent so I relented. "I'm not sure, only the other man he was with came back into the ballroom. He must have stayed in the back half of the manor somewhere." The guards behind Thomas reigned in on the crowd, corralling us towards the exit. The gap was closed.

"We need to get outside, maybe he went out a back or side exit. We certainly can't go back the way I came from," he said, glancing over his shoulder at the security guards.

"What about Leon?"

"Same thing. We have to hope he's made it out elsewhere. He was caught up with a couple guards, but I think he'll be alright as long as he can get out before the rest of the security force arrive and really lock the place down." He sounded less than confident.

We merged with the throngs of people funneling out into the entryway. The sooner I could get out of this stuffy faceless hell the happier I'd be. Thomas and I did our best to worm our way through the crowd, gaining each inch forward by an 'excuse me' here and an 'apologies' there. Within minutes, we breathed the cool night air once more on the threshold where we'd first met the man we were after.

The masses of annoyed socialites spilled out into the lawn, some taking their masks off and others loudly berating the guards as they closed and locked the doors behind them, complaining about wanting to contact their chauffeurs who weren't expecting to pick them up until much later in the night. Their words fell on uncaring ears, of which mine were included. I searched the faces of the guards who'd remained outside to keep the peace, not finding the missing Morris Fletcher.

"Is that-?" Thomas spoke up behind me and I turned from the guards. Pulling out of the lot nearest the manor, was a blue coupe. *The* blue coupe. The car rumbled by; gray gloved hands turning the wheel, over which stared a slate gray mask from beneath a gray hat. Both having the same idea in an instant, Thomas and I broke into a run; heading for my car. The lot was down the way, past the marble fountain and along the drive that ran from the boulevard to the mansion. Thomas stretched far out ahead of me in no time, thanks to my heels. I stopped momentarily to pull the damn things off, carrying them with me, not wanting to have a 'Cinderella' moment at the stupid Glasspier estate party. Small rocks dug into and embedded in my feet as they pounded down the asphalt towards the lot, sending tears to the corners of my eyes; I just kept going.

We'd been looking for Fletcher, but the Gray Man was the next best thing I figured. Where had he been the whole party? Surely he knew we were there, so why hadn't he come to find us if we were supposedly on the same side, like Leon and Thomas were so convinced? Sure would have preferred a friendly chat in the ballroom over having to chase him down. Thomas beat me to the car, heels or no heels, and was leaning against it catching his breath. There was no time to catch mine. Thomas tossed me the keys and I rushed to get behind the wheel.

With key in the ignition, I turned it over. *Click.* Nothing. I backed it off and tried again. Another click. "Come on!" I shouted at the damn thing, giving it another few attempts. Nothing. Letting loose with a string of expletives that caused Thomas to blush, I turned the ignition over in what I knew would be my last attempt before the battery gave up. It groaned in protest and sputtered to life. Without a word I threw it into gear and pulled out onto the drive.

The blue coupe was gone. I drove the length of the boulevard twice in full, seeing only a stream of expensive cars leaving the estate grounds and the evidence of Conrad's protest; a patch of trampled down grass and a few broken sign posts was all that remained. Had the security force driven them off? I hoped he was alright. My attention returned to the dark streets of north Glasspier, where the Gray Man and his coupe had once again lost us in the night.

"Do you think Leon made it out?"

"Haven't seen his car leave, but he could have while we were burning gas up and down this strip." Thomas shrugged in response. "And there's no way we're getting back inside to pull him out either." He pointed at the entrance to Manor Drive on our third pass and I saw that it was flashing red and blue with police lights. Thomas was right, the estate had to be well locked down by now. If Leon *had* made it, he'd want us to regroup back at his place. Without a word, I turned at the next exit left and the stupid, rickety car that'd made us lose the blue coupe rattled and squealed its way back to McCreary Investigations.

Chapter 37 - Symposium

Thomas

I breathed a pent-up sigh of relief at seeing Leon's black sedan parked in its usual place on the curb in front of the agency and Dottie's shoulders too noticeably relaxed behind the wheel in recognition of his safety. We'd made it. Now the question was: was it worth it? We got out and I led Dottie to the door. No lamps betrayed any sign of life from within.

As we stepped into the quiet blackness of the agency, the only light came from the street lamp outside passing through the blinds and casting angular shadows into the room. With a glass of dark liquid in one hand and a blood-soaked rag in the other, Leon stood staring out into the quiet street. His stag mask and outer jacket had been discarded, the former resting with broken antlers on the coffee table and the latter draped over the back of an armchair. Hanging there, I could see there were shards of glass protruding from a ripped left shoulder and the back of the once brilliantly golden suit jacket was now stained with earth and blood. Leon turned from the window, letting the gap in the blinds close with a rattle and revealing a visage that'd seen better days. Aside from general scrapes and bruises, his left shoulder had been recently wrapped in fresh gauze; a sight that made my own ache dully where the bullet graze had mostly healed.

Leon parted his split lip in a grin. “You made it. Were you followed?”

“I don’t think so,” I answered, but it came out sounding more like a question of its own. I hadn’t even thought about the possibility of being followed. We had been the ones attempting to do the following after all. In all the excitement and car troubles, the thought hadn’t crossed my mind. Leon stepped away from the window, moving towards his chair and grimacing at the effort.

“Lock the door,” he grunted, while rummaging inside the hanging jacket, sending a small shower of glass fragments clinking to the floor. I turned the deadbolt over and finally had the notion to remove my mask, exchanging it for my glasses and taking my seat. Dottie tossed her mask unceremoniously onto the table beside Leons before sitting. Drinks were poured and a beige folder was placed before us on the table by Leon. “Go on, take a look,” he said. “I want to hear what you think before I make any statements that might color your view.”

I leaned forward and turned the document open, taking a long look at the contents inside. Keeping my expression blank and my tongue held, I passed the file to Dottie. She looked it over carefully too, before laying the sheets of paper out on the table.

“Everything’s there,” she whispered incredulously, “how did you find this?”

I too was baffled. A file containing all the proof we needed was just laying around somewhere in the Glasspier estate? The signed statement even implied that he and Jake had made contact at some point.

Keeping his voice even, as if not to imply anything, Leon stated: “The Gray Man gave it to me.”

That turned my doubts into full blown suspicion. Sure, the Gray Man had seemed to be on our side so far, but why orchestrate having us be at the party if he was just going to hand it to us anyway? Unless… he was trying to maintain some kind of plausible deniability. Everything he’d done so far kept him anonymous and at a distance. Was he trying to stay detached from the investigation for some reason?

Dottie made a start before I could, “You met the Gray Man? Where? What did he say? Do you know why they ended the party early? Was it something to do with him?” Questions tumbled out one after the other – seemingly her patience had finally run dry. I couldn’t blame her; I was equally curious about what had happened before I’d arrived at the scene.

Leaning forward gingerly, Leon set his glass down before relinquishing an account of all that he’d seen. “After you got that guard out of the way, I eventually ran into the Gray Man. It was brief, but he gave me that.” Leon pointed to the file. “Also said something about choosing me – and that he was being paid by someone. I would have pressed him for more, but I heard something. Foxglove. She killed Thomas Glasspier. Poisoned him. And I had to shoot Silas…”

It wasn’t news to me, I’d been there and seen the aftermath after all, but hearing it said out loud was still something else altogether. Glasspier was such an idealized and untouchable figure in the collective world psyche that it was like hearing someone had shot and killed God.

“Glasspier… dead?” Dottie stared at the table, eyes wide as if she was picturing the scene playing out before her in miniature. She turned her head slowly towards Leon. “Then… Natalie Scarlet. It was her, wasn’t it. A woman in red?”

“Yes. You met her at the Den?” Leon asked, and she nodded confirmation, “although that’s not her real name. She’s Barbara Wakeman.”

Wakeman. The night at the airfield felt like so long ago. “So their disappearance was tied to our case after all?” I spoke the thought aloud, directed at nobody in particular.

“Not sure. She’d been killing long before the party, and who knows, she might keep killing after it. It can be hard to stop once you start…” Leon trailed off and lifted his glass again from the table.

“So she got away?” Dottie asked with an inflection that was, dare I say, hopeful?

“Not sure about that either. I was too busy getting my ribs kicked in by Glasspier’s security. Not sure where she got off to during all that; might have been caught. There were more of 'em coming when I made my exit out the window."

"But you're saying Thomas Glasspier may have just been caught in her crossfire?" I asked.

"Maybe. But the Gray Man did seem to be aware something was happening. Maybe he orchestrated it too? I don't know. There's just too many maybes."

"Sounds like the Gray Man is behind even more than we thought. I don't know if we can still count him as our ally in all of this. Your hunch about the masquerade was right, but what if it was only so because the Gray Man planned for it to be?"

"That's what I'm afraid of. He's helped us, but can we even believe these documents are real? If he's gone through this much trouble with everything else… it's all uncertain. We have the evidence we need, supposedly, but I don't want to go off half-cocked in the courtroom with it if someone is setting us up."

There was a lull in the questioning after that, where we all nursed our drinks and let our imaginations run. I tried to imagine how Barbara might have made her way out of the manor, evading the guards, or maybe deceiving them. One thing was for certain: tomorrow's paper was going to be one for the history books. Dottie broke the daydream with a new line of thought.

"There's one more thing. I haven't brought it up yet, because I can't see where it fits into everything, but I think it's our next step. Thomas, you said that we were looking for that guard, Morris Fletcher?"

"Yes."

"Why?"

Unsure of that myself, I looked to Leon.

"Silas said to," he started to explain, but Dottie jumped in.

"I thought you-?"

"Shot him? Yes. But after that, he was dying – trying to tell me something about Morris Fletcher. All I could get was something about him planning something that would 'ruin everything'."

"The harbor. Tomorrow night," Dottie said solemnly. My blood went cold. What? How could she possibly know about that? My hands folded over on each other uneasily in my lap as she elaborated, directing her statement at Leon rather than me. "I followed Fletcher. During the party. He took someone in a black mask into a back room and was talking with him. They were saying something about a second shipment at the harbor tomorrow, and… a train? Strangest of all, one of them mentioned Russians."

Upon hearing that, Leon let out a sigh of exasperation and leaned back into his chair. In that instant I almost came clean about my involvement with The Blight, but stopped myself. Being outwardly affiliated with a criminal organization would be a death sentence for mine and Leons partnership. Something had to be said now though, or I'd be under even more suspicion for seemingly withholding information. I decided instead to take a middling approach, hoping that Dottie wouldn't out me any further. "I know what she's talking about. What they were talking about."

Leon raised an eyebrow. "Glad you both found the party worth your while; I wouldn't have wanted to have all the fun."

"Well, it's not that exactly… I was actually involved in the *first* shipment. And I'll be at the one tomorrow night, it's a side job I'm working, just bringing a ship in."

Leon stared a hole into my head at that confession. "What do you mean *involved*?" he asked slowly.

I thought about my next words carefully. Maybe Leon could get the information he needs, and The Blight could still pull off their job at the same time. I was in a precarious spot. "It's just some extra money I'm pulling in from the yard, piloting the tugboat for a ship that's coming in late. I don't get any more involved than that and I don't ask questions."

"Maybe you should," Leon retorted, "isn't that our whole thing here? Asking questions?"

"I had no reason to suspect a fairly routine job to be related to your twenty years in the past homicide case."

"Well now you do." He was still staring. "Can I count on you to watch our backs there tomorrow night?"

"We're going there-? Of course. Yes. I'll be on the water though."

"What happened at the first one?"

"A ship came in, with no markings on it, right on time at midnight. Heard foreign voices as they were unloading it, could have been Russian I suppose."

"What is *'it'*? What were they unloading?"

"I'm not sure, it was under coverings. It comes in at midnight again, that I do know."

"We'll be there at least an hour before then," Leon declared, finally breaking eye contact with me to ask Dottie. "If you're willing. I'll be going regardless."

"Of course I'll be there," Dottie quickly assured, "if you think I'm going to sit out what might finally be the last piece of this puzzle you haven't been paying attention." Leon nodded approval while she added: "Oh, but could you give me a lift? I promised Angelo the car tomorrow night… and besides, I wouldn't trust it to get us out of anywhere in a hurry."

Leon agreed, and that was that. Dottie hadn't brought up my dealings with The Blight and I'd at least bought myself another day of time with Leon. There was an exchange of information; Dottie giving Leon her apartment address, and Leon giving me Conrad's number. There was something I wanted to ask him personally, assuming he wasn't in custody given the state of his rally when we left…

The usual goodbyes were said, with promises to see each other on the morrow. I slung on my leather jacket and went for the door, but Dottie lingered in the sitting room. Usually we took our leave together, but tonight she made no effort to follow behind. *She's going to tell Leon.* The thought screamed through my head like a runaway train, and just like a runaway train – there was nothing I could do about it. My hand was already clasped around the door handle, and being unable in that moment to think of any justifiable reason for turning back, I pushed forward and stepped out into the night.

The dark streets were ideal for mulling things over. With the keening whine of the motorcycle beneath me and the cool night air rushing through my ears, I ran through some possible scenarios in my head. If Leon knew that I was tied up with The Blight, he'd surely drop me from the investigation, and probably as a friend too. It'd be a shame. Leon's escapades really helped the time pass while I was between trips, but I knew he had a reputation to keep up for his profession. Streetlights flashed overhead, and I reminisced back to the night that Dottie had appeared on my doorstep and we'd confided our pasts. I thought for sure that night she'd question me about my outburst at the airfield, but she didn't. Instead, we understood each other. I finally found someone who could understand my loss of Maria, and she – her loss of Charles. Sure, circumstances had changed now that my job seemed to be intersecting with the case, but I hoped that even if Leon could no longer associate with me, Dottie at least might.

By the time I arrived home, it was nearing midnight. I didn't really care if I woke Conrad up or not; there was something I needed to ask him. Something that couldn't wait until the day of the final shipment. The dialer spun beneath my finger and the line rang for only a few seconds before being picked up.

"Hullo?"

"Conrad, it's Thomas. I hope I didn't wake you, but it's important."

"Nah, didn't wake me. How could I sleep after what I did today? Been keeping eyes out for police."

"What you did today? It was just a rally, right?" I put my original question on hold.

"The rally yes, quite a success by the way. You remember ol' Jason Fullom, don't you? From that creepy house you two dragged me to? Even he showed up to join. But no. What has me worried is that I gave the big man himself a piece of my mind. *That's* what has me watching over my shoulder."

So Conrad had a confrontation with Glasspier before he was murdered. Bad timing. "Well, I hate to say it, but you might be under even more suspicion than you know. Keep an eye on the news tomorrow and keep your head down."

"Why? What do you know? Did some-"

"I shouldn't say too much. You never know who could be listening. Besides, that's not why I called." Conrad, surprisingly, relented and fell silent. I'd already rehearsed what I was going to say on the ride over, so I got into it without a pause. "Have you noticed any odd shipments passing through, or maybe even being dropped off at the steel mill? Any trains rolling through at odd hours perhaps?"

"No, can't say I have. Why?" I heard the flick of a lighter beside the receiver on his end.

"You will tomorrow. Just after midnight. I need you to work late, come up with a reason to, or just hide somewhere in the mill. We need to know *if* the train stops there, where the cargo is being taken."

"What are you, my manager?" he laughed once and descended into a small coughing fit.

"This could concern you. This could concern us all. Maybe even the whole city. Someone is planning something and I have to be at the harbor during it; we need your insider eyes on the place."

"Sure, I reckon I can come up with a reason. I'll be there. I'd better be getting paid for my overtime though." He gave another short laugh and we hung up after a quick farewell.

Tomorrow was the end. One way or another, I knew I likely wouldn't be involved in the case any further. I left the telephone and wandered absentmindedly into the dark kitchen; pouring myself a nightcap as I searched in vain for a way to keep my two worlds separate. Sleep wasn't going to come easily tonight.

Chapter 38 - Reflections

Dottie

Memories of the masquerade flashed by in a nonlinear blur; a whirlwind of glitz and glamor stained by the darkness that seeps from the underbelly of this entire city. The circling trays of dark red wine; the blood on Leon's face. The buzz of a hundred infuriatingly snobbish voices betting on horses; the pounding in my ears as I ran from the Glasspier estate in those damned heels. The crescendo of bow on string as the orchestra began another waltz; the roar of the engine in the blue coupe as it disappeared yet again in a cloud of dust and fumes. Thomas Glasspier; the unmistakable star shining through a sea of obscured faces and hidden intentions, the unofficial king of the city, crowned by a circlet of steel and exploitation. Thomas Glasspier; the man murdered by a woman scorned – and I couldn't help but secretly applaud her for having the spine to do what so many have surely yearned for. All the memories of the night drowned my head in a fog of second-guessing, only made worse as I drowned them further in another glass of Leon's whiskey. Masks, whispers behind closed doors, and secret identities that almost click into place before slipping from my grasp – all fanning the flames of more burning questions that seem to only be soothed by the liquid burn of alcohol. I took another drink, staring out into the space that Thomas had until recently stood.

"Something on your mind Dottie?" Leons voice cut through the whirlwind. I was stalling. I'd have a lifetime to reflect on the masquerade, right now, I had to warn Leon.

I started tentatively, "Yes… I was hoping I'd never be put in this position. I was hoping to just continue on, pretending that I didn't know, after all, he's been able to keep it from being a problem this far…"

"Who has? Keep what a secret? What are you talking about Dottie?"

Best to just rip off the bandage I supposed. "Thomas. He's working for The Blight."

Leon closed his eyes and rubbed his temple with his free hand. He sat like that for a while, before eventually waving his hand in a way that I took to mean 'out with it'.

"When you were… away, at the airfield that night. He tried to get those guys to stand down by proving that he was one of them."

Leon looked hopeful at hearing that. "So he was bluffing then. Lying to save our skin."

"No. I'm sorry Leon, but he wasn't."

"How do you know." He didn't phrase it like a question. More like an accusation. I could understand why he was upset. I was too. I didn't want to see our new-found posse break apart. But I couldn't let him go into the endgame blind to this.

"He has one of their coins," I said, doubling down. Leon made no indication of the weight of that statement having made any impact on him, so I continued, "The Blight only gives those to their members and friends – if just anyone found one, they wouldn't recognize their importance."

"So how do you know about them?" Leon asked, "if they're so special – and you're just anyone?"

"The places I go tend to be rife with the type of men that carry them," I told a half truth, "places I go for information for *you,* I might add. " There was no sense in bringing my brother into it. Leon's tense features relaxed a bit, and he rose gingerly from his seat.

"Thanks Dottie. I want to trust Thomas, I really do, but you and I both know how it is in this city." Sensing our big night was nearing its end, I too stood and gathered my things.

The car put up a small fight as usual, but soon I was on my way home in the lonesome wake that followed a day of socializing. Funny how that emptiness still crept in, even when the company you'd been entertaining for most of the day had been loathsome. I hoped I'd made the right call. Either way, after tomorrow Thomas would have been outed as a gang affiliate regardless unless he abandoned his job. Maybe I should have given him the chance to… No. Leon deserved to know what he was getting into. Sooner rather than later. And even if he could no longer associate with him, I hoped I that might still be able to – and not just because I was really looking forward to him fixing that starter.

The apartment was dark when I got home and Angelo was asleep. My interrogation would have to wait until tomorrow it seemed. I couldn't complain, I was exhausted. I changed out of the uncomfortable formalwear and despite all my worries about what tomorrow might hold, I was asleep the moment my head hit the pillow.

Sept. 27th 1947
Saturday
Glasspier,

It was much later than I'd anticipated when I woke to frail sunbeams filtering through the curtains. The faint sounds of the city too filled the apartment, but from within, all was quiet. I ventured to the kitchen, drawn to the scent of a breakfast cooked some time ago but still lingering in the air. Eggs and toast left for me – an Angelo special. Beside them, was a small note.

Dots,

Here's a little thanks for the car. Be back late tonight. Don't forget the garbage.

-A

I cursed under my breath. The job was *late* tonight, why had he gone out so early? I glanced at the clock on the wall, doing some routine math based on how many minutes slow I knew it to be. Just before noon. I knew it was no use trying to find him, wherever he'd gone; he always shut me out from that side of things 'for my own safety'. But apparently he had big plans for the day, so now I did too: wait around the apartment hoping he'd stop by before Leon came to get me. I busied myself with picking out a sensible outfit for the harbor stakeout – no heels necessary this time, thank god.

Chapter 39 - Arrangements

Leon

Leons Journal
September 27th, 1947 10:20
Entry #313

I should have known it would happen again. Can't expect not to shoot somebody eventually carrying a gun in a city like this. Like trying to stay sober and going to the bar every night.

Last night, I dreamed of The Stag. I knew I would, after what'd happened at the masquerade. But this time it was different. Normally, it's me versus him, with flashes of blood and snow. Sometimes I have my Ka-bar, other times I see through the eyes of a lion or some other beast. Sometimes it's mixed with the events of before I got lost in those woods; the German boy driving his knife into my gut. Not this time. This time I saw through the eyes of The Stag. I saw myself through its eyes, ravenous with hunger, stalking through the snowfields and briar; felt that pain in my stomach as I always did, but this time – I was the one driving in the knife.

Thomas Glasspier Jr. in Critical Condition Following Annual Estate Party! Foxglove Killer Prime Suspect in Attempted Murder!

In my office, putting my journal aside, I appreciated another sensational headline from the Herald, but for once – I was actually invested. Glasspier wasn't dead after all, although he might end up that way by the sound of it. I tried to read through the fluff and shock value over my morning coffee for a sense of what the authorities might really know. The article made it clear that the 'Foxglove Killer' was to blame, but made no mention of her identity. She was still at large and unknown; I wondered if she'd found a better way out of the building than taking a swan dive from the second story. I continued reading, getting caught up on events that I was a part of and in the end, it wasn't the caffeine, but rather the last paragraph of the piece that really spiked my heart rate.

Two men: one in a black half mask, and another in a golden deer mask were also reported to be at the scene of the crime, according to Glasspier security officers, and are wanted as accessories to his murder; along with the killing of Glasspier head of security Silas Stevenson. Silas is survived only by his mother, Penelope Stevenson, permanent resident of Blossom Valley Hospital. (More on pg. 3) Authorities and citizens alike are encouraged by cash reward to report with any information they might have that leads to the apprehension of these suspects.

At first, I set the paper down and sipped the dregs of my coffee as contentedly as a bruised-up man wanted for murder really could be expected to. It was fine; they hadn't seen me, just my masquerade persona. A further thought dispelled that hollow contentment. *Dammit*. There *was* someone who knew the stag and she could implicate the whole lot of us, not just me. It would've actually been better if they'd just seen my face – at least then all they'd have to go on would be a police sketch. My hand wavered over the handle of the top left drawer on the desk. Inside was the easy answer to the problem. No. I leaned back, forcing out that notion. I'd only killed Silas because if I hadn't, I wouldn't be sitting here right now contemplating killing an old woman for the crime of selling me a suit. I didn't even know her name and she only knew my first. If she pieced together who I was, I'd just have to tell the truth and plead self-defense. My father hadn't raised me to solve all my problems with *.45* slug – only some of them.

I left my office in favor of the sitting room, putting some distance between myself and that grim solution. I switched on the radio and switched to a drink harder than coffee. The mayor was on, halfway through an address about the events of last night. I listened for a while, but gleaned no new information. Wesson was artfully doing what politicians did best: talking in circles and expressing condolences without any real plan of action. I turned the dial off and placed a phone call.

I met Cruz up at the Byway Bar on 7th around 16:00. It was twice as clean and twice as expensive as the Gold Pig, with a slightly more agreeable patronage. Was coming here the mark of a condemned man enjoying his last days of freedom? Possibly. But it was an arrangement I'd been meaning to make for a while now, regardless of venue. My brawl and flight from the manor had just expedited things. I got there first and called for two whiskey sours, busying myself by watching the crowd circling around the craps table. My old partner arrived just after the top of the hour; walking quickly and taking the stool to my right.

"Finally got outta there," he breathed, taking quick to the whisky, "like hell trying to amputate myself from that office chair." He set the glass back onto the bar top, and wiped his mouth. "How've you been keeping?"

"Well, I'm on the right side of the ground for now, but there's still time." I answered, lighting up a cigarette to contribute to the haze in the room.

"Jesus man, that well? I saw all the shit in the news today. That you?" He whispered the last part.

I didn't answer, taking a draw instead and blowing a fan of smoke, which was answer enough.

"Hell, you *are* lucky to be on the right side of the ground. On the right side of the pen, too."

"For now."

"Anybody able to make you?"

"There's one. No reason I can see why she wouldn't sing either. I reckoned this would be a final supper of sorts for us, before the buttons come knocking," I admitted, downing the rest of my sour.

"Who is she?"

I hesitated, then figured there was no point in keeping it a secret. She already knew, and Cruz already knew. What difference would it make if Cruz knows that she knows. "Lady at The Red Dress down on Harlow. Don't even know her name."

Cruz blinked in shock. "The Red Dress? I passed by there on the way here – it was being put out. There was a fire. Didn't think anything about it, you know how this city is, but do you think?"

Someone burned down The Red Dress? I didn't for a moment consider it was an accident. "Hell of a coincidence. But I swear I-"

"I know it wasn't you. Wouldn't have been sitting here so glum, like a man on the gallows if you'd done it."

"She make it?"

"Didn't look so."

We drank in silence for a while after that; him finishing his first and me starting my second. I hadn't a stroke of luck yet and had no reason to think this was the start. It was the Gray Man, or the person he worked for. It had to be. He'd been watching over us the whole way and that wasn't something I necessarily liked; even when it was in my favor. I also didn't much like the idea of somebody being burned to death for my benefit. My cigarette went out with a hiss in the ceramic tray on the far side of the counter.

We made some idle talk as the evening stretched on, him about his fraud case, and me about anything but the Marlowe case. The clack of billiard balls punctuated his anecdote about a careless intern, to which I made a disparaging remark about him even having one in the first place. Our laughter died away along with the light outside, as the sun slipped lower behind the skyscrapers out the window. That was another thing I enjoyed about the Byway. It wasn't crammed into some small lot between buildings; it sat at the end of 7th Street, offering a few of the fading crimson sunlight out its western windows. It was nearing time to retrieve Dottie. Nearing time to start our stakeout of the harbor.

"There's one more reason I wanted to meet tonight," I started, "and it doesn't have to do with being outed by the seamstress." Cruz didn't say anything; his good-natured expression slowly slipped into his drink. "Keep an eye on your telephone tomorrow. If I don't call by this time, go to my office. There's a journal, it'll be locked in my bedside stand and it'll explain everything. Can you do that?"

Cruz responded slowly, "Why are you talking like that? You've been in dodgy situations before, surely you can handle another."

"Surely. Yes. But just in case…" What was it that had me so on edge about this? At first, I just chalked it up to the investigation coming to a close, but no, there was more than that. It was the fact that everywhere I'd gone so far, everything I'd done, had been planned by the Gray Man and his benefactor. Everything until this. This wasn't something handed to us, it wasn't something we were supposed to know about. The only other time I might have gone off script was at the airfield… and look where that'd gotten us.

I stood up from the stool and settled our tabs.

"I'll be seeing you," Cruz said, extending his hand, "you'll be alright, you always are." I shook it.

"I hope so," I said, nodding to him and rising for the door. Halfway I stopped and turned. "If you *do* have to break into my journal, just rip out a few pages as you see fit before it gets entered into evidence. You'll know the ones."

He squinted in question, but nodded his agreement nonetheless. I turned from him again and walked out into the orange glow of twilight.

Dottie was outside the apartment building when I arrived. She stood, purse and cigarette in hand, breathing the shapes of the city into silhouettes beneath a street-lamp. She was wearing more practical clothes than I'd ever seen, and the dusk was heavy on her jacket-clad shoulders; with only a faint glow remaining of the meager sun. She pulled the door open and climbed inside. The yellow headlights tracked a path through the bustling streets of a Saturday night in Glasspier; neon signs blaring their messages into the gloom. I pulled onto a side street a block from the pitch-black harbor and killed the engine.

I didn't need to explain why we were here so early to Dottie; she knew the plan. Finding a vantage point was the first step. I retrieved my binoculars from the glove box after she stepped out and we made our way casually down the sloping street towards the shipyard. As far as I could see in the afterglow of sunset, there were some low-rise buildings spread throughout the yard, alongside stacks of big box shipping containers scattered here and there. Although I couldn't see it, I knew the railroad ran to the south most wharf. We veered that direction, going slow in the uncertain light, keeping low and quiet.

I'd liked to have perched atop one of the buildings, but as we drew closer, I could see they were rounded structures with no good handholds. Instead, I selected a stack of metal shipping containers about four high. I climbed up first, the natural overlap of the boxes providing hand and footholds, and reached a hand down to help pull Dottie up after me. On top, we had an unobstructed view of the main jetty and the land surrounding it – save for the darkness of course. I hoped the cloud cover would dissipate and allow the moonlight through by the time midnight rolled around. If not, I was going to be wishing I had the money for a night glass.

I wrapped my coat tighter around myself and Dottie did the same with hers, both of us trying to minimize contact with the metal of the container as we laid prone on it. I set my binoculars out in front of us and we stared out silently over the port, taking in the salty breeze and shivering from the cold and the anticipation

Chapter 40 - The Stag

Leon

Thirty minutes to midnight a single beam cut through the blackness of the shipyard like a small sun, burning bright in our night adjusted eyes. The sound followed, rising steady over the gentle lapping of waves against the docks. It was a sound I was familiar with. Thomas. His motorcycle careened through the yard towards the piers, weaving between containers and dry-docked boats alongside railcars and a dormant engine. He dismounted nearby a small building shaped like a rectangle set on its end and went inside, reemerging shortly after with something in hand.

Fifteen minutes to midnight a lone tugboat pushed off from the dock, chugging its way out into the harbor. The air had dropped a few degrees since we'd arrived and I fought back shivers as we watched Thomas beneath the starless sky. The one benefit the cold provided was the shrinking away of the cloud cover, which allowed the moon occasional purchase to shine through. Still didn't feel like much of a benefit laying atop that steel box.

Five minutes to midnight brought the others. The Blight. Three cars, pulling quietly into the shipyard one after another, taking the same route Thomas had. A score of men emerged from them, four to each car, and they began preparations. Three went for the train, one climbing up into the engine and the other two readying one of the boxcars in tow behind it. A gap in the cloud cover momentarily bathed the scene in faint moonlight and allowed for a quick visual stock to be taken. I searched the faces of the men. None were covered. No Gray Man here, not yet at least, unless he wasn't in costume. My scrutiny fell on the vehicles they'd arrived in – no blue coupe either. But was that Dottie's car? Sure as hell looked similar. I didn't dare whisper to her, with how near the men were to our lookout spot. I could feel her breathing quicken. She tilted her head towards the water.

Straining, I could just make out a dark mass on the horizon, perceptible only by the faint glow of light behind the clouds that it passed in front of. The men on the shore stared out towards it too, without even a whisper among them. Time passed in a crawl. The cold sank deeper into our bones and we all waited in mute anticipation for Thomas to bring the ship in. I was used to laying long periods in conditions like this; Camp Ritchie had seared it into my soul – if I still had such a thing. Poor Dottie though, shivering and shaking beside me like a naked Quaker at the North Pole; I willed the ship to move faster for both our sakes. It crawled ever closer and finally, agonizingly slowly, it came to a stop beside the dock. Or was it technically a jetty? Whatever, it didn't matter. I was just thinking about anything and everything I could to take my mind off the cold. Low voices, in a language familiar to me, carried above the waves made by the two vessels coming into port. Russian.

What the hell was a Russian ship doing in Glasspier's harbor? It wasn't a massive one, but large enough, and its presence alone was enough to set my jaw on edge. Whatever it was bringing in, I was sure it wasn't good. Right on cue, the crew aboard the ship busied themselves with offloading a large load of… something. In the intermittent light, the best I could make out was a vaguely rectangular mass resting on a pallet of some kind. It was lifted by a combined effort of the Russians and The Blight, and carried slowly off the docks and toward the train. All in all, it took about twenty minutes by my estimate to move whatever it was into the train and for the Soviets to file back into their boat. On the plus side, the sudden intrigue had made time pass a hell of a lot quicker, and I'd almost forgotten I was supposed to be freezing. I was reminded, as the tugboat piloted by Thomas took the vessel back out to open waters and the activity in the shipyard came to a lull.

The men buttoned up the boxcar and most piled into their vehicles again, while a few lingered in the briny air, smoking and watching the water. It was another agonizing wait. My gun dug into my ribs, and Dottie's teeth started to chatter idly while we waited for some kind of action. The moment the gang cleared out and the train pulled away I intended to follow it. Even if it took me far out west, past the Mississippi. Although if it got that far, I'd probably just hop aboard the rattler myself and see what it was carrying.

By the time the tugboat groaned back into the port, bitter pin pricks of star light were shining out in the darkness beside the nearly full moon. The sky was nearly clear and it was nearly one o'clock. Thomas disembarked the dinghy and walked evenly down the pier, his shoes clacking dully through the crisp air on the half-rotted timbers. He approached one of the men still standing about in the yard, whispering a few quick words, before climbing aboard the train. Now we really had a man on the inside. Or did we? Shoving my doubts out of my head I focused again on the cars. Damn, that one really *did* look like Dottie's two-door, it even had rust in the same places along the wheel wells. Within seconds, all the doors were shut and the engines rumbled to life. Except one. I heard one of them fight for a bit before sputtering to life. Just like Dottie's did. I turned to whisper a question to her, but the hiss and scrape of the train coming to life drowned out my words. It was time to move.

Wordlessly, we slid one after the other off the backside of the stack of metal containers. Myself first, then Dottie, as I helped lower her down to earth again. We shook the cold from our aching limbs and kept to the shadows, making a zig-zag path through the shipyard and back to my car. Behind us, the train clanked into motion and the motorcars flanked it on its path away from the harbor. There was only one direction they could be going – west, so I wasn't too worried about being able to track them. My sedan came into view up the street and I figured we were more than far enough away to converse.

"Dottie, that two-door down there looked an awful lot like yours. Even sounded like it." I shot a sidelong glance at her as we hustled down the street, but she kept her eyes fixed on the car, not saying anything at first. I was about to ask her directly: 'was that your car?' when she finally broke.

"My brother was there." We'd reached the car but stood facing each other on either side of it without getting in, looking across the roof. "Angelo. He had the car tonight. And he had it back there," she confessed, not meeting my eyes.

Were all of my friends tied up with The Blight? Next I'd learn that Cruz was the head of the mob.

"I don't know why he's here; I never know what he's up to with his friends. I prom-"

"Just get in." I cursed and yanked my door open. We didn't have time for this, there was a train to catch.

Catching the train proved easy. It rumbled along the otherwise barren rails, resolutely heading west. The trick was staying far enough back that the convoy of cars escorting it wouldn't take notice. I did my best to keep up with the sparse traffic, occasionally looping a block in order to not get ahead of my quarry. Dottie was quiet and staring out the window towards whichever direction the convoy happened to be as we wound through the streets and alleys towards the steel mill.

The mill at night had an eerie quality to it, with its massive columns and stacks looming silently over the city. A few red lights flashed on various buildings, along with some overhead security lamps dotting the expanse around the main structures. The tracks ran through the south side of the mill, between a gap in the chain link fencing that sectioned the place off from the slums. I wheeled the car around the outskirts of the mill, alongside the fence as the train passed through. But it didn't pass through. Instead, a long hiss and screech echoed through the chilly September night before fading away into the ambient sounds of the city. It'd stopped. Whatever the Russians had brought over in secret was for Glasspier Steel Company. Either that, or something else was being picked up. Regardless, we needed to get inside.

I wheeled the car around, back towards where the tracks passed through the gate in the fence; hurtling down a desolate side street lined by decaying shanty homes.

"They stopped in the steel mill," Dottie whispered to me rhetorically, "can we follow?"

"So long as we catch the gate," I grunted with the effort of whipping the wheel around to pull sharply off the little alley and take a ninety degree turn towards the railroad tracks. I floored the pedal, hearing the roar as the RPMs spiked and a clatter of loose gravel kicked out from behind the car. We closed in on the gate and I could see that it was open. I let off a little. The small guardhouse beside the gate appeared dark and vacant and the gate itself was slid open allowing entry via the tracks. "Hold on." I clenched my teeth and pulled the wheel to the right, popping the car up onto the railroad ballast right before we reached the chain link. It rattled fierce and I fought to keep our heading. No sooner had the tires ridden up onto the tracks, did they depart from them, as I maneuvered back to the left the second we'd made the gap in the fence. I was on the brakes soon after, pulling the car into hiding behind a stack of steel girders. The headlights vanished in a gasp, followed by the engine shuddering to a stop, leaving only the whirring hum of fans winding down. The doors clicked open and we stepped out into the indifferent night.

We wound through a yard similar to the one at the harbor, myself in front and Dottie tailing after me. Instead of dry-docked boats, there were steel cylinders that I couldn't identify a use for and more metal shipping containers, along with piles of what I assumed to be slag of some kind. The railroad tracks ran perpendicular through it all and we followed their trajectory, keeping to the deeper shadows near the containers. From above, I imagined we'd look like ants navigating a maze thrown together by some higher being. Hearing low voices, we stopped at the edge of an open space where the engine and its boxcars were strung out along the rails running in front of the mill. The vehicles were parked alongside, between the boxcars and the scaffold structure of the steel mill's main building. Just breathing here, I could feel soot stifling my airways and I fought back a revealing cough.

The gaggle of men had spilled from their vehicles once more and were pulling the doors of the rust-stained boxcar open, which issued a sharp metallic wail. A flickering overhead bulb provided enough light on the area for me to see Thomas was off to the side and leaned against the train observing, but speaking with no one. Maybe he *was* only marginally involved. The men got to work at sliding the palette and its contents carefully from the boxcar onto the ground beside the rails. Two of the men from the group broke away, heading to our left towards a stack of shipping containers near the edge of the large open area. One of them was tall with broad shoulders, and the other was the opposite, swimming in a black leather jacket that was one or two sizes too big.

Dottie touched my shoulder and pointed, whispering, "Angelo."

So one of those two was her brother. I couldn't make their faces from here, but based on stature I had a guess. They undid a lock on one of the containers and pulled the doors open facing the clearing. Even if it hadn't been too dark over there to see anything, the angle was wrong; I couldn't tell what was inside. The two disappeared into the crate. Back over by the train, the object on the palettes was still covered in some kind of tarpaulin and they didn't seem intent on changing that fact for the time being.

One of the men nearest the object stooped down and raised something from the dirt, causing a small cloud of coal dust to rise into the air between him and the direction Angelo and the other man had gone. A wire. Or a pair of wires. Instantly, all doubts were cleared from my mind in regards to what the shipment was. Explosives. I whispered an expletive, causing Dottie to look curiously between me and the covered bomb. I carefully pulled my lighter from my pocket. It was chrome, scratched and dulled, but still chrome. I angled it to catch the light from the overhead in the clearing, flashing it once at Thomas' eye level. He made a surprised start, no longer leaning against the railcar and instead squinting towards the shadows that housed us. A look of recognition dawned on his face and he glanced towards the others, who were starting the process of hooking up the wires to an exposed corner of the still otherwise fully covered payload. I jerked my head in the direction that the wires ran, before slinking back away from the clearing edge, pulling Dottie's arm to follow.

"What are we doing?" she hissed as we moved along the outskirts of the clearing.

"It's a bomb. Or some kind of unused wartime explosives if I had to guess. We *need* to find where those wires run."

Dottie looked like a ghost in what little light there was to see her by. "Who would do this?"

I didn't answer. I was asking myself the same thing. It was an entire targeted attack on Thomas Glasspier and his industry. It must have taken years to plan. I didn't like the man myself, but we had to stop this. People's livelihoods were at stake, not to mention the city's economy and infrastructure. Glasspier was a tough city to get by in, but blowing up its biggest industry was only going to make things worse. Once I was sure we were out of sight, I cut left, back towards the tracks in hopes to intercept the cable run on its path away from the clearing.

I wasn't an explosives expert – my realm of expertise was more counter-intelligence, but I knew that whoever was pushing that button had to be a ways away from the blast site if it was going to be a big enough bang to take out the mill's main structure. I drew my small pocket flash and started going over the dusty ground. Sure enough, a dull silver gleam caught my attention running alongside the tracks. I pointed it out to Dottie and we walked the line further west.

We didn't have to go much further before it veered away from the tracks into the midst of a group of old boxcars sitting beside the rails. I saw the line snake into one of the cars which had its sliding doors opened and a faint glow emanating from within. My hand itched for my pistol as we approached, but the faint taste of bile at the thought of shooting someone again stopped it. So, armed with just the flashlight, I glanced back at Dottie and stepped up into the boxcar. Inside, a man dressed top to bottom in all gray was standing, hunched over a makeshift table with a dim lantern and a slate gray mask resting on it beside him.

Hearing the boxcar creak beneath my feet, he whipped around. No longer was the faceless man faceless. Our guiding hand, our guardian angel, the blue coupe driver, the one behind it all, the Gray Man – I recognized. I recognized him from the ticket check at Glasspier's party. Morris Fletcher. The man Silas claimed was going to ruin everything. I believed him now, seeing a detonator switch on the table.

For a second that felt like a lifetime, we both stood in shock. Him, presumably at being found, and me, at the realization of the two separate entities in my mind being one and the same. He made the first move and lunged forward, grabbing hold of my coat lapel and bringing a heavy fist into my jaw. I registered a throbbing pain in my head and a cry of shock from Dottie behind me as I stumbled from the blow. The shift in weight from my reeling pulled me from Fletcher's grasp and I steadied myself against the steel wall of the boxcar before lunging back at him. We grappled, fists searching for openings to hammer into soft flesh and I got a couple good licks in before a sharp pop echoed through the tin can. My ears rang. Fletcher stumbled back, releasing the hold he had on my sleeve and I took the opportunity to throw him forcefully back into the darkness of the far side of the boxcar. He let out a pained shout and then all was quiet, save for the ringing that was fading away in my ears and the sound of my own heavy breathing.

I retrieved the flashlight I hadn't even registered dropping from the floor and turned to Dottie. She stood still on the ground just outside the boxcar, with her purse emptied out beside her and a small silver gun still smoking in her white knuckled grip. She was full of surprises tonight. She lowered the muzzle, trembling a little but looking resolute and I'm sure she was finding, like I did, that the second time was easier. Still a hell of a shot, with me and Fletcher moving around like that, I had half a mind to check myself for holes.

"Thanks," I breathed, and reached out a hand to help her into the boxcar. I shone the light to the back of the space where I'd thrown Fletcher and moved to interrogate him. I hoped I'd have more time with him than I did with Silas. The boxcar creaked and groaned beneath my steps as I approached where Fletcher stood, or rather, where he hung. I could see now what the boxcar had been housing: rolls of rebar. He'd been impaled on the ends of a roll, which now supported his weight as his feet struggled helplessly beneath him to stand, trying in vain to lift himself off the metal piercing through his abdomen. *The forest*. No.

I tried to focus on his face. A trickle of blood was running from the corner of his mouth down onto his gray collar. But beneath all that, I could picture his intestines wrapped around the rebar, protruding outwards from where they belonged. I'd only seen it for a second, but it lingered in my mind. A floating vision, like a ghost, pulling my consciousness back to that forest. Back to The Stag. I stepped closer and took a handful of his bloodstained shirt.

"Who paid you to do this? Who paid you?" I snarled.

"The Stag," he said, his mouth not matching the words that came out. He continued to speak through a mouth that had drawn closed in a grimace: "There's blood on the snow. Do you remember it? Do you remember the blood and sinew, how it felt between your teeth, how it tasted?" He was smiling now, with lips that still weren't moving. "I know you do. How could you forget?"

I looked down at hands that weren't mine anymore.

How could you forget The Stag? It's golden pelt.

IT

The blood spread around it: red seeping into the whiteness of the snow. **WAS**

proud golden beast in my teeth " -Leon!"
I had too!

A

-knife digging in, red and white so hungry…

I had to. I had to. I had to. I had to. I had to. I had to. I had to. I had to. I had to. I had to. I had to. I had to. I had to. I had to. I had to. I had to. I **STAG** forest of gold and red and white and gold and red and white and gold and red and white and a lion

A hand on my shoulder. No?
how?

There hadn't been. It was. No it wasn't. A Stag. *The Stag.* No. A silhouette. I chased it, but it wasn't.

"Leon please," with tears.

"I don't know what to do."

I didn't either. It wasn't. Wasn't a beast. Wasn't a stag.
blood trail. I could see it. See *him.*

you know this. Do you?

A woman's voice? There hadn't been a woman's voice…

until sundown. I chased. The man. *The stag?*

No. The Man.

"It's me. You have to-" "Thomas too-"

A man stood before me. He was worn down, out of breath, exhausted. I chased him. I'd caught him. He was a stag…

No. That's not true. The man, a German soldier. A boy really – just like me: Leon Bauer.

-No, he's dead.

He wasn't then. The German stood before me, at the end of a blood trail. Through the snow, we'd arrived here, each of us sealing the fate of the other. I clutched my knife and approached him. Not a beast. Not a stag. A German soldier. Antlers branched from my head. He wasn't the stag. I was the stag. I'd created it. I'd become it. Behind the mask, beneath the antlers – the stag was a fiction. A falsehood. It no longer existed. I'd killed it. Just as I'd killed that German soldier in those woods. My breathing steadied. My blurry vision came slowly back into focus.

Before me stood a man. Not the German. It was Thomas. Thomas Langston. My friend. I was in the boxcar again and my pistol had found its way to my hand. He was between me and Morris Fletcher, who was still hanging by his guts from the rebar. Thomas stood between us with a pistol in one hand and the detonator in the other.

Chapter 41 - Loyalties

Thomas

"Put the gun down," I said, in as calming a manner as I could, given the circumstances. Leon had seemed out of his head, but something had changed in these last few seconds and I was beginning to recognize my friend again. I think he was recognizing me.

"Put yours down. The detonator too," he replied, raising his gun slowly to point at my chest.

I raised my own to match it, my left hand still clutching the switch. I had to do this. We could both win here. I could succeed where Fletcher hadn't – and The Blight would surely see my worth. Leon and Dottie could walk away. They still had the evidence they needed and the steel mill's fate was irrelevant to them. I just had to convince Leon.

"No, stop!" Dottie cried, as we both leveled our pistols.

I did my best to ignore her, although it was difficult because she too had a gun. Thankfully hers wasn't pointed at anyone. Yet.

"There's that look again. You had the same one in Glasspier's suite at the party when you found me. Fear." Leon released a deep sigh; the kind that comes from the soul rather than the lungs. If there were such a thing. "I thought this city would be full of opportunity to start over, but it just made me a killer again. I killed Silas or he would have killed me. I had no choice. Do you know what was in his will? Did you see it in the paper? He left everything to his dying mother. He wanted all of his remaining assets to go towards paying for her care. That's why he continued to live in this damn city with all its killing. What reason do I have?"

"What reason do any of us have? We're all here, whether we intended to be or not, and we have to make the best of our situations. All of us. That's what I'm doing and that's what you're doing whether you realize it or not. I have to do this."

"No. You have a choice. At least you *have* a choice, mine was taken from me. It was kill, or be killed. The violence, the cycles of it, the corruption and bloodshed – it must stop somewhere. Everything I've done up to now I had to do. That's what I told myself, but there will always be another reason to kill. To save myself. To save others. It's why I killed that stag… no... not a stag… that German soldier, it's why I killed Silas, and it's why I'm prepared to kill you; even though I swore to myself I never would again."

"If I don't do this, The Blight will kill me anyways. You can walk away. Both of you. I'm not killing anyone, it's just a building. There shouldn't be anyone inside at this hour." Other than maybe poor Conrad… I'd asked him to keep an eye out, but now I was wishing I hadn't. The Blight had me ride along anyway, so now it seemed he was just going to become collateral damage. But I didn't need Leon to know that. He also didn't need to know that I'd already been responsible for calling in a favor to have one building burned down today. That was to protect all of us. This was to protect me. What was one more?

"You might not be killing anyone directly, but what about their livelihoods? Families will starve if you remove the city's biggest employer. And fuck The Blight. We can take them on together."

The detonator was heavy and slick in my hand, heavier than the gun somehow. This was getting nowhere. Leon was too stubborn. Usually that was part of his charm, but right now it was only serving to tighten my finger around the trigger. And Dottie seemed to be standing with him, but at least her pistol wasn't raised. Maybe I could sway her, if I couldn't convince Leon.

“There’s no good or bad, just people doing what they can to get by. Some do it with a heavy conscience, while others are completely heartless. Dottie, do you remember what I told you that night? And what you told me? That rainy night you found yourself at my door? You told me-”

Chapter 42 - Halfway

Leon

For the second time that night my ears rang within that boxcar. The clatter of a gun hitting the floor was heard only dully amidst the echoes of the gunshot. Thomas stopped mid-sentence to stare down, with eyes wide in shock at the hole torn in his suit jacket. I too looked down in shock at my pistol – I hadn't fired. I snapped my head to Dottie and she looked just as surprised as the rest of us. Her pistol had never been raised. Thomas' knees buckled beneath him and I caught him, preventing him from falling onto the cold steel. I clasped my hand around the detonator, preventing it too from falling from his faltering hands. His gun clattered to the floor. I lowered him gently down to lie beside it. Behind him, I could see Fletcher, still impaled and staring upwards with glassy eyes. He'd managed to pull his coat aside, revealing an empty holster on his hip. A gun lay at his feet.

A ring of crimson was forming on the chest of Thomas' well-tailored dress shirt and all I could think about was how disappointed he'd be in having it stained. Stupid. It was all stupid. The whole case. I never should have accepted it. I put pressure on the wound, a bullet hole meant for me, but I knew it was no use. His eyes already had that dreaming look to them that people got when they were halfway between this world and the next.

“You… can still walk away,” Thomas mumbled, “told them I’d take care of it… won’t be coming to check for a little while yet…”

I was aware of Dottie kneeling beside me. We weren’t going to let it be for nothing. We’d see it through. We’d stop them. We’d find out who planned the attack and we’d stop them.

Chapter 43 - Nothing

Dottie

No. I kneeled beside him. The floor of the boxcar was cold, he didn't deserve it to be like this, in the end. It wasn't supposed to go like this. They were supposed to argue, like they always did, before both cracking grins and finding a solution that they never could have on their own. His head rolled to the side and I placed a hand on his cheek, steadying it. He stared up at me with damp eyes.

"...Maria..." he whispered, just like the night he'd shown me her sapphire. The prayer of a dying man.

I knew what he meant. For all the cynicism this city fostered, we both held onto a similar hope in the back recesses of our heart. There was nothing else to do but hope. Nothing. Nothing I could do for him. So I let go.

Chapter 44 - Summer's End

Thomas

The day was coming to an end and so was the summer. It was coming to an end beneath a sky full of clouds, billowing leisurely to herald autumn. Open water around us, sails mimicking the rolling clouds overhead, distant white shores on the horizon, and my hand clasped around the box in my pocket. Long before the coin-

-my back was cold. I could… feel the cold, sinking in-

The low sun painted the clouds in orange, pink, and crimson; gulls squawking in the warm sea breeze and my heart beat faster in my chest as I kneeled down-

-she was kneeling beside me, why… was she looking at me like that… it was dark overhead, red steel-

Maria. "Maria." Short blonde waves of hair above a silken white blouse that rested soft upon her shoulders; everything golden in the rays of the setting sun. The sapphire shone in her eyes, refracting the light. Everything glowed. The sun, the sparkling blue around us, her hair, the sapphire, her eyes. Yes, most importantly, her eyes. She smiled. I'd do anything, I'd do anything to see her smile. She breathed, wordlessly, and held my face-

-a hand on my cheek, it was all so dim, but I could feel it, soft and understanding-

Summer was nearing its end, but the moment stretched outwards for an eternity. Bending and warping over itself but never breaking. There was nowhere else, past or future: there was only then. I could stay there forever. With her. Don't fade, please. I could… stay here forever-

Chapter 45 - The Spark

Conrad

I'd heard the second gunshot and hurried down the stairs out of the mill into the storage yard, having half a mind to call the police. But after what I'd read in the papers and what Thomas had told me over the phone, I wasn't looking to get mixed up with them. I never was, to tell the truth. I approached the pack of boxcars sitting abandoned off the side of the rails, particularly the one with the light coming from it. The Somerset Line stored them here and in exchange, we stored stuff in them. Some had been here so long that weeds were growing up beneath them into the wheels. Speaking of wheels, there was a blue car parked behind the boxcar with the light – hadn't Leon mentioned something about a blue coupe back when this all started? I tried to place exactly what he'd said, but there were more important things to worry about at the moment.

I pressed myself against the side of the boxcar. It was quiet within. Were those wires running into the doorway? In one motion I pulled myself up inside. *Fuck.* Was that? Yes. Thomas was laid on his back with eyes closed and a small, dark puddle forming beneath him. And was that someone hanging in the back? I didn't stare long; I'd avoided the war for a reason after all. Well, a couple reasons.

Other than the two bodies, there was a small table made from an old board and two sawhorses with a dim metal lantern sitting on it, along with a crushed-up metal and wood object of some kind. Fragments of the same type of material were on the ground beside Thomas. I wasn't the sharpest spike in the railyard, but I quickly put three and three together. The wires, the bodies, the car, the far-removed location of the boxcar, and of course – the shattered remains of what I was sure had been a detonator.

I heard a distant cry go up, back towards where the men had been starting to move the explosives towards the mill. I hung out of the door of the boxcar, staring into the night down the alley of identical steel boxes, trying to see what the shouting was about. It was the far end of the yard; too dark and too far away to tell what was happening, but I had a guess. Leon and Dottie were making their escape: and they'd been seen. *Shit.* A hundred different outcomes flew about in my head, most of which ended with them getting shot and then me getting shot, before they set everything back up and blew the place to pieces. Of course I could run, and then only *they* would get shot – but the mill would still probably get blown apart. The ends of the wires lay detached from the ruined detonator on the floor. In all my ideas of how this might go down, there was only one possible option where everything could work out in our favor. Maybe.

I grabbed the metal lantern. No. It wouldn't work. The wires were too long for a battery of this size, there'd be too much resistance. I wracked my brain for a solution. Maybe the lantern could work, just not like *that.* I jumped from the boxcar, rushing behind it to where the blue coupe sat. I tried the door. Locked. I tried the window with the metal lantern. That seemed to do the trick. I reached through and popped the door open, pulling the hood release seconds after. Around the front of the coupe, I propped the hood open and located the battery. I didn't have the proper tools for the job and there wasn't time to get them, so I opted for brute force. Yanking on the battery and its cables, I wrestled it from the engine bay amid a shower of sparks. My moment of triumph was clouded with doubt. Would this even work? My knowledge of the logistics of explosive ordnance detonation rattled around in my head while I re-entered the boxcar: and there wasn't a lot. Gunfire popped in the distance, in the direction of their escape. Was it too late? And if it wasn't, were they far enough from the blast radius? I pictured where I'd seen them park their car from my vantage point on the third floor. It was about as equidistant from the explosives to the east as this boxcar was from them to the west. I pulled out my work gloves and put them on. I just hoped they'd done the math on their bunker site, because I sure as hell didn't have time to.

They hadn't gotten the explosives in position beneath the mill yet when I'd left to investigate the gunshots. All of this was hinging on that fact, along with my imagined idea of how large the blast would be in relation to this boxcar being a safe point. I suppose it was also hinging on whether or not this improvised detonator was going to work. But there was no more time for debate. I gathered up the ends of the wires, holding each above the terminals of the battery where it sat on the floor of the boxcar. Could I really do this? The train would be collateral, but that was easier to replace than the mill. Easier to replace than Leon and Dottie too. Wasn't that what I always said anyway? That revolution starts with the people – with the individual. A few more cracks of gunfire burst in the distance. I could do better. I took a deep breath and pressed the ends of the wires to the battery.

There was a moment after the spark and crackle of energy ran down the cable where nothing happened. I waited. There was more gunfire – gunfire that was abruptly dwarfed by a deafening thunder that shook the boxcar and the very ground it rested upon. I clasped my gloved hands over my ears and saw dust and debris rushing by the open door of the boxcar before I clenched my eyes shut and pressed myself to the floor. It was over just as soon as it started, but I lay prone on the floor for a sixty count before daring to open my eyes and remove my hands from my head. I could immediately hear the wail of sirens from all corners of the city in the distance. The echoes of the blast rattled around in my head and made my ears buzz.

Peering tentatively out of the boxcar, I was met with a yard turned into hell-scape. The mill was intact, save for the windows, which had all been blown inward; but where the train had once sat in the clearing was a smoldering wasteland of ash and twisted metal. I found it hard to imagine that anyone could have survived. I didn't hear any more gunshots at the very least that was for sure, and I strained to see through the cloud of dust and smoke for any signs of life. It was just too damn hazy to tell. I left the boxcar shakily in the aftermath, adrenaline at an all-time high. I *really* didn't want to be around when the badges arrived at the scene, so I started retracing my route back towards the building. I was going to pass through the mill as quickly as possible to come out on the north side, away from the blast site, but I just had to know. I had to know if it was all worth it.

It was dark inside the place, but I'd tread these metal walkways a thousand times. I found my way back to the third floor in no time and rushed to the south window. The glass lay shattered in small fragments before the gaping frame and crunched beneath my boots as I approached. From my vantage point, I could see red and blue lights descending on the yard but there was one pair of lights that only shone red – heading east along the railroad grade. I drew out my box of Lucky Strikes and my lighter, which sparked to life beneath the end of the one I selected from the packet. The smoke mixed with the haze of ash still rising from the yard and down the line the set of tail lights faded out of sight into the black horizon.

Chapter 46 - Empty

Dottie

Sept. 28th 1947
Sunday
Glasspier,

I sat alone at the table and felt the gauze bandage on my left arm where the flying debris had lashed a thin red line into me last night. It was going to scar, but that was better than the alternatives. I felt drained, and not from the injury. The apartment was quiet. Only the tick of the clock and the low ringing that hadn't left my ears yet filled the silence. I'd stayed up far too late; far too late waiting for something that I knew would never come. It was just like last time. The quiet desperation of waiting in vain for someone who you knew wasn't coming home. And now, I was waiting again. Waiting for a newspaper to land outside the door tomorrow that would remove all doubt, or rather, all hope.

It wasn't the injury, or even the lack of sleep that had me feeling empty, like a coffee pot with only the dregs left in the bottom. It was the emptiness of the apartment. The same emptiness I'd felt in that old house Charles and I had just made our first down payment on. The feeling of something missing, something that left you with no option but to pick up the pieces of your old life and try to go on – no matter how much you wanted to just lie on the floor amidst them and never get back up. Something that left you completely empty, with no more tears left to cry.

I wiped the dampness from beneath my eyes for the hundredth time since climbing into Leon's car after the blast. We were behind the car, ducking fire from The Blight before we'd been thrown to the ground, cut with shrapnel, and deafened by the explosion. Angelo and the others were much closer to the train. I'd already run through the scene a thousand times, in a thousand different ways, trying to imagine a version where anyone could have survived being that close to the bomb. None of them came close to believability. And the continued absence of Angelo only made each one seem more impossible.

On the table before me, a few things lay scattered about. An ashtray with a neglected cigarette smoking away, my pistol – short one bullet, the note that Angelo left for me the day before, and a large envelope with its contents laid out beside it: eight by ten glossies from my photoshoot. They'd come out well, very professional. They had a certain look to them – like I'd made it. Sure didn't feel that way. It all felt so pointless and silly now, after all that'd happened, and I found myself not wanting anything to do with them.

I sat that way for a while, chewing idly on a cigarette that tasted like wet newspaper and thinking about opening a bottle of whatever was strongest from the cupboard. Although, standing up to do even that sounded like an insurmountable effort. But finally, something forced me to rise: the phone rang. I raised it from its cradle expecting either Leon – or the police.

"Hello. Is this the residence of Miss Dottie McFarlane?" asked the voice on the other end.

I recognized it, and nearly slammed the receiver back down. It was Mr. Barry. "Yes," I replied flatly against my better judgment.

"This is Jon. I wanted to apologize for the other day, but not until I had something to show my sincerity with."

I didn't say anything.

He continued in my silence, "Tonight, you sing at the Crown. If you'd still like to, of course," he added hastily. "I set it up, because I remember you saying how it was your dream to perform there; as a way of saying I'm sorry. Should you choose to, you'll take the stage at nine, and no – I won't be there. This is for you."

I couldn't count the number of times I'd told Angleo that someday the Gold Pig would be ancient history and I'd be singing in the Crown. It was my dream. It was everything I'd been working towards. But that was before. Before spending afternoons with Thomas and Leon had become a regular pastime. Before the case had torn everything apart.

I realized I was letting the silence stretch on for too long. "Yes. Thank you. That means a lot. Some things have come up recently, but I'll think about it." That was all I could choke out but it seemed to be enough. Mr. Barry wished me well and success with the show and then I was plunged back into the quiet seclusion of the lonely apartment. I snubbed out the cigarette in the tray and grabbed my coat.

I no longer had a car, so I hailed a cab to the agency. It deposited me on the front step of McCreary Investigations and idled out front, per my request. Standing in front of the door, I was met with a sign that read 'CLOSED' hanging from the door handle. From what little I could see inside, it was dark, and Leon's black sedan was absent from the curb. Maybe he'd taken it somewhere discreet for repairs? All the glass had been shattered after all, and it'd taken more than a few bullets. Somehow though, I didn't feel like that was high on his list of things to do in the wake of last night. Would he be staring into the bottom of a bottle somewhere in the city? No, I knew from experience he had plenty enough to get by, and knowing him, he'd want to be alone. Where would Leon go to be alone? I returned to the waiting cab and climbed inside.

Leaning forward, I told the driver: "Take me to 201 Carmen Avenue."

Chapter 47 - Shedding Velvet

Leon

The attic was how I'd remembered it. Dusty, quiet, and sparsely furnished with the last remnants of a long-forgotten family. It was the perfect place to drink myself under. It was where this case had started – and now, where it would end. I sat on the floor, leaning against the wall and taking long swigs from my flask. The case had run dry, but at least the liquor hadn't yet. There was nowhere left to go with it, the last possible link to whoever had orchestrated everything died in that boxcar last night.

I suppose we did have everything we needed to launch a case against Thomas Glasspier and Jenny would just have to be satisfied with that. But I wasn't. I wanted to get to the bottom of who'd set us up from the beginning and so zealously waged war via proxy against Glasspier and his empire. At least we'd saved the mill. Kind of. I wasn't sure why the explosives still went off, despite us destroying the detonator; I guess we just got lucky that they weren't in position yet. Still, the Somerset Line engineers couldn't be happy…

And all of this, at a cost. Thomas was dead and Dottie lost her brother. Last time I was here, it was with Thomas. What had he been asking me about? Ghosts? He always did have a flair for the macabre, even back when we'd first met and he'd hired me to help him find that supposedly cursed necklace. Only thing cursed about it was the hell we went through trying to get it back. I took another drink, recalling some of the only fond memories I'd made since the war – memories that all seemed to include the three of us. Well, it was just two now. And that was *if* Dottie even wanted to be mixed up with me anymore… I wouldn't blame her if I never saw her again.

I pulled my journal from within my coat and thumbed through it absentmindedly. I thought I might write something, but no words would come. It was around then that I heard the wooden creak of the ladder with whatever hearing I had left over from last night. Instinct was to go for my gun, but I wasn't carrying anything today save for half a fifth of whisky and a whole lot of regret. Whoever it was, I'd just have to talk with them person to person – without my go-to intermediary.

Chapter 48 - The Journal

Dottie

'You look like hell', was my first thought at seeing Leon slumped against the wall in the attic. So I told him so, although I was sure that I looked twice as bad myself. What can I say, his manners had rubbed off on me. He acknowledged me with a jerk of his head and a raise of the flask he was nursing as I walked past him to the far end of the attic where an old wooden chest sat deteriorating beneath a small window. I noted faint streaks in the thick dust on the lid of the chest, indicating that it'd been touched more recently than the rest of this place.

"Is this where the pictures came from?"

He nodded, rubbing his temple with his free hand, the other clutching his journal.

"You know, this is my first time here. You left me to babysit Jenny, remember?" I raised the lid and dug around in the chest a little, although there wasn't much to see. Just a couple of kids books and some mouse droppings.

He sighed and slowly spun the cap back onto his flask. "I know. I'm sorry." He leaned his head back against the wall. "I'm sorry for it all. For getting you wrapped up in this. I was just used to working with a partner, with Cruz. Maybe I'm not cut out for solo practice yet… I *wish* that babysitting Jenny was the extent of your involvement in this case. Maybe then your brother would still be alive…"

With the two books in hand, I gently closed the lid and sat across from him, my back leaned against the opposite wall. I was fighting back tears again. "You can't blame yourself for that. He knew the risks of running with that crowd. I tried to convince him out of it a couple times, but it kept the lights on – and you know how guys like him are. They think they're invincible. Thomas probably did too…"

Leon grimaced and stared out the dirty window. It was quiet in the small space, so I examined the covers of the books, *Tarzan of the Apes* and *Outlaws,* imagining a young Charlotte reading them to Jake. That wasn't helping my composure any, so I glanced back up at Leon and blinked hard.

"Here," he said, sliding the flask across the floor to me, "to Angelo and Thomas, men of action."

I drank to that.

We reminisced about how the three of us met, chasing down a necklace thief. I hadn't realized that was Leon's first solo case after leaving Trusted Eye to start his own firm; but it did explain a lot. That case had been a mess too, although I couldn't blame Leon – the city and the people in it were a mess. I guess it was a detective's job to sort out the jumbled messes of people's lives and make sense of them. Shame it seemed like this one was just too far gone to be sorted out.

Soon the flask was empty and I was feeling a little warmer. The conversation died down and Leon resumed absentmindedly thumbing through his journal. He had a torn expression, like he was weighing two equally bad options. I kept quiet and let him work through it on his own. Finally, he held the journal up and talked apprehensively, "You know, last night was the first time in a long while I've slept soundly? I had a realization in that boxcar, and I think it made this unnecessary going forward. It was just avoidance the whole time."

I held my tongue, not sure what he was getting at. The journal unnecessary? I'd seen him write in it before, case related stuff I assumed. Was this his way of saying he was giving up being a private eye?

To my surprise, he tossed it into the space between us, sending a small cloud of dust rising from where it landed. It was a small, black leather bound that had seen some wear. I leaned forward tentatively, looking at him for approval.

"Just promise you won't think less of me," he whispered in a low voice, "I haven't even read the first entries since I wrote them…"

I leaned forward again and lifted the journal carefully. "Fine. But here, you read something too, I don't want you staring at me like that," I said, and tossed him the cowboy book.

Gently opening to the first page of the worn journal, I couldn't deny my curiosity. On the inside of the cover, a scrap piece of paper had been taped seemingly in post, after the journal had already been started. I began there:

I started this journal as an attempt to lay the wounds of my mind to rest. I thought, rather than idly picking at the same scab day after day, it could serve better to carve the whole wound open and bleed out onto the page so to speak. A bloodletting. To purge the darkness from myself and into this leather and paper vessel where it might be forgotten as the wound closes. The finality of it is what appeals to me the most. Permanent lines drawn into the shapes of what lurks within my subconscious – lines that turn the boundless and shifting madness into a tangible, contained thing. Maybe that doesn't make any sense. That's fine. It only needs to for me.

What was this? Some kind of therapy? I knew Leon had been through some horrible things in the war… I continued to the first actual entry.

January 23rd, 1944
Entry #1

My name is Lionel David Bauer. It's 14:38 on January 23rd, 1944. I'm in Glasspier, at the General Hospital. It's been forty-six days since I was extricated from the Soviet wilderness. I have not been lucid until yesterday. The last thing I remember was being very hungry and tracking down a large stag. I don't remember much else, just flashes of white and the taste of blood.

They won't give me many details, but they said that they found me, unconscious, in a survival lean-to, next to the mangled body of a German soldier. I have several broken ribs, a fractured ankle, and a gangrene infection in the wound I sustained in Poland. They tell me that I was most likely going through withdrawals from the medication the Soviets had given me before I escaped, which accounts for the lost time.

They're not telling me the whole truth.

"Your name isn't really McCreary?" I asked, looking up briefly from the page.

"No, I thought it would help me fit in with all the Irish Catholics in the area, like yourself and Conrad."

"I'm only Catholic by heritage."

"You and me both."

Leon opened up the *Outlaws* book and I returned to the journal.

January 25th, 1944

Entry #2

I slept for most of the day yesterday. My ribs are healing nicely, but the nurses are worried that the infection in my stomach wound will spread to my heart. I will be disappointed if I survive getting stabbed, being partially disemboweled, and being stranded in the Soviet wilderness for a month just to die in a hospital bed five hours from the farm I grew up on.

The food here is much better than rations; even if I've had trouble keeping some things down. I was served a steak yesterday and immediately threw up everything I had for lunch. The nurses said I kept saying "It's stuck in my teeth" – or something along those lines. They were asking me what I meant, but I didn't know.

My hands were damp on the smooth leather of the journal as I continued to read. I wanted to stop, to throw the book back at Leon and try to forget what I'd already read. But no. Leon wanted me to know this. He finally trusted me. He'd just done what he had to to survive. It wasn't his fault. Besides, he wasn't in his right mind at the time.

The next entry was obviously written with a shaking hand and there were some places where the pen had been pushed so hard into the page that it'd pierced through. There was no date and no entry number.

> *I know what happened. I killed that stag and I ate him.*
> *I ate him.*
>
> *I heard what the nurses called me. They were talking in whispers, thinking I was asleep, but I heard it. They lie. I'm not. It was a stag. I'm not what they called me. I'm not a cann*

"-son of a bitch!" Leon exclaimed, and I nearly jumped out of my skin. He was staring hard at the cowboy book. "Look at this!" He rushed to my side with the book, laying it over the top of the journal in my lap and pointing at the page. Underlined by his finger, were three words. A title and a name. *Sheriff Miles Wesson.*

It seemed Leon might not be the only one who'd forged a new identity.

Chapter 49 - Plus Expenses

Leon

Sept. 30th 1947
Tuesday
Glasspier,

It was two days since the attic and I stood on the corner of Jackson and Bluff with a briefcase in my hand, smoking and waiting. Steam rolled out of a sewer grate down the alley behind me, like the very fires of hell were burning under the concrete beneath my feet. From what I'd seen in the last couple of days I didn't doubt it. Across the street, stood a grand official looking white building sandwiched between skyscrapers. The Glasspier 'Mayor's Office of Operations' to be precise. I hadn't called ahead to make an appointment – I was planning on a walk in.

At 12:30, right on schedule, Mayor Wesson emerged from the front of the building alongside a handful of other suit-wearing aristocrats. I recognized his dark hair, clean face, and choice of pinstriped suit. They strolled down the street, talking in voices that I couldn't hear over the sound of car horns and rumbling engines. I crossed over, walking confidently up the steps of the white building and into the lobby. You could go just about anywhere if you did it with enough confidence and looked the part. Nobody looked twice as I climbed up two flights of stairs to the third floor. I walked with the confidence of knowing where I was going – because I did. Yesterday, after an enlightening visit to Bluebird Orphan Home and a call to Jenny, I'd given the place a once over making sure I knew where the mayor's office was.

The middle office of the third floor was where I was headed. Luckily, most of the building seemed to be out to lunch, because the door was locked and I'd need a few minutes uninterrupted with it. Listening for a second, I heard nothing from the other side so I drew a pick and tensioner from my pockets and got to work, keeping an eye out for anyone that might be coming down either direction of the hall. It was a tougher lock than the ones previous, but I kept my head and soon the knob clicked open. I went inside and closed the door, locking it again behind me.

The office was full of dark rosewood paneling and furniture, with a large desk sitting front and center on top of a red and navy floral-patterned rug. Around it were wooden chairs with dark green cushions on the visitor side and a high-backed leather executive chair on the other. One end of the room had windows with white sheer drapes and the other had shelves and cabinets housing awards and various other trinkets. Behind the desk was a large black and white picture of Glasspier's harbor, some thirty to forty years ago by my guess, framed on either side by tall bookshelf sentinels. I had an hour to get set up, but I'd only need half that. I laid my briefcase on the desk and popped it open.

Inside was a gift courtesy of Jenny. She'd been happy to put up the dough as an expense per our initial agreement when I told her that after today, the case would be closed. Closed on this side of the courtroom at least. The object in question was a brand-new Dictaphone, in a smooth gunmetal-gray rectangular casing, with a Lexan plastic belt instead of a wax cylinder – the kind that would be permanently etched and most importantly: admissible in court. I pulled it from my briefcase and set it on the carpet beneath the desk, running the wire over to a plug in the wall. It wasn't too noticeable, and it would be even less so with his focus directed elsewhere. Lastly, I pulled open a drawer and hooked the receiver into it, facing upwards, before sitting in the mayor's chair.

I waited. I placed my automatic on the desk in front of me and waited. While I waited, I imagined what sort of man it took to plan everything he had. What sort of man it took to get where he was and still not be satisfied; the sort that would carry a vendetta to this length over so many years. Had he been wronged? Surely, yes. But Dottie and I intended to hold both him and Thomas Glasspier accountable for the things they'd done. With that thought, I heard the sound of footsteps outside in the hall. I hoped he'd come in alone. He had yesterday. With that hope, I reached for my pistol, resting the bottom of the magazine well on the desk and pointing the barrel towards the door. A key scraped into the lock on the other side and the handle turned.

"Hullo, Jake," I said, as he entered the room, "shut the door behind you and lock it."

He reached for the handle quickly in surprise, but then his eyes narrowed at the gun in my hand and he slowed his movements; doing as I requested. The lock clicked and he turned his back to me, casually removing his overcoat and hanging it on the spindly wooden rack standing beside the door. I kept both my eyes and my gun trained on him while he did so. A cigarette dangled precariously from his lower lip. He approached the desk slow and I gestured for him to sit.

"Put that thing away. Guns are loaded by the devil and unloaded by fools," he said in a smooth but warning tone, staring not at the pistol, but at me.

"Don't make me have to do anything foolish and it shouldn't be a problem."

He took the cigarette from between his teeth and broke into one of his charismatic grins that I remembered from his swearing in ceremony. Only this time, he smiled more like a fox that'd gained entry to the chicken coop; with perfect dazzling white teeth. Beneath the table, I clicked the Dictaphone on with my foot like I'd practiced a dozen times last night in my office. It was only good for about fifteen minutes – and I wanted to make sure that I got everything. He sat down across from me.

"You're good Mr. McCreary. Very good. It's why I picked you. Although it seems you were a little *too* good. How'd you find me out? Really, I'm curious. Having Fletcher as an intermediary was supposed to avoid this very situation. I thought I'd thought of everything."

"Sheriff Miles Wesson ring a bell?" I pulled the *Outlaws* book from my inside jacket pocket with one hand and dropped it on the table in front of him. His smile grew wider and he reached tentatively for the small paperback, holding it with an almost serene look in his eyes.

"So that's where I got the name from. I'd forgotten about this. I suppose the name just had a certain panache to it, don't you think? Must have stuck with me." He placed the book carefully back in front of where my pistol rested, unwavering. "Yes, I do think I recognize the cover. My mother would have read it to me. She was determined that I wouldn't grow up to be some ignorant sleaze like her husband." He paused and his eyes grew dark, as though he were remembering that night. The night he'd crawled through the dirt beneath the house and been born again into the world as an orphan. "I suppose my *real* father just jump-started things that night he sent Silas. Forced me to grow up fast and value my life and my wits. That's the only thing I have to thank him for. Well, that and his money."

I didn't say anything, hoping he would continue to spill. He was a talker and a smooth one at that. He was one of those people you just couldn't help but to like. Unfortunately for him I could help it – I knew what he'd done. It was just the confession and the details I wanted from him now.

"Money?" I asked, prompting him when he closed his mouth.

"Well sure, mayoral campaigns take some serious funds."

"Why would Glasspier fund you? Wouldn't that defeat the purpose of him trying to kill you years ago, putting you in the spotlight now?"

"Oh come on Leon, think. I know you're smart enough to put that together. Surprised you haven't already, the way you put everything together for that necklace thief case. The day that story graced the papers I knew you were the one. Don't make me lose my admiration for you."

Okey. I could think. Thomas Glasspier funded Wesson's mayoral campaign, but why? He'd never taken any public interest in politics before and I couldn't imagine Wesson had any talking points he cared about enough to get involved under the table. That was it. Under the table – there had to have been a blackmail angle. Wesson found out somehow that Glasspier was his real father and blackmailed him for money to fund his bid for office.

"Those documents Fletcher gave me at the masquerade – one of them was fake. You found out somehow that he was your father and struck a deal: in exchange for you keeping quiet he'd fund your rise to power. The death certificate for Jake Marlowe was fake – so that Thomas Glasspier would be the only one to go down in your little ploy and the world would be none the wiser about your real parentage."

He beamed. "There he is! Very impressive. Yes I found out, can you imagine? Spending your whole life trying to find your real father and it turns out he's the richest man in the world? I knew it the moment I met him at one of his earlier parties, but Morris was so helpful in getting Silas to come clean with confirmation… shame what happened to him. Morris, not Silas. I hope he rots for what he did to us. But let's put that unpleasantness behind us. Can we get to business? I know why you're here."

I let the silence stretch on again, giving him the opportunity to fill it with why he thought I was here. And sure enough, he did. I could tell he was the type of guy that felt in control as long as he kept talking. I was the type that felt in control when I had a gun and the other guy didn't. It made for easy conversation between the two of us.

"You're here to strike a deal."

I stayed quiet. Let him think that all he wants.

"I'll admit, there was one thing that I didn't count on. I thought my father would be the one paying you off, not myself, hence having Conrad as a failsafe. But it seems he won't be needed after all. Oh well, either way, it's my father's money," he laughed. "So what's your price? What's your price to only present the evidence in that document Fletcher gave you?"

"Two things. There were two things you didn't count on," I grumbled.

"Oh? What's the second one? Do enlighten me."

"Your father survived. Miss Foxglove failed to kill Thomas Glasspier," I said, but as I did, the wrinkles of confusion crawling their way onto Wesson's face made me doubt his involvement in that aspect. "You paid her too, didn't you?"

"No. As a matter of fact I didn't. I never wanted a posthumous trial. I wanted to see the light die in my father's eyes as he watched his empire of dirt crumble around him. It was supposed to be a war on two fronts, not three. On his reputation and on his industry – not on his life. Foxglove wasn't something I'd accounted for, but lucky for us, she failed."

"Us? There is no us," I said thickly.

The foxlike smile turned into a wolfish scowl; his perfect teeth disappearing behind a frown. "Don't be stupid. Everyone has a price. Name it and it's done."

I thought about Dottie, and how outraged she'd been at the corruption we'd uncovered. How it'd affected, and in some cases ruined, people's lives. How badly she wanted justice – and how I'd promised to help her win it. I thought about Jenny, and how her sister had been the unfortunate catalyst for all of this. I'd made a promise to her as well. I remembered what I'd told Thomas in the boxcar: 'the cycle of corruption and bloodshed must end somewhere'. This would be a start.

"I know why you did all of this. To keep yourself on top. You couldn't reveal Glasspier's crimes without revealing your own. But if you got somebody else to… well, then you could have your cake and eat it too. Glasspier falls and you stay on top. But here's the thing: I don't care if you stay on top and I've already got my price."

"Already got your price?" he fumed, rising from his chair in anger. "From who? It'll be your word against mine in court! What evidence have you got?"

"You're right. It'll be my word against yours. And since you're so good at talking, you shouldn't have anything to worry about." I shot him a patronizing grin, picturing the immutable lines being carved into plastic beneath the table.

He lowered his voice to a threatening tone. "Everyone in this city sells their soul sooner or later, I just made sure I got a good price. This is your chance to do the same."

I stood to face him at eye level. "I've already named my price – and not to you. Thirty a day, plus expenses."

Chapter 50 - Epilogue

Dottie

April. 21st 1948
Monday
Glasspier,

I left my apartment wearing a two-piece charcoal suit with a cream-colored collar and low-rise leather heels. The sun rose proud over the tops of skyscrapers and smokestacks and it was the first day of the year that really felt like spring. It was also the first day of the trial. I got into my car and it purred to life in an instant; carrying me down the sun-drenched streets of the city. Leon wanted to go over some of the details one last time and head down to the courthouse together; an idea to which I was not opposed. The route was second nature to me by now, and soon my sedan rolled to a stop along Belmont Street.

I stepped out of the car, taking in the sign above the door at the agency in new light. I'd developed a habit of shrugging off Angelo's offers for help over the years, saying that 'I could handle myself'. I still believed it, the sentiment of it at least, but there was no denying now that having someone watching your back was essential in this city. Leon had realized it too, and the sign above the agency reflected that. I smiled once again, seeing those bold golden letters hanging overhead that read: 'McCreary and McFarlane Investigations'.

Acknowledgements

Glasspier was written starting in April of 2023, but began as an idea in the summer of 2022, in the form of a tabletop RPG set in a realistic setting as opposed to the high fantasy D&D that our group usually played. The game ran in the winter of that year, wrapping up as spring rolled around – which is also when I began seriously considering the notion of writing it into a novel. Its initial storyline shared most of the same beats and characters as the book that would come to follow, with some significant changes made to fit the translation to novel format. For those that participated in that original game: I hope that the necessary changes serve to enhance the story along with the main characters so lovingly crafted by you.

It is those four, listed below, whom I must extend the greatest thanks for their various roles in bringing that initial story (and eventually this book) to life in the unique format that is collective storytelling via tabletop RPG.

- Kaitlyn Speigl, for just about everything: the fantastic character art found within the pages and on the back cover of the book, editing help for the early versions of the manuscript, and of course: the creation of the character 'Dottie'.

- Laura Sliva, for the creation of, and subsequent immense contributions to Leon's character, especially in the form of his journal entries. Also, for always being willing to be a sounding board for my ideas.

- William Holder, for the creation of 'Thomas' (Langston, not Glasspier).

- Zachary Stanley, for the creation of 'Conrad' and his pamphlet manifesto.

I must also thank my family. My parents, James and Cathy, for always supporting my interest in reading, and also my sister Rebecca, for some editorial help on the early manuscript.

Lastly, a thank you to Susan Bin for providing the amazing cover art.

Milton Keynes UK
Ingram Content Group UK Ltd.
UKHW010814220424
441551UK00001B/215